Mist O'er the Voyageur

by

Naomi Musch

SMITTEN
HISTORICAL ROMANCE
LIGHTHOUSE PUBLISHING of the CAROLINAS

MIST O'ER THE VOYAGEUR BY NAOMI MUSCH
Published by Smitten Historical Romance
an imprint of Lighthouse Publishing of the Carolinas
2333 Barton Oaks Dr., Raleigh, NC, 27614

ISBN: 978-1-946016-61-4
Copyright © 2018 by Naomi Musch
Cover design by Elaina Lee
Interior design by Karthick Srinivasan

Available in print from your local bookstore, online, or from the publisher at:
ShopLPC.com

For more information on this book and the author visit: http://naomimusch.com/

Brought to you by the creative team at Lighthouse Publishing of the Carolinas (LPCBooks.com): Eddie Jones, Karin Beery, Pegg Thomas, Shonda Savage, Brian Cross, Judah Raine, Jenny Leo

Library of Congress Cataloging-in-Publication Data
Musch, Naomi.
Mist O'er the Voyageur/ Naomi Musch 1st ed.

Printed in the United States of America

PRAISE FOR *MIST O'ER THE VOYAGEUR*

With all the excitement and danger of the rough and tumble fur trading era, *Mist O'er the Voyageur* is packed full of adventure and a sweet romance. Travel along with Brigitte and Rene into the wilderness of the wild northland. This is a story you won't soon forget.

~**Michelle Griep**
Award-winning author of *The Captured Bride*

A Northwoods adventure told with authenticity and grace, *Mist O'er the Voyageur* draws you into a wilderness peopled with remarkable characters and a way of life seldom captured on the page. Naomi Musch shines in this stirring tale of longing, belonging, and the quest for truth.

~**Laura Frantz**
Author of *A Bound Heart* and *The Lacemaker*

Brigitte, a true *femme du nord*, her Métis compatriots, and her challenging nineteenth-century world of the northern wild are so engaging that I feel I am living the adventures of my French Canadian ancestors. Naomi Musch writes with her signature insightful brilliance and nimble use of expansive, precise vocabulary for the period and place. Her command of historic and geographic detail transports readers to Brigitte's time of rugged, unforgiving Canadian wilderness and waters of the Lake Superior region, and connects us with the canny, brave Métis people of whom Brigitte is part. Naomi Musch challenges the reader with insightful character development, and compelling human conflict and cooperation throughout. *Travail exceptionnel!*

~**Thomas Wayne King**
Author & descendant of durable French Canadian women and men of mixed heritage

The determination of a young woman, the courage of the French Voyageurs, the strength and majesty of Lake Superior, and the steadfastness of a man trying to hold them all together. Mist O'er the Voyageur transports to the reader back to a time when the line between civilization and raw wilderness was difficult to discern. Naomi Musch paints the reader into the story with her vivid descriptions and accurate details.

~**Pegg Thomas**
Author of *Her Redcoat*, part of *The Backcountry Brides Collection*

What an adventure! Naomi Musch has woven together a vibrant tapestry of history, setting, and character that drew me right in to a different world. Amazing talent. Captivating novel.

~**Linda W. Yezak**
Author of the award-winning Circle Bar Ranch series.

Naomi Musch has woven a mesmerizing tale that immerses readers into a dangerous adventure from the start. With believable and honest characters encountering situations true to the period, this suspenseful story captivated my attention and didn't let go until the end. Musch's depth of research enabled her to transport readers back in time. I highly recommend this novel to lovers of historical romance.

~**Sandra Merville Hart**
Author of *A Musket in My Hands,*
A Rebel in My House, and *A Stranger on My Land*

Acknowledgments

This story has been a long time coming, and by that I mean I wrote the first draft almost a decade ago then tucked it away, only to pull it out now and again for ponderings and rewrites. Meanwhile, as I published other novels elsewhere, I waited to determine what the Lord might have in mind for this story of my heart.

When I met Pegg Thomas via social media, I really had no idea she was dipping her feet into the world of editorial management with Lighthouse Publishing of the Carolinas. We seemed to have a lot in common, both being farmers from the Great Lakes Region—Wisconsin and Michigan respectively—with other similar interests that stretched from writing historical fiction to gardening, canning, and camping, so we became acquainted. (Since then, we've also discovered we're the same age and both played trombone back in the day.) Without God directing our paths to cross and Pegg's willingness to take a look at my novel, this story would still be waiting on a computer file with an uncertain future. She also recognized the changes needed to strengthen the tale and make it more perfectly fit the LPC Smitten line. Thank you, Lord, and thank you, Pegg!

Others, whose sharp eyes and insights also helped to shape and smooth the story, include my editor Karin Beery and the rest of the Smitten team who have made many things come together perfectly, including the gorgeous cover.

Outside of LPC, I truly wish to thank Ann Treacy who has been my writing friend for over twenty-five years and has a keen eye for detail and history. She has been actively supportive and encouraging, offering feedback in many of my writing ventures. (Read her YA novel *The Search for the Homestead Treasure* for another taste of upper Midwest historical adventure.)

Lastly, but of great importance, I'd like to share my deep appreciation to my husband Jeff and our clan of adult offspring who encourage me to continue with this writing gig, and they don't even mind when I slip bits and pieces of their lives into a character on occasion. If they did mind, they'd probably put up with it anyway. God is good, and He's *so* good to have shared their lives with me.

DEDICATION

To the Upper St. Croix Writers in beautiful Solon Springs, Wisconsin, the best and most eclectic writers group in the northland. For all the wonderful hours of critique, encouragement, and ideas; for direction, support, and camaraderie; for Tuesday mornings filled with relaxing laughter and sidetracked tales of humor, hope, and adventure, I can think of no other group of writerly souls to whom I would rather dedicate this story. God bless, write on, and keep on being the engaging, insightful, and inspiring bunch that you are.

CHAPTER 1

"The year came when I regretfully took leave of ma petite
fille *for her instruction with my own sister and with the
sisters of the Congregation of Notre-Dame."*
— Journal of Etienne Marchal, Voyageur

Montreal, May 1807

Brigitte Marchal gripped the handle of her wicker basket tighter, wishing to stall, but the nun beckoned her without looking back.

"Come along with the basket, Brigitte." The good nun wended her way between market vendors and traders hawking their wares and bushels of vegetables and baked goods. Rough-edged crates of small squawking and squealing livestock caught at her gown.

Brigitte ducked her head and hurried behind the nun's billowing veil and dark robes. Steps later, the nun halted, and Brigitte bumped into her. Sister Agathe turned around, her pale brows arched. "Whatever are you doing? Come walk beside me."

Brigitte peeked over the nun's shoulder, her gaze darting this way and that across the market square. Her heart pounded as she released her breath. Tristan Clarboux had disappeared. Perhaps he'd slipped away on one of the side streets or into a shop. "I am sorry, Sister. I was distracted by … by the flowers." She glanced at the vendor across the cobbled street.

"Come along. We must get our eggs and fish before there are none left to be had." The nun dabbed at her forehead with the sleeve of her habit. "My, but it is warm today."

Brigitte stepped to the sister's side and scoured the square once again. *Cher Dieu, do not let him see me.* But it was no good. There he was, her unwanted suitor, standing outside the potter's. His gaze settled on her. She scooted closer to Sister Agathe, crowding her.

"Did you not hear me say how warm the day has gotten?" Sister Agathe gasped. "Whatever is the matter with you today?"

"I am sorry. I did not mean to rush you."

Tristan stepped before them and inclined his head. "Sister. My dear Brigitte."

The nun paused, compelling Brigitte to check her stride, though it would have been impossible to maneuver around the young man blocking their path.

He reached for Brigitte's hand and drew it upward. She slid it free before it touched his lips and clasped it around the basket handle.

The good sister smiled. "Monsieur Clarboux. How good it is to see you. You are faring well and doing your best to stay cool on this sweltering day, I trust?"

"*En fait*, mademoiselle." He nodded at the nun, but his gaze slid toward Brigitte with a gleam that made her chest tighten. She had heard the rumors about his philandering ways, even if the nuns and her aunt had not. His lips stretched into a thin smile. "I hope you have not forgotten my invitation to the *masque* tomorrow night. You will not let me down, I hope."

"My aunt ..." She looked to the nun for support.

Sister Agathe's eyebrows rose nearly to the hood of her wimple. "There will be chaperons, will there not? Our dear Brigitte must not roam to such parties without supervision, though I am sure her interests are safe with you."

Brigitte clamped her mouth shut.

"*Oui*. My father and mother will attend, and my sister will ride with us in the carriage."

Sister Agathe bobbed her head, sealing Brigitte's fate. "Very good. We must look out for our dear girl while her aunt is convalescing. That gentlewoman would keep you on your toes, monsieur." She shook her finger at Tristan. "Do not forget to bring your sister, and I'm sure you will be rewarded by God."

"Until tomorrow." He smiled again at Brigitte, a smile her

numb lips could not return. Tristan bowed and sauntered away.

She pulled her gaze away from his back. "Shall we get the fish, Sister?"

"*Oui.* Come. The others will have begun preparing the noonday meal. Our tasks have taken such a long time this morning." She patted again at the dampness on her brow.

Now that the threat of meeting Tristan had passed, Brigitte strolled beside Sister Agathe, searching for a way to explain her apprehensions.

The nun stopped before the fishwife's stall. "What have you for us?"

The fishwife chased away the flies over a basket of whitefish. "You will not find fresher among the stalls today."

"How much? Keep in mind I have little to spare." Sister Agatha almost always compelled the marketers to generosity. Brigitte looked away as they haggled over a price.

Tristan's father was rich. Were his gifts to the church the reason Sister Agathe assumed Tristan a safe match for Brigitte? Or did she favor him because he was the only man who'd shown an inclination to court Brigitte?

He had spied Brigitte at mass, and she had avoided his glances. Why did he even pay her any notice when there were so many more beautiful ladies in his class? Yet she had caught his eye somehow.

A cooling breeze blew through the booths, assailing her nostrils with the scent of fish. Fitting, as now she was caught in Tristan's net.

Sister Agathe exchanged an English and a Spanish coin for the fish. Brigitte carried them in her basket while the nun moved on toward the butcher's stall. Father and son greeted Sister Agathe with a smile.

Brigitte smiled as well. With all the time she spent caring for *Tante* Eunice, and coming so often to the convent, how would she ever meet someone else? What other man might offer for her and make her future secure once her aunt passed? The butcher's son?

She curled her nose. He always smelled like a market hog left too long in the sun. Besides, he hardly seemed to know she was alive.

She adjusted the basket while the nun laid a thick portion of fatty pork inside and folded a stained cloth over it. The nun then directed them to the final stall where she counted out eggs, laying them atop the pork one-by-one.

When the farmer turned his back to them, Brigitte summoned her courage. "Sister, I do not wish to seem ungrateful or offensive, but I had so hoped to avoid attending the party. It will be nothing so grand as a real *masque*, like I have heard about from the ones who came from France."

"Seven … eight …" Sister Agathe paused to look at Brigitte. "I know you worry for your aunt, and you are good to come and help us as well, but you must do the things that young people do. You cannot spend all your time with us old ones."

"I do not regret my time spent serving others. It is only that …"

"*Oui?* What is it?"

"It is only Tristan, Monsieur Clarboux …" She glanced about warily, in case his eyes and ears might be close by. "I am unsure of him."

The nun chuckled and turned up the street. Brigitte hastened beside her, the full basket in tow. "Do not worry much about it. It is sensible for a young woman to be nervous when a young man decides to court her. I am sure your *tante* would tell you the same."

"I have heard things said of him, that he … that he has enjoyed the company of many young ladies." There. She'd said it.

The sister paused. She gave a heavy sigh. "I am certain that most young men enjoy the company of a lady or two before they settle on the one they choose." Brigitte glanced at the sister's red face. Beads of sweat speckled her nose. "Nevertheless, you must not miss such an opportunity, Brigitte. You must think of your future." She huffed as they walked on. "I dread to say it, but you must prepare yourself for your aunt's departing."

"*Oui*, but I hardly know Monsieur Clarboux or his family."

Sister Agathe chuckled. "Then you must attend the party so you will get to know them better. I am sure you will find you like him very much." She gave Brigitte a wry grin. "He is a very handsome young man, *non?*"

He was handsome enough, but should Brigitte trust such outward appearances?

The nun continued up the street. "Come. Let us return to the convent before the meat spoils. You will wish to return to your aunt's house with plenty of time to prepare before Monsieur Clarboux's arrival tomorrow." Brigitte walked along, lagging half a pace behind the nun, when Sister Agnes added, "You would be foolish—even ungrateful perhaps—not to accept a *soupirant* such as Tristan. He is not without prospects in his father's shipping company. He can offer you security. Should he offer for you, then likely it is God's will that you marry and make a home together."

It was no use. If the nun thought him God's will for Brigitte, how was she to explain the nettling feeling he gave her? If only Papa had returned after *Oncle* Robert's death and *Tante* Eunice had not fallen ill.

Brigitte had not heard from Papa in three years. He had likely joined Brigitte's mother in the grave. If he would only return to see her again as he used to, she would have no need to consider Tristan, or any man for that matter. She would return to the Upper Country with Papa. She frowned, refusing to delve further into such a thought.

Brigitte sighed, wishing she could twist the stifling muslin scarf from her head and let her black braid swing freely. The day was warm indeed for so early in the year, and thoughts of marrying Tristan suffocated her.

At last, they broke free of the market and found brief spells of shade along the road back to the convent. Eager to return home, Brigitte picked up her pace, moving a step ahead of the nun. As they turned the corner beneath an oak tree, she stopped and clutched the sister's robe. "Look."

A man stood upon the convent's door stoop. A trapper, or maybe even a *coureur de bois* from the looks of him. Broad-shouldered, dark and burly, wearing a white muslin shirt and buckskin leggings. A *ceinture fléchée,* or arrow sash, woven in hues of bright red and blue circled his waist.

He bent over a basket.

Brigitte's heart shot into her throat. "He intends to leave *l'enfant.*" She could barely restrain herself from dropping her basket and running to him. She would shake him until his eyes bulged. He must be shameless! Abandoning his responsibility in broad daylight on the nunnery stoop of the Congregation of Notre-Dame.

Desperate women and battered wretches starving on the streets sometimes abandoned their babies at the convents. Most did not survive, though a lucky few were given a vestige of hope on the doorstep of the Grey Nuns'. Indignation flamed in Brigitte's breast.

Sister Agathe touched Brigitte's arm. "I will speak to him. Come."

He did not notice them until they broke free of the shade. When he spotted them, his head jerked upward. Brigitte glared at him as they drew near.

"Monsieur, may I help—*Ah!* Monsieur!" Sister Agathe's firm tone fell away and delight took its place. Brigitte shot her a look. Sister Agathe beamed and clasped her hands.

Darkness fell heavier over Brigitte's soul. This man—this *father*—would leave his babe to die in the sweltering sunlight, not even bothering to bring the infant inside the convent's cool walls, yet the good nun would not rebuke him?

Murder of unwanted infants was most common among mothers in Montreal, but everyone knew it was at their husband's, father's, or lover's behest that it was so. Serving girls, household *domestiques*, left with little recourse when taken advantage of by their masters, often left their infants to die, or more often, gave them up to the river. Brigitte's blood steamed.

Sister Agathe rushed forward and bent to retrieve the child. "You are here once again, and what is this?" She lifted the child from the basket. It mewed like a kitten.

"I know not. I only discovered the creature a moment ago."

"So you say." Brigitte stepped forward, her chin raised in challenge.

"Brigitte!"

She stepped closer, her fists curling around the handle of the fish basket. "The babe could have died in the sun."

He picked up the babe's basket. "Such would have been most unfortunate."

Her eyes widened. "You pretend you know nothing of this child you have no doubt fathered? You are without conscience." She spat at his feet.

He jumped back, his brow drawing down into a black line. "*Espèce d'idiot*. I am not the baby's father. Tell her." He looked sharply at Sister Agathe.

"Brigitte, *non*. Surely not. This is Monsieur Dufour, our friend these many years. You remember."

Dufour. She jerked her chin up and studied him.

"He is a *bienfaiteur*."

A benefactor. She eyed him again. She could not recollect having met the man.

Sister led them both through the door into the relief of the convent's cool interior. She held the infant close while Brigitte and the trader followed, carrying the now-empty child basket. He set it on a long, timber-frame table, the lone piece of furniture in the wide stone foyer.

Sister Agathe faced Brigitte. "Perhaps you should see to *le bébé*. Monsieur Dufour will assist me in taking our goods to the kitchen." Brigitte avoided looking directly at the trader as he took the basket of fish and produce from her. Sister Agathe handed the newborn to Brigitte. "Once we have tended to the child's needs, we will deliver it to the care of our Sisters of Charity at the *Hôpital Général*."

Brigitte was more than glad to take the child and get away from the stranger. She'd heard stories aplenty of the traders in the west. Of the voyageurs who transported goods, and the *coureur de bois* who traded illegally apart from the North West Company, making alliances with the natives. The native women they took as wives or simply used.

Her father had been such a man, yet he had always spoken of Brigitte's native mother with love. It was so hard to remember her now. Brigitte had been a girl of only seven summers when her mother died. When she was nine, her father took her from her mother's people, the Ojibwa, to Montreal to be raised by his sister, *Tante* Eunice, and her husband, Robert. They had seen to her education at the convent.

Brigitte bit her lip as she hurried the child to a whitewashed room. The sparsely furnished room contained a washstand with pitcher and bowl, a chest of linens, and a narrow bed upon which she could change the babe's swaddling and feed it before it would be taken to the Grey Nunnery.

Brigitte cooed as she washed and changed the abandoned infant girl. Such little comfort there was to offer the tiny soul. She wrapped it in a blanket as her thoughts burned. If the man downstairs had not fathered the child, who had? Some poor farmer who could not feed another mouth? Or might it be a man who thought the child a nuisance? A rich man, perhaps someone like Tristan Clarboux? She had seen these kinds of things often enough.

The baby let out a weak cry, and Brigitte nestled it close. "Shh …"

Brigitte had learned to care for children, to read and work figures, to produce food in the gardens, to cook, and launder—to improve herself as a desirable candidate for marriage. Even so, how could she ever give herself to a man like Tristan Clarboux, whose smile did not reach his eyes and whose nearness felt akin to that of a spider's? How could she bring children into the world with such a man? Surely she was not wrong to trust such an instinctive feeling about him. No matter what his father could offer in gifts to the church, the notion of belonging to Tristan repelled her. As long as her aunt breathed and the nuns did not encourage his suit further, Brigitte would carry on until someone else offered for her. Or until Papa returned.

"Brigitte." Sister Therese spoke in a soft voice as she slipped inside the room. "I will take the child now."

Brigitte nodded and handed her the baby, her heart aching for the abandoned whelp. The room smelled sour from the infant's fouled clothes. Would this child live, or would it die like so many others whose mothers had given up hope of caring for them? Likely it, too, would not take many breaths in this cursed world.

"Sister." Brigitte stalled the young nun's departure. "Do you know anything of the man called Dufour who is downstairs with Sister Agathe?"

"Monsieur Dufour? *Oui*." Sister Therese smiled. "He brings gifts upon occasion. I did not know he had returned."

"He is a good man, then?"

"*Oui*. René Dufour is a good man." She nodded and left with the baby as quietly as she had entered.

Brigitte dropped the soiled linens into a pail for soaking then wound her way to the kitchen, where three nuns worked to serve the afternoon pottage. Her step caught at the sight of the trapper seated at the table.

Sister Louisa handed Brigitte a bowl and tilted her head at their guest. "Give this to Monsieur Dufour, *s'il vous plaît*, before you are on your way."

Brigitte set the bowl before him. His gaze drew upward and caught hers. She looked away, but not soon enough. His stare found purchase, searing her with its intensity.

"Brigitte, will you take the board and take inventory of the pantry?" Sister Louisa asked as she continued filling wooden bowls. "Your hand is so much neater, and I simply do not have time."

"*Oui*." She turned her attention to the task but felt the occasional glances of Monsieur Dufour as she pulled a slate from the shelf and moved past the table to the pantry. She began scratching out the list of items remaining on the shelves.

He cleared his throat, and her head came up before she could stop herself. "You can write." His voice was deep, resonant.

"*Oui*. Naturally. I have been schooled by the sisters."

"You must be a great help to them."

The unexpected compliment caused her to miss a letter. She erased her mistake, and, blowing away the dust, rewrote it legibly. "I try to be. They are good to me, so I come to help from time to time for as long as they allow it."

"You are not a novice, or planning to become so?"

She had considered becoming a nun when she first began her schooling, but God had placed no such calling on her heart, so she soon gave up the idea. Still, it was no business of the trader's. "Life is filled with choices." He grunted. She paused and looked at him. "What? Why do you growl?"

Monsieur Dufour set his spoon down. He gave a small grin. "Did I growl? I apologize. You will likely marry then, or take a position?"

"Likely." She thought of Tristan, and the chalk fell to the floor. She stooped quickly to retrieve it.

"Do I make you nervous, mademoiselle, or merely angry?"

She turned her back and looked again at the shelves. "Neither. I do not even know you."

"This is true. I am only making conversation. Being polite. You have nothing to be angry or uneasy over concerning me. I swear to you, I know nothing of the child in the basket."

He sounded genuine. Sincere even. Conviction punished her. Perhaps she had been too quick to judge. Hadn't she been told often enough that she tended to such? "I beg your apologies, monsieur."

"It is all right. I, too, was unhappy to see *l'enfant abandonné*."

"It happens more frequently than you might suppose, and so often the infants do not survive."

"Then you are justified in your sadness. And perhaps your anger." His voice softened.

She turned and glanced at him. His features did not seem so dark as she first imagined. His eyes were soft, his face above the beard weathered by the sun. "You are a friend of the Sisters of Notre Dame. How is that?"

"I was a child in Montreal. My mother—God rest her soul— saw to it that my brother and I were brought up with prayers and Scripture. I am most often away now, making my trade in the Upper Country, but I come back now and again, every third or fourth year. It is a small thing for me, when I return, to give a gift in memory of the woman who raised me."

Brigitte nodded. "She would be pleased, I am sure."

The trader picked up his spoon and finished eating while Brigitte returned to her inventory. She completed her task and stepped out of the pantry as he rose to take his bowl to the waiting tub of wash water. Their paths intersected.

Her gaze lingered on him. A leather whang clubbed dark, thick hair at the back of his head, and a beard covered his face, but his eyes were actually blue and bright, like the colored glass in the chapel windows when the sun broke through. "Forgive me for saying, but you do not look like the traders I usually see in Montreal. The clerks and agents dress much finer ..." She dropped her gaze as a flush raced through her. "I am sorry. I should not say such things."

"It is all right. You are correct. I dress as the voyageurs because I prefer simplicity."

He puzzled her. Most men, even the boys her age signing up with the company as *engagés* or apprentice clerks, stuck out their chests and put on airs over their positions with the company. Grand adventurers they thought they were, off to make their fortunes. Most never returned. Those who came back, men like this one, usually wore fine coats and tall beaver hats. If Monsieur Dufour had come to the door dressed better, perhaps she would not have been so hasty in her conclusions.

Such thoughts! Did not the wealthy and privileged abandon their children as easily as the poor? She had seen it so.

She relaxed her shoulders. "My father is a voyageur. He brought me here from the lake country."

"Away from your mother?"

"She is dead, though I lived with her people for a while."

"Which people?"

"Ojibwa." She pressed her hands to the side of her dress. "His name is Marchal." She bit the corner of her lip and watched for his response.

His glance flickered, but he said nothing.

"You do not know him?"

"I am sorry. I do not."

Brigitte hugged her waist. "I am afraid, sometimes, that he is dead or has forgotten me. It has been a long time since last he came to Montreal."

"It is a hard life." He sighed. "The journey is long and tiresome."

The journey to Montreal she remembered as arduous. She and Papa rode in a big canoe for a long, long time with voyageurs who sang and cursed and left a rank smell imprinted on her memory. "*Oui.* I am fortunate to have been provided care in his absence."

His gaze scanned her face. Finally, he nodded and moved away to deposit his empty dish into the tub. "If I should ever meet this Marchal, I shall tell him that his daughter is well."

She dropped her gaze. "Thank you, monsieur."

"*Au revoir*, mademoiselle."

"*Au revoir.*" She looked up as he departed, and an ache pinched her chest. With his back to her, his shirt and sash made her think again of her father, but she swallowed the reminder away as her gaze lifted to the dark queue of hair that touched the base of his muscular neck. And for some reason, her thoughts flickered to Tristan who made such a pale comparison.

The following evening, the sun hovered over the housetops to the west, yet Brigitte was too busy to enjoy the lingering rays of day's end. She emptied the slop bucket out the back door and hurried inside to tidy up her aunt's small kitchen. She had succumbed to the notion of attending the party with Tristan Clarboux. As much as the idea galled her, it would be best not to concern *Tante* Eunice right now.

She slipped into her aunt's bedroom, and the old woman stirred. Brigitte stroked the woman's cool brow. "Are you awake, *Tante?*" From a pitcher on a side table, she poured fresh water into a cup.

A thin smile appeared on her aunt's pale lips as she opened her eyes. She struggled for voice. "Are you ready for the party?"

Tante Eunice hadn't noticed that Brigitte still wore her stained work dress. She slipped her hand behind her aunt's neck and offered a sip of water. "I am getting ready now. Angelique will be here soon to sit with you while I am gone."

"She's a good girl." Her head settled back into her pillow.

Brigitte nodded, but her aunt's papery eyelids had closed again, and her mouth dropped open in a soft snore.

Brigitte climbed the narrow stairs to her small bedroom and slipped out of her soiled apron and dress. Dipping a cloth in the bowl on her washstand, she wiped the day's dirt and sweat from her face, neck, and arms, and whispered a prayer. "*Cher Dieu,* I do not wish to attend this *masque.* Please do not let *Tante* Eunice suffer while I am away. Perhaps I am selfish. My life could be worse." She remembered the abandoned baby girl. "*Cher Dieu, laissez vivre l'enfant.*" She set aside the cloth and crossed herself. "I will call her Renée," she whispered. One day, should Monsieur Dufour return, she would tell him of his namesake.

She donned and buttoned her clean dress. She would not likely see the trader again when or if he returned. He himself had told her that he only came to Montreal once every several years, just as Papa had done. Look how Papa had disappeared. By the time Monsieur Dufour next visited the nuns, she would likely be married and raising her own family. *Only not to Tristan Clarboux.* A shiver raced up her arms as she tugged her cuffs straight.

"I pray it is not so," she whispered.

CHAPTER 2

"One cannot answer for his courage when he has never been in danger."
— François, duc de La Rochefoucauld, Prince de Marcillac

Brigitte brushed the wrinkles from her light blue gown. The dress was not elaborate, but it was pretty in its simplicity, with pleated sleeves and bits of lace around the collar and cuffs. She doubted the other guests would be dressed so commonly. "It is good enough for Tristan Clarboux," she told herself. Yanking her hair free of its binding, she brushed it before weaving a new braid that she wound at the base of her neck.

Coming down the stairs, she found Angelique nestled in a chair, working her darning needle through a frayed sock. "You are here. *Très bien*."

Angelique's blue eyes brightened against her pale face. She rested the darning in her lap. "Oo, la, la. So pretty you are."

Brigitte flicked the skirt of her gown. "It is my only nice dress. You have seen it many a Sunday."

"*Oui*. But Monsieur Clarboux has not. To think he wants to marry you." She sighed. "Are you not happy?"

Brigitte pursed her lips and bent to tie the silk ribbons of her leather shoes. "You are mistaken. He has said no such thing. He merely escorts me to a party."

"But I was here when he came to speak with Madam Tremblay, to seek your hand." Angelique covered her mouth. "Oh! It was to have been a secret. I should not have spoken."

Dieu merci! Tristan had spoken to her aunt of marriage? At least she'd been forewarned. There was time to plan her refusal. Brigitte straightened and laid a hand on the younger girl's shoulder. "Do not trouble yourself. No harm is done. I do not intend to have

Monsieur Clarboux."

"*Pourquoi?*" Her darning tumbled to the floor. "He is handsome, is he not? And very rich. Do you not find him desirable?"

"In truth, Angelique, I do not."

"I do not understand." Her white brow wrinkled. "His father is like a king. I see his carriage on the street. He is a prince!"

"Please do not go on about him so."

Angelique scooted back in the rocker and retrieved her darning. She pushed the needle through a woolen sock. "*Aie.*" She stuck her finger in her mouth, her look turning sullen.

"Now you have hurt yourself."

She wiped the damp finger on her apron. "Mademoiselle, who better could you hope for? I wish that such a man cared for me."

"I know not that he cares for me, only that he pursues me."

"Is it not one and the same?"

"Indeed not. I wish that it were."

"I do not understand at all."

The rattling of a carriage outside spared Brigitte from explaining. How could she explain something merely instinctual to the day-dreaming girl? "I do not wish for *Tante* Eunice to be disturbed, so I will meet Monsieur Clarboux and his sister outside. *Au revoir.*" Settling her shawl around her shoulders, Brigitte slipped out.

Tristan stood a few steps away. His gaze swept her head to toe with only a flick of his eyes toward the closed door beyond her.

Brigitte brushed at the fringes of her shawl, avoiding his eyes. "My aunt is not resting well. I do not wish to disturb her."

"Well, then." He hooked her arm through his, clasping it against his side as he led her to the carriage. She couldn't have withdrawn it if she'd tried. He released it to help her aboard, and Brigitte slid onto a cushioned seat. Tristan's sister, Camilla, sat opposite, her voluminous green gown, with its gold cording and lace-trimmed accents, filling the space. Tristan positioned himself beside Brigitte, pressing his shoulder and leg against hers in such a way that heat rushed up her neck. Camilla flitted a glance toward Brigitte before turning her gaze out the window.

"You look absolutely … endearing." Tristan's breath brushed her neck. Of course she wasn't beautiful. Next to Camilla, she looked like a pauper.

Brigitte leaned forward, hoping to free her shoulder. "Your gown is beautiful, Mademoiselle Clarboux. It matches your eyes."

Her attention drawn, Camilla gave Brigitte a small smile. "But I always liked brown eyes. They are so … so warm."

Brigitte gave a tiny nod. "*Merci*."

Camilla continued to study her. "Do you not think so, Tristan? Aren't her eyes lovely? They are trusting, wouldn't you say?"

Brigitte started when Tristan's hand wrapped around hers. "Yes. Didn't I say she looked endearing?"

Camilla gave a small harrumph as she turned her gaze out the window once more.

Breathe. Brigitte needed but one breath at a time to make it through the uncomfortable evening.

Some minutes later, as they pulled onto a brick-lined drive and up to the expansive home of the Clarboux family, Camilla handed Brigitte a blue feathered mask. Brigitte slipped it on. Tristan's black mask did little to disguise him, but that seemed hardly the point as the *masque* wasn't to be a full-blown affair.

Entering the house, heads of partygoers in wigs and powdered faces turned their way. Brigitte imagined their thoughts as their gazes slid over her. *This must be the Métis girl Tristan fancies.* Soon enough, their attention was captured by the lovely Camilla, and Brigitte drew in a breath, releasing it slowly. Tristan guided her through the room. Passing by those already gathered, he nodded a greeting but did not linger to introduce her. He led her past a trio of violinists warming up in the corner and drew her toward the bottom of a long staircase where his parents stood.

"Mother, allow me to introduce to you Mademoiselle Marchal."

Lowering her mask, his mother smiled, removing the severe lines from her brow. The older woman stood taller than Brigitte, but seemed more diminutive somehow, frail almost, with thin arms and slightly stooped shoulders. Perhaps it was Tristan's father standing next to her who made his wife seem so small. Tall and broad-shouldered, age had developed a bit of girth around his middle, and his hair had grayed, but he kept it in a thin queue rather than cover it with a wig. He was still handsome for a man his age and size, and Tristan would likely favor him as he grew older.

"So, this is the girl." Monsieur Clarboux eyed her from top to bottom. How his face would redden behind his mutton-chop whiskers if he knew what she thought of his son. Heat flooded up her neck, as much at having those thoughts discovered as at his sharp perusal over her. His gaze was so like Tristan's. Sister Agathe wouldn't give a smoked ham in the marketplace such a review. "What is your age, my dear?" he asked.

Brigitte's hand stole to her throat. "I am nearing twenty."

"Not quite past your prime then." He grinned at Tristan. "Eleanore, what do you think? Does she pass your inspection?"

Tristan's mother blushed. "Wh-why of course."

Brigitte shrunk inside. It was bad enough being put on display, but to be discussed like quality mutton?

"Really, Father. Isn't it enough that *I* admire her?" Tristan smiled at her.

The violinists struck a waltz. His father reached for Brigitte's hand. "We shall see. May I lead you in your first dance?"

Tristan released his hold on her and turned to his mother. Other couples swooped around the floor. Monsieur Clarboux's heavy palm settled on her waist as the other pressed against her hand.

Brigitte had only danced once before, on her sixteenth birthday. Her aunt and uncle had given her a special dinner with a few friends of the family, and an old gentleman from the marketplace joined them with his fife. Angelique, along with two younger sisters, had twirled about the floor with Brigitte, but it was not like this. Brigitte willed her mind to follow the elder Clarboux's lead.

He grinned. "It is obvious you have grown up among commoners and nuns."

She glanced to the musicians rather than look at him. "You forget my savage ancestry as well."

"Soon enough, you will become accomplished. Tristan will know what to teach you." His fingers plied her waist, edging closer to her hip as he pulled her about.

She cringed. "I suppose if one thinks such skills are important. I never thought dancing to be such a necessary part of my studies."

He guffawed. "You will find many such things important soon enough."

"I am certain I do not know to which things you refer, monsieur. Is it not important to know how to tend children and cook meals? To read and know sums? To care for the ill? Is it not important to learn kindness to others and respect to God?"

"And husband?"

His gaze seared her, and once again she looked away, the weight of his meaning pressing down on her as heavily as his hand on her waist. *"Oui.* And husband."

"You do not plan to become a nun and have God as your husband." His statement held no question, only certainty.

No, she did not intend to become a nun, but she would not satisfy him by acknowledging such intentions. "It remains to be seen. I was not always in the nun's school or my aunt's home, and I had not known my circumstances would lead me to either. Who can tell what choices I may make until they are presented?"

"You are at an age, mademoiselle, when such a choice may come sooner than you expect." He squeezed her hand tighter.

By the time the dance ended, Brigitte breathed better, but her palm was damp with sweat that was not her own, and her hairline tickled with misgiving over Monsieur Clarboux's remarks. Tristan must truly intend to press her into courtship.

As if beckoned by the thought, he appeared at her side and led her into another dance. He moved as smoothly as he could with her untrained feet inhibiting him. An apology rose to her lips, but she bit her tongue. Let him think her a clod. Perhaps he would give up on his attentions.

Instead, his lips stretched into a thin smile. "There was a moment yesterday in the market when I thought perhaps you meant to refuse me. Perhaps you only worried about the gala, *non*? Yet, as you can see, you are well accepted here and have quite charmed my parents. You will become more comfortable at these events in time. You will see."

She wanted to tell him she had no intentions of becoming comfortable, but what good would it do to anger him now, here in his home? She tripped over his feet, and he steadied her, smiling still.

For the next hour, Tristan kept her near his side or within reach on the dance floor. His gazes grew warmer. "You are not too tired, I hope. You are not used to so much dancing."

She shook her head. "No, I am not used it."

"Let us sit for a while."

She followed him to a pair of empty chairs near the back of the room. She took a seat and watched Camilla dancing with a man wearing a white dove's mask. "Your sister is very graceful."

Tristan shrugged. "She is skilled at the art of dancing and other such forms of coquetry."

Brigitte blushed, thankful that the heat she already felt would hide it. "She was friendly. I might like her."

"If you knew her better?" He reached for her hand and pressed it gently. She looked at him. "Perhaps you shall."

Brigitte tried to convince herself of some goodness in him. Was she wrong, even now, to hold him in such contempt? What if, like René Dufour, she'd judged Tristan too harshly? Perhaps her misgivings were unfounded. Perhaps the gleam she'd noted so often in his eyes was nothing more than admiration. He'd never been anything but civil, if not entirely chivalrous, and what experience of men did she have?

Oui, perhaps she should give him the benefit of her doubt. She would not consent to marry him, but mayhap she could at least give him time and some small attention. She allowed herself to offer him a generous smile.

He tucked her arm in his again and drew her to her feet. "Why, I do believe that is the first smile I have seen from you in a long time. For a while, I feared I had lost my advantage."

"It would be rude of me to seem unappreciative of having been so entertained on such a lovely evening."

"You must be thirsty. You have taken no refreshment. Come."

He led her to a table dressed in fine array, with laced cloth, sparkling china, and a glittering candelabra. He poured her a beverage, which she sniffed cautiously.

Tristan laughed. "It will not harm you."

Blushing, she sipped the spiced apple cider.

"Ah, here is Camilla. I will leave you with her momentarily. There is something I must attend to."

For the first time since Brigitte had danced with his father, Tristan left her side. She sighed and drank down her cider.

Camilla stepped closer, her own wine goblet cradled near her chin, her eyes brilliant. "You have warmed to my brother." She sipped and glanced toward Tristan's back as it disappeared between guests.

"He has been … attentive."

Camilla's brow lifted. "I am sure. Does this please you?"

"Please me? Why …" She shook her head. "I—I do not know what to say. I am uncertain about him."

"I sensed earlier that perhaps you did not seek his attention. Was I wrong?"

"*Non*. Not wrong."

"You have instincts. Instincts are best often followed."

Brigitte gasped, then slammed her lips together.

"You are surprised I say such a thing because I am his sister? Do not be. I know things about him a sister should not know." Camilla applied a rigid smile to her lips as she looked away. "I would be free of him, but I find I cannot be free at an innocent's expense."

Brigitte's lips parted in shock as the taste of cider turned to acid on her tongue. Her mouth dried. She could think of no sensible reply. Sealing her lips, she followed Camilla's gaze to where Tristan reappeared among their guests.

"Do you find yourself charmed by him now?" Camilla dipped her head elegantly and backed away as Tristan approached.

Stars crowded the sky overhead as Tristan escorted Brigitte to his carriage. The air had cooled and, like a balm, soothed her over-warm skin. Only a short time more and she would be home again where she belonged with *Tante* Eunice.

Tristan offered his hand as she ascended the carriage step, the ruffles on his wrist brushing hers.

"*Merci.*"

He tipped his head and allowed her time to arrange herself on the seat. Her conversation with Camilla niggled at the back of her thoughts, and she released a long breath. She had managed the evening as best she could. Soon she would be safely home.

The carriage tilted with Tristan's weight as he settled into the seat across from Brigitte. He rapped on the ceiling, and the carriage lurched away from the curb. "I hope you are not too fatigued from the evening, Brigitte. I sometimes find the dancing tiring, when one would rather spend time in another's quiet company."

Brigitte twisted sideways. Her chaperone. They mustn't leave without Camilla. "We've gone without your sister—"

"I thought it unnecessary to withdraw her from the party. She is quite taken with Monsieur Bonnet. He did not seem inclined to part her company either."

Brigitte's heartbeat picked up speed. "But my aunt—"

Tristan reached across the small space between them and covered her hands with his. She curled her fingers as a shiver raced down her spine. "It is of no consequence. Your aunt need not know I brought you home without a chaperone." His gaze rested on her as he raised her hand to his lips and lingered.

The curtains of the coach were drawn closed. Her heart beat guiltily. "Tristan—"

"Shh, though I do like to hear my name on your lips."

She pulled her hand free and reached for the door. "We must not return without my chaperone."

"Careful." He put out his arm and stopped her from opening the door. "You must not fall." The next moment, he was off his seat and cushioned next to her, his body heat warming her. "You worry so." He took her hand again and urged her to relax against the plush cushions. "You will soon be safely home."

The carriage moved slowly. So slowly that the wheels beneath them and the horses' shoes made hardly a sound on the cobbled street. A tiny lantern wobbled on its hanger in the corner of the carriage, as light beams and shadows bounced over them. She breathed to calm the racing of her heart. After all, what was she to do? Race into Tristan's house crying out for Camilla to attend her? She gave him a hesitant glance.

He smiled, his face inches from hers. "That is better. We left early. Your reputation is in no danger on account of the hour. I would keep you from returning to a sick house longer if I dared." Raising her fist to his lips, he opened her fingers and traced a trail over her palm and up her wrist, pushing back the lace of her sleeve.

She pulled in a sharp breath and tugged at her hand. "Tristan, you must stop." A cold fear wormed into her as he raised drooping eyelids and moved closer. His breath washed over her in warm wisps as he pushed a tendril of hair back from her temple. Her heart throbbed against her ribs. He must hear it! It pulsed against her eardrums. Her hands fell against his chest with nowhere else to go. "Tristan, I forbid such behavior." She pushed against him, but he was like a rock, immovable.

He grinned. "Brigitte." Before she could breathe, his mouth pressed against hers, crushing her lips until she tasted blood. She struggled beneath his grasp, but he only pressed his body closer, squeezing her until air grunted from her lungs.

Waves of anger washed over her, drowning out the cold fear. When at last he broke the kiss, she cried out and shoved him backward. Arms free at last, she slapped him hard enough to sting her palm.

His eyes widened. His chest rose and fell as rage twitched across his features. With a glare, he struck her in return, his hand slamming across her cheek with a jolt that made her see white. Then black. Tristan had turned out the lantern.

He clutched her shoulder in one hand and yanked her against him. His other hand pinched her jaw. The bruising force of his kiss brought tears to her eyes as she gripped his arms, pushing against him. Never in her life had she been kissed by a man, and now, with Tristan smashing his mouth against hers, the very violence of it nauseated her. Her neck and jaw ached. When she thought she might suffocate, he released her and shoved her back into the corner. She sobbed and crossed her arms before her face, thinking he would force himself upon her further. When she dared to peek at him, he rubbed his ruffled sleeve across his mouth.

"Soon you will not push me away, mademoiselle."

She shuddered and gulped on another sob.

"Do you doubt it? We will be wed, then we shall both see how pliable you will become."

She wanted to spit at him but feared what he would do. Her cheek throbbed. She sniffed back her tears. "I will never marry you."

He leaned forward, and Brigitte pressed deeper into the corner of the carriage. "You will see. You will do all that I ask, and more."

CHAPTER 3

"All alone, she stood, holding in her weeping. Seldom had I seen such bravery in one so young."
— Agathe, Sister of the Congregation of Notre-Dame

Brigitte quaked as she hastened up the pathway to the house. Her hand shook on the door latch. She fumbled, but the door swung inward, and Angelique reached for Brigitte's arm, tugging her over the threshold.

Angelique lifted a chamber stick. Standing in the candlelight, her eyes grew wide. "I am so glad you have come. Madam Tremblay needs you."

"Something is wrong?" Brigitte removed her shawl and hurried through the house as Angelique followed behind, the candlelight throwing shadows on the walls. "What happened?"

"She awoke and cried out. I found her gasping for breath. Then she went to sleep again, but even in her sleep she struggles so." Tears choked Angelique's voice. "I tried to wake her and could not. I was so afraid. I held her hand and spoke to her and prayed you would come home."

Brigitte rushed into her aunt's bedroom and looked down on the shrunken cheeks and chalky flesh. Her shame and fear over Tristan's ill-treatment fled away. She took the candle from Angelique's quivering hand, casting a halo of light over the older woman's form. Her aunt lay still, her breath uneven. "I thank you for staying with her. Bring me some water and a cloth. *S'il vous plaît.*"

Angelique nodded and fled the room.

"*Mon Dieu*, show me what to do." Brigitte set the candle on the nightstand and pulled a stool close. "*Tante* Eunice, can you hear me?" Brigitte laid her hand on her aunt's brow and smoothed back wispy white hair. Her lips looked cracked and dry.

When Angelique returned, Brigitte bathed the old woman's skin. She squeezed droplets of water onto her lips, but *Tante* Eunice did not awaken. Her breaths were so slight, Brigitte's chest tightened, almost as though she herself would soon forget to breathe. *Tante* Eunice must not leave her. Not yet. Not now.

Angelique touched her shoulder. "Shall we pray for her?"

Brigitte blinked away a tear. *"Oui."* Together, they fell to their knees beside the bed and prayed.

Angelique rested fingertips on Brigitte's shoulder. "I will stay with you if you wish."

"Oui, just tonight perhaps. I will sit with *Tante* Eunice while you rest. Go to my bed. I will fetch you if I have need of you, but at least one of us should sleep."

Angelique wiped her eyes on her sleeve and nodded, rising to her feet. "I hope she does not die."

Brigitte stood, and the girl wrapped her arms around her. "We have prayed. It is all we can do."

Brigitte did not wake Angelique during the night as no change came to her aunt. Brigitte dozed in a chair by her aunt's side, but nightmares stalked her. Her bones ached from the chair, and perhaps from the dancing, as well as the unpleasantness of the carriage ride home.

Tante Eunice must not die. However would Brigitte manage without her? She could not live at the convent without becoming a novitiate. She was too old to continue her schooling, and when the other students returned later on in the summer, they would take over the market tasks and kitchen work Brigitte sometimes helped with. Even the garden weeding and harvest would be well in hand.

Whatever funds her uncle had left upon his death must be nearly depleted. Her aunt had hoped to see Brigitte settled with a home of her own and a husband to provide for her. Since there was no one else to care for her or marry her ... Brigitte swallowed against the tightening in her throat. She would be at the mercy of Tristan Clarboux. Now she understood the depth of Camilla's ominous warnings.

In the dawn, Brigitte stared out her aunt's bedroom window. Perhaps she might remain in the house, care for it, take in sewing or any work she could find.

Tante *Eunice must not die. I am not ready to lose her, God. Have mercy. Have mercy!*

Brigitte went into the kitchen and built a small fire to boil water for her tea, to wash life into her face, to bathe her aunt's dry skin. The morning was cool, but the sun would warm the day soon. She poured water from a pail into the kettle hanging on the hook above the hearth. Then, as she set cups and the box of tea on the table, Angelique entered the room. Brigitte offered her a tired smile.

"Mademoiselle." Angelique gasped. Brigitte stiffened. Angelique stared at Brigitte's face.

Brigitte raised a hand to the tender flesh of her cheekbone. The bruise must be something livid. She turned her back. "It is nothing."

Angelique scurried around the table and stared again. "It is a wound."

Brigitte shook her head. Angelique reached for a cloth and drenched it in the nearby pail. She approached Brigitte to tend her with it. Brigitte pushed her hand away.

"Allow me, mademoiselle, please. You must."

Brigitte lowered her hand and allowed the girl to administer the cool cloth to the painful bruise.

"What happened to you?"

Brigitte averted her eyes as Angelique held the damp cloth against her skin. She didn't want to burden Angelique with her troubles concerning Tristan. "I fell against the carriage, actually. Stupid of me."

Angelique sighed. "You must have given poor Monsieur Clarboux a fright. At least Madam Tremblay has not seen." She lifted one corner of her lips as she removed the cloth and turned away. "You must take care to watch where you are going."

"*Oui*. I must."

Angelique placed her hands on her narrow hips and sighed. "Do you wish me to stay longer so that you may rest?"

"*Non*." Brigitte shook her head. "I cannot sleep now. You go home. Your *maman* will wonder what has become of you."

"I will come again later. Perhaps Madam Tremblay will feel better soon."

"Let us pray so. I thank you for staying with us last night."

"Goodbye then."

"*Au revoir*, Angelique."

Brigitte drank her tea alone. Her friend's hopeful words did little to take away Brigitte's fears that the last of her family lay dying, and she would be left alone to fend off the evil of Tristan Clarboux.

René Dufour ran down the list of supplies he'd acquired for the voyage. Lead shot, flints, trade beads, point blankets, sugar, coffee, flour, raisins, dried apples; cloth in scarlet, blue, gray, calico, and flannel; thread, finger rings, buttons, awls, knives, buckles, tin pans, copper kettles, washing soap, tobacco. What remained to be gotten? Beaver traps, seeds, the inevitable rum. So many supplies, but he wouldn't have to move them all himself.

Newly hired men, *mangeurs de lard* or pork-eaters, as they referred to the seasonal voyageurs, would transfer the cargo to the waiting Montreal canoes at Lachine. Each *bateau* would carry 3000 pounds, including crew. René would organize them, making sure the voyageurs didn't lose their cargo in the rapids or on the swells of the great lake. Such work required skill, sound judgment, and good food. His stomach rumbled.

He hoisted a small pack onto his shoulder and stepped from the warehouse into the street. Blinking against the brightness of the sun, he whistled as he strolled toward the market stalls where the smell of warm bread called him to breakfast.

Habitants crowded the streets this morning. Tomorrow, on Sunday, the world would quiet, but today the markets flourished. He steered around women in shawls carrying baskets on their arms and past men in tall beaver hats. His beaver plews wore elegantly on the heads of the *bourgeois*, yet he was comfortable in his shirt and leggings.

Stepping back for a group of children that scurried across his path, he paused to buy an apple from a vendor. He tucked it into his pocket to savor later, after his bread and meat.

"Oof!" His step faltered as a slight woman jarred into him.

Startled eyes, like a deer's in flight, dashed a glance at him, but barely long enough to utter a hasty, *"Pardon,"* before she sprang around him and hurried on.

She must have just come from across the street. René stared after her. He frowned. Could it have been the little mademoiselle from the nunnery? Surely it must have been she. He gazed at her back as she wound through the crowded street. Her long black braid swung as she turned a corner. *Oui*, so like a frightened doe she looked. Was it he who caused such fear? She had seemed not to recognize him.

His breakfast forgotten, René followed. He reached the corner where she'd disappeared and looked about. Ah, there, in her gray homespun dress and her telltale braid. Once, twice, she caught her breath, looked left and right before hurrying on.

A bell from one of the churches rang in the distance, its rolling gong calling out a reminder to the devout. *She goes to the convent.*

The girl turned another corner, disappearing again.

Non. Non, she does not.

He adjusted the pack he shouldered. "You wear me out with this running of yours, mademoiselle," he murmured, hiking uphill, beads of sweat gathering on his brow. Then, just as he thought he would be wiser to return to his work and give up the chase, he turned the corner, and there she stood, pressed against a stone building, panting for breath.

She jerked around, her eyes wide. He held up his hands in a calming gesture. "I apologize."

She stepped away.

"Stop." He reached for the sleeve of her dress, halting her.

She darted a look at him. Breathing hard, she puffed at a wisp of hair that fell across her discolored cheek. "M—Monsieur Dufour. What do you want?"

She did recognize him.

He let go of her sleeve. "I saw you running. I recognized you from our conversation several days past, and I wondered if there was some trouble." He raised his brow as he watched her, waiting for her response.

Her gaze flitted past him up and down the street. She shook her head, hesitated, then nodded. "*Oui*. There is trouble."

"Some assistance is needed perhaps?"

Her gaze came back to him. "If you would be so kind as to see me home."

"I am happy to do so. Lead the way."

She moved up the street. René walked beside her. What must she fear that led her to accept his help? He glanced down at her as she clenched and unclenched her hands in the folds of her skirt. "Are you in harm's way, mademoiselle?"

She sighed and looked up, catching his gaze before staring ahead. "*Oui*. I believe so." She gave a curt tilt of her head directing them down a side street leading to the edge of the district. "I am hoping to avoid someone who wishes to ... to marry me."

René clucked his tongue. "Ah, a pursuer has made himself a nuisance."

"More than a nuisance. My aunt has died. I come now from her funeral. He was there. He knows I am alone now." Her voice quivered.

René narrowed his gaze at the fading bruise on her cheekbone.

"You do not wish to marry this gentleman then."

"I do not." She nearly spat the words. "I hate him."

"Surely he would not press such a suit if he had no hope of winning your favor."

She stopped and pinned him with her brown-eyed stare. "He cares nothing of my favor. He ..." She touched her bruised cheek, and a flush infused her neck, enriching her dark skin.

René's throat tightened. "Never mind. You need not explain."

They continued walking another block until they reached a corner where a small stone house sat surrounded by a picket fence. A worn footpath led to the stoop. Two white-framed windows in need of new paint faced the street, and an upper story dormer looked out to the side road. Flowers edged the path, and a small, well-tended vegetable garden graced the corner of the yard. Likely the girl's work. The girl turned into the cozy yard while René stalled outside on the street.

She paused and turned to him. "Monsieur, you are most kind to assist me. Might I offer you some refreshment?"

Dare he enter the house? He had other things to which he must attend. Perhaps she continued to fear for safety here in her own home. He stepped off the street. "*Oui*, mademoiselle. I would welcome a drink of water."

She licked her lips and turned to the door, leading the way inside. "Please, sit." She moved toward the dry sink where a pail and dipper stood on a sideboard.

He lowered himself onto a straight-backed chair next to a bare wooden table and settled his shoulder pack on the floor. She ladled water into a tin cup and handed it to him.

"I am indebted." He took the cup and swallowed down the drink. His throat had been dry indeed.

She took the cup from his hand. "More?"

He shook his head. "*Non*. I am refreshed. *Merci*. I will be on my way and allow you your peace."

"It is I who am indebted, Monsieur ..."

"Dufour."

"*Oui*. I remember, Monsieur Dufour." She leaned against the dry sink and folded her arms over her waist. "You are preparing to return to the west?"

He nodded. "*Oui*. Very soon now. I intend to leave Lachine before week's end."

"Where will your travels take you, if I may ask it?"

"First to rendezvous at Fort William. Then to a post in the western Lake Superior country. It is a rugged land."

She nodded. "I remember."

"Do you?"

"Some of it. As I said when last we met, it is the land of my mother's people. Perhaps my papa still."

"It is a shame you cannot go to them again, now that you have lost your aunt. But you are learned in the ways of your aunt's people now. You will live better here than you could in such strange country." He lifted the pack over his shoulder and stood. Part of him wanted to remain in the coolness of the house speaking of pleasantries, but he had tarried as long as he dared. He must be at Lachine in a few hours, and she was safely at home. He turned toward the door.

"It does not sound so strange."

He turned to her once more, but she stared at the place he'd been sitting, a strange light burning behind her dark eyes. "Do not think otherwise. It is a wild country. Little is likely as you remember."

"You do not know what I remember."

"You remember your childhood. Life changes for the older ones. There is much work, little pleasure."

She shrugged. "Perhaps that is so. Still, it is my mother's home and once was mine."

He moved to the door. "It is good to have met you, mademoiselle."

"And you, René Dufour."

He glanced back and caught the dip of her head. "And what name shall I remember you by?"

"I am Brigitte."

"Brigitte Marchal. See? I did not forget. I will pay attention should your papa cross my path."

"Thank you again. For everything."

"You are welcome."

He stepped into the bright sunlight. He had gotten her safely away from the suitor she feared. She should not give herself to such a man if it were he who caused the bruises. She was wise to stay away. Soon enough, there would likely be another to speak for her. She was a comely girl, after all. But she should choose soon. Worse things happened than to marry out of necessity. Of that, he was certain.

Brigitte spun on her heels and hastened into her *tante* and *oncle's* bedroom. Dropping to her knees before an old trunk under the window, she moved the lamp and doily lying on top and lifted the lid. The hinges creaked with age, and out of the recesses of the trunk rushed the smell of old leather, gun oil, and *Oncle* Robert. Strange how it yet lingered.

His hearty laugh and twinkling eyes swirled to life before her. She grasped the upper layer of clothing, folded with care and packed with memories. She caressed it to her chest like a babe and breathed in the welcome aroma. Tears crept to her eyes, blinding her in the dim room. How she missed them both.

She rose to push the curtains back, hugging the bundle tight. Standing in the shaft of light, tears swept down her cheeks. Alone. With only the specter of Tristan before her. She dashed the back of her hand across her cheek and sucked in a breath.

Brigitte bent to the trunk again. Setting the clothes aside, she dug deeper. *Oncle* Robert's pipe, a beaver hat, and other sundry articles brought more memories.

At the bottom, she discovered the things she sought. Two shirts, two pairs of leggings, trousers, two handkerchiefs, and two *braillets*. In a larger bundle, a hooded *capot* and sash. She looked over the two breechcloths and set them aside with the other articles. Digging to the bottom of the trunk she found two woolen, green-and-red striped point blankets. Her relatives used these Indian trade blankets on their bed each winter. A single two-point trade blanket like them hung over the foot of her bed also.

She laid the garments on the bed so recently vacated by her aunt. Unfolding them, she studied their sturdiness. They'd stored well. They would only be slightly too large. *Oncle* Robert had not always been so generously proportioned. As a young voyageur of twenty, he'd been at least eight inches taller than she, but not a great deal heavier. The length of the leggings and trousers might prove her only difficulty, but she was adept with a needle.

Stowing the other things away once again, she took the costume and went to work. Licking the end of a stiff piece of heavy thread, she pushed it through the eye of a needle. God willing, she would make the clothing wearable again, and, with fortune, she would find a way to be at Lachine before week's end, traveling a *voyage en bateau* with René Dufour.

CHAPTER 4

"Bon voyage! Bon voyage, mes voyageurs!"
—Habitants of Lachine

R ené Dufour stood before the counter inside the supply depot. "I have no room for more axes. Give me more shot instead." He pocketed his list as the white-haired clerk wandered down a long row of shelves.

René whistled as anticipation hummed through his body like it always did when departure grew near. With eight to ten men assigned to each thirty-six-foot boat, his crew was nearly complete. The three Montreal canoes would carry several tons each of trade merchandise back to Fort William, where traders like him and his brother would be outfitted for wintering at a trading post in the interior.

The clerk returned and handed a heavy bag to René, then set a large pot on the counter. "Here is another kettle like the others I gave you. You have credit enough from the agent if you want it."

"I will take it." René took the kettle and the fifteen-pound bag of shot and left the building. Claude's wife would like a new kettle. His brother had risen from apprentice to clerk just as René had done several years earlier, managing the flow of merchandise in and out of Fort St. Louis, a busy trading post at Lake Superior's head. René hoped things had gone smoothly for Claude this past season while he had been away.

"You there." He caught the attention of a young *engagé* and handed him the items. "Take these and put them with the rest. See that everything is secured for tomorrow. We will leave at an early hour. See to it you go to sleep without first putting fire in your belly. Tell the others. I may wake them without warning. Tomorrow we begin putting muscle on those sticks of yours." He gave a nod toward the boy's thin arms.

As the crew followed orders, René shook his head. These voyageurs, so many of them boys, freshly cut from their mothers' apron strings, would sing and shout when they departed. Sometimes they would whine and fuss. Before long, the seasoned woodsmen, those like René himself, would give these youngsters a short course in manhood.

René grinned as he moved past each canoe, double-checking for leaks and to see if the supply bales had been properly secured. Another young one strode past, ignoring him. René glanced after the boy, taking in the short stature and slim build. That one would tire quickly, but his size was good for the cramped canoe.

The youngster stood before the door of the company depot. René straightened to watch. The boy rubbed his palms against his trousers and blew out a breath. René remembered the day he had signed on to work for the company. He had not suffered such nervousness. The lad on the warehouse stoop touched the latch of the door. His shoulders rose and fell before he pushed it open then stepped inside. "You find your courage," René murmured. "As we all must."

The following dawn spread like warm, lapping water across the earth. Seasoned voyageurs and new *engagés* moved quietly among the boats and wares, their barely checked energy humming through the group.

Wives, sweethearts, and children stood along the shore, some weeping, others embracing their departing men, murmuring their sad farewells.

René stood on the bank near the boats. Pressing his index finger and thumb into his mouth, he let out a sharp whistle. The cacophony of voices fell silent. "Voyageurs of the North West Company!" he called out. "You have been warned, I hope, of what lies ahead." His gaze swept across the voyageurs, pausing to penetrate the freshest among them. "Your romantic notions of adventure can be put away. You will be hungry. You will grow tired.

You will learn to live with wet on your skin and cold in your bones. Remember that if you fail to bear your weight, you will likely die.

"Your mothers and sweethearts will not be present to scold or take care of you. Your father's teaching is passed, and now you must be men." He grinned, then shrugged. "Perhaps you may even come to enjoy your freedom."

A few chuckles broke out among those gathered, and René caught sight of a woman swatting her husband with her handkerchief.

"Some of you have been to the lake country before and have learned what that means. My friend Jacques, who is to be our guide, has wintered many seasons in the interior." He cast a grin at a grizzled man in a sweat-stained shirt and trousers, a colorful *ceinture fléchée* wrapped about his thick waist. "If you have questions, you may bring them to me or to him. However, he is not obligated to answer you."

René scanned the crowd, looking each man in the eye. "In each *canot* you will heed your *avant* who stands at the front of each boat to guide you. You will do as we instruct. I am captain of the lead canoe. Jacques is captain of the rear. In the middle, your *avant* is Monsieur Munion."

Munion, a short man with dark eyes and hair, a barrel chest, and a broad smile, leered at the men, followed by a gruff belly chuckle. René swept a hand toward the only men seated in the boats thus far, the steersmen. "Your *gouvernails* you must also hearken to." Each steersman lifted his paddle from the stern so the crews could identify their leaders. "I trust you have each found a place for your personal provisions. Now you must say farewell to this civilized land—to those you love—and take your places."

Someone began a song as they hastened into the canoes. Several others joined in the singing.

René watched them clamor for their positions, wobbling the heavily laden boats with entry. Water rose to the gunwales as they settled inside. Besides the men's personal effects, each canoe carried supplies, equipment, and eight-hundred weight of grease and dried food for the journey, all stacked in tightly bound bales filling every available inch of space around them. René raised a brow at the new *engagés* awkwardness, but he did not doubt they would grow sure-footed. Fear of swamping and daily practice would teach them to make their adjustments with grace.

Jacques barked commands at several in the rear canoe. René's gaze fell on the young *engagé* he'd seen yesterday, now seated in the center canoe. He was one of the smallest of the bunch. His face hadn't yet grown a whisker.

René strode slowly along the bank and rested a foot on the edge of the canoe as the lad wrestled to position himself alongside his seatmate. "I see you have decided to join us."

The boy looked up briefly, then tucked his chin low, his pretense at calming youthful nerves and excitement obvious.

"How old are you?"

"I—I am eighteen."

"I would have said fifteen."

Dark eyes flashed up at him before falling downward again. "Eighteen, monsieur."

René removed his foot, looking up and down the line. "I am René." He shouted the words loud enough for all to hear. "I do not stand on anything more formal. You may call me René, or simply Dufour if you wish."

He stalked away. René had worked the merchant ships for three years, from the time he left school at sixteen. At nineteen, he'd signed on as an apprentice clerk with the North West Company and spent four years in Upper Canada. Living alone, without hearth or kin, in a land as foreign as any, he'd learned to manage his fears. This lad would too.

Brigitte's hands trembled. She gripped her pole tighter, hoping to still her shaking, but her heart raced in her chest as sweat greased her hands.

She had known she would meet René eventually, but she had prayed it would not be until they'd gone far from Lachine. Here, if she were discovered, she could still be put off the boat.

But he did not recognize me. He is too busy to notice. It will be fine. I must simply do my part. There are some here younger than I, and one at least as small. I have nothing to fear. Nothing to fear.

She finally stilled her shaking enough to peek at the man. He strode up and down the length of the three *bateaux*, covering nearly a hundred feet of shoreline. She watched as he examined each boat with a stern eye, seeming to miss nothing, and yet he had missed her.

His gaze flashed past her again, and she looked away, tugging down her cap.

The captains and crew settled into their places, blocking her view of René. Each *gouvernail* called out to his crew, and poles dipped into the water, hers included.

The boat lunged and turned against the current. René shouted from the lead *bateau*, and the boats straightened their course. Hankies waved in the air, and the men broke into a *chanson de voyage* as cheers rose from the shore.

> *"Derrière chez nous, il y a un étang*
> *(Behind the manor lies the mere),*
> *En roulant ma boule.*
>
> *En roulant ma boule.*
>
> *Rouli, roulant, ma boule roulant,*
> *En roulant, ma boule roulant,*
> *En roulant ma boule..."*

With each push of the pole, the crew developed a more

synchronous rhythm with the song. In a dozen strokes, they had developed a steady momentum. Brigitte's spirits lifted as the singing continued. She smiled, caught as much in the swell of adventure as in the fact that Tristan Clarboux would soon be nothing more than a bad memory. As the crew sang the refrain, she joined in, the words coming out barely above her breath but the tune capturing her.

After twenty minutes of steady poling, the singing died down. The good folk who'd seen them off had long disappeared from view. Fatigue already challenged the fresh crew. Brigitte's arms ached, and her palms stung.

Twenty minutes. How could she manage sixteen hours a day for weeks? The foolishness of her decision settled on her with a new weight. *It is better than marrying Tristan.* That thought alone filled her limbs with renewed vigor. She paused only a second, long enough to deepen her breaths, before plunging her pole against the rocky river bottom again.

Time passed, and her shoulders burned. Her legs cramped in their unchanged position in the bottom of the boat. Her stomach growled. Why hadn't she taken more time to break her fast that morning? Because she had been too anxious to eat. Now she simply must suffer.

As the sun glimmered through the leafy boughs of the trees, she thought she might drop her pole. Then the village of Ste-Anne-de-Bellevue came into view. She pulled in a breath of relief. A rest lay at hand, for the voyageurs would not begin their journey without seeking a blessing from their patron saint.

Within minutes, they had moored their boats. From the front of her canoe, a hat was passed back. Brigitte pulled out one of the coins she'd been paid when she was given her equipment by the company and deposited it in the hat with those of the others. The money would be given to the priest. He, in turn, would pray for a prosperous voyage and a safe return to friends and families.

For them, God. Not for me, for I shall never return. An unwelcomed image of Tristan crept into her thoughts. Had he gone to her house to find her yet? Did he realize she'd gone away?

Hopefully, her ruse would last, and the truth would be discovered too late. Better still if it was never discovered, for who knew how long the arm of the Clarboux family reached?

Perhaps they would think her a fool and not bother.

She followed the others as they disembarked, heading to the village's church. The church bell chimed, and her thoughts turned to the Congregation of Notre Dame. What would Sister Agathe think when she learned of Brigitte's deception?

She'd left a note for Angelique, another lie telling her she'd gone to stay with the nuns for a time. She only hoped the girl found the note before Tristan did and that her disguise kept her safe. *Help me escape, dear God. Do not let Monsieur Dufour or any of the others discover me.*

Weariness threatened to beat Brigitte down. Their prayers at Ste-Anne had given short reprieve, and they had been poling, paddling, and towing in the hours since. She had only to imagine some mistake she might have made to lead Tristan to her, and her arms gained strength.

"*Pose!*" The *gouvernails* finally called for a halt once they'd passed into the stretch of water the steersman called the Lake of Two Mountains. "After our rest, we will veer for the mouth of the Ottawa River."

Brigitte took a long breath. Her arms rested limply against her sides. The canoes glided one by one to the forested bank. Men laid aside their poles and paddles, groaning as they disembarked and towed the *bateaux* ashore. She was not alone in her agony at least.

A voyageur about her own age who had been positioned two places ahead of her caught her eye and sighed while he flexed his arms. "It will be hard to start again," he said, reaching into the pouch around his neck. He pulled out a chaw of tobacco and a pipe.

She nodded, not trusting her voice.

He glanced at the leather bag hanging around her neck. "You have tobacco?"

Brigitte curled her lip and shook her head.

He extended his pouch. "Have some of mine."

"*Merci, non.*" She kept her voice as low as she could. Better she sounded like an immature boy than a girl. She opened her satchel and pulled out a dry biscuit.

He grinned and bobbed his head. Lighting his pipe, he sucked hard, and a halo of thick smoke rose up around him.

"I will stretch the kinks from my legs." Brigitte tipped her head toward the woods and left him standing there with his smoke. Most of the men seemed more anxious for their tobacco than to relieve themselves, so she used the moment to find privacy.

Going deeper into the forest but staying within hearing should they be called back to the boats, she hurried to find relief. Mosquitoes droned about her head and attacked her exposed skin. She swatted and jerked at their bites, hurrying to finish. Securing the string on her uncle's trousers and adjusting her shirt and sash, she hustled back, only to stumble upon men taking care of their business not ten feet from the shore. Silencing a gasp, Brigitte lowered her eyes and hurried on.

They set their first camp near the upper end of the lake. There the voyageurs received their regale—a keg of rum.

Hoping to fit in, Brigitte took a cup and pretended to enjoy the small sips that sloshed against her pinched lips. The smell alone turned her stomach. The fellow who'd offered her his tobacco smiled in her direction and lifted his cup in a toast as he sang. She couldn't help but grin and finally chuckled, taking up his joyful spirit.

The voyageurs drank into the night. Brigitte stepped around wrestling matches and avoided conversations. On the edge of the camp lingered one of the *bourgeois* partners, the captains, and René. She spied him, resting on his blanket, his hands tucked beneath his head.

She edged along the encampment, looking for a place to unroll her bedding, making a wide berth around René as she moved away from the rest of the party. She arranged her bed against the trunk of a tree where she could look out. Settling herself on her blanket, Brigitte kept one hand on the knife tucked into her sash until, blinking into the dancing firelight and shadows, she was unable to stay awake any longer.

The call to move on came well before dawn. Brigitte's body ached with stiffness as she returned to her position in the *bateau*. The fellow who'd toasted her last evening gave her a weary glance, chagrin stretched over his features as he climbed into his place. Then she saw only his back as he picked up his paddle.

"Hup! Hup! Hup!" The call traveled up the line of *bateaux*.

"Pull!" The *gouvernail* of her canoe shouted. With a few calls and shouts traveling up and down the line of *bateaux*, they fell into rhythm, paddling and poling up the Ottawa. The men who had been drinking last night were slow to join in the singing today.

As the early morning mist burned away, the river dazzled in the sunshine. The voyageurs' endless chorus drowned out the screaming in her muscles.

She soaked in the sublime freshness of the air and the coolness of the water dribbling from her fingertips each time they touched the water. The speed of the passing swirls of deep, blue eddies mesmerized her, as did the flashing bright colors of the voyageurs in the high-ended *canots de maître* on either side, behind, and ahead of her. The hours melted away.

"Are you awake?" the steersman called out from the rear of her *bateau*. "You had better be. Hear that song?"

She strained to hear above the voices. Not music swelling from the lips of the voyageurs. Rather a rasping growl from the throat of some demon in the river.

She dipped her paddle in time with the others but stretched to peer around the shoulder in front of her. The water grew shallower.

"Poles!" the *avant* called. She set her paddle aside and pushed her pole into the river's bottom. The current pushed harder against them. Sweat popped out on her brow, but she dared not pause to wipe it away. A breathless glance again caught the canoe ahead of her as it beached along the riverbank. A few small cottages dotted the shore, but woods stretched beyond. Her own canoe swam to a stop. Panting from the exertion, she disembarked along with her companions.

"The Long Sault!" a voice called.

She looked behind her as the last canoe pulled along the shore. The voyageurs began hauling out their packs and securing them on their shoulders. Brigitte watched as the experienced men stretched their tumplines across their foreheads to help them steady their loads.

"What do you wait for?" Georges Munion, *avant* of her canoe, laid a boot against her backside. She lunged forward, losing her balance and landing in the dirt. "Unload. There is no other way around the Long Sault."

Heat flooded her face, but she nodded. She rose and lugged one of the packs out of the boat, almost toppling over yet again. Taking a breath, she dragged it, aware that the others lifted theirs onto their shoulders. Only some of the young men, fresh *engagés* like her, struggled to lift the heavy packs. Yet, with reddened faces, they eventually managed. She did not.

How will I carry the load? I had not thought of the portages.

A voyageur strode past, sneering at her. "What's wrong? Did you forget you were not signing on a pleasure boat ride?" He laughed and moved on, two huge bundles on his shoulders.

"How long is the Long Sault?" another young voyageur called out.

"The Carillon Rapids are twelve miles. But we can take it at a dog trot, eh?" The man let out a hoot of laughter.

Twelve miles. She would have to carry these packs for twelve miles? A new fear gripped her. She would be discovered, certainly, and they were not so far gone from Montreal that she could not be left behind.

If they leave me, I can make a home here.

But it was not far enough from Tristan, nor would she find her father here.

Slowly, the loads were all drawn up, covered, and secured beneath oilcloth. Brigitte joined the others setting up another camp in the enclosure of trees and equipment. She helped turn over the canoes, standing them on their tall ends to provide a bit of shelter. She straightened, legs and arms shaking with exhaustion.

From the corner of her eye, she caught a glimpse of René. Come what may, she must find a way to carry those packs. Come what may, she must not let him discover who she was.

CHAPTER 5

Huzzah, huzzah on the river. You can hardly hear me.
Huzzah, huzzah on the river. You don't hear me at all.
—Youpe! Youpe! Sur La Rivière

Brigitte's stomach growled. She retrieved her bag from where she'd set it against a tree and reached inside to pull out another biscuit. Her last. Her legs quivered. She shook first one, then the other.

"I am starved as a bear. Aren't you?" The friendly fellow from her boat approached.

She deepened her voice. "*Oui.*"

"Perhaps in a few days, we will be used to it." He smiled and stuck out his hand. "I am Gervais."

She looked at him. A broad smile on a thin face accented by a few freckles and startling blue eyes greeted her. A queue of thick red hair stuck out of his cap. He was pleasant-looking and seemed genuine.

She shook his hand, mimicking her uncle's firm grip. "'Tis a pleasure to meet you. I am Bénédict." After St. Bénédict, since it meant *blessed*. Truly, she prayed for God's blessing on her precarious plan.

"Bénédict. Let us hope we survive our adventure, eh?" He laughed as though such a feat had the most unlikely chance of success and was yet to be endured as the happiest joke.

"And this Long Sault." Brigitte offered a cordial smile.

Up the shore, a cook fire came to life, a *chaudière* settled over it. Several men stood around the big pot, adding salt pork and a few vegetables. Some men gathered in groups to talk as others went into the woods, collecting fuel for the fire. Some stretched themselves on the ground and fell asleep. Still others cast lines into the river, hoping for a fish for supper.

She followed Gervais's gaze as it wandered to two men heading toward the river. "I have no line," he said.

Brigitte fidgeted in her necessary and pulled out a small spool. "You may use mine."

"*Non*. I will carve the end of a stick for a spear for some fat trout, eh?" He grinned again.

Brigitte warmed to his idea. "I have never speared a trout. I would like to try."

His eyebrows lifted. "Let us find some sticks."

They roved together into the brush as Gervais cut and trimmed two strong branches. He measured their weight in his hand. Seeming satisfied, he dropped cross-legged onto the ground and pulled his knife from its sheath. Careful to be as casual in her movements, Brigitte followed his lead.

"Get the ends as sharp as you can."

"All right."

Together they sat on the ground, whittling their spears. She'd whittled for pleasure with her uncle before. He'd taught her how to carve a spoon, and she'd watched him carve two-pronged forks. A spear couldn't be much different. Easier really.

Before long, Gervais was satisfied with the results. "Come. Let us give it a try, shall we?" She followed him to the water's edge. Gervais strode along the bank until he found a spot to his liking. Balancing on a length of log that stretched from the bank on one end and sunk into the river on the other, he stepped across it to reach a series of boulders. Brigitte followed, finding purchase above the swirling water.

She stared into the pool, allowing time for her eyes to adjust to the sunlit depths. Eventually, a movement caught her eye. A tail waving slowly from beneath the edge of the next rock. When the body emerged, she plunged in her spear. The fish disappeared.

"I missed." She smiled, anxious to try again.

Gervais took a stab in the water. "Ach! Too slow."

Minutes passed, but no more fish appeared.

Gervais gasped.

She glanced his way. With his tongue clenched between lips in concentration, he steadied his spear and gave it a mighty shove. As his feet slipped on the rock, he leapt, landing in the water up to his knees, splashing her.

He stood in the midst of the pool and laughed. "I have scared away our quarry." He shook his head as he climbed up the embankment. "Too bad, too. It was a big fish."

She chuckled, turning with care as she made her way back to the bank. Setting her foot upon the log, her gaze swept up to see René's boring down on her. He frowned, and she burned under the scrutiny leveled at her.

She ignored the tension winding in her gut and watched her footing as she climbed off the log, grunting as she leapt off, hoping for a masculine sound. He held his hand out before her. She looked at it and reached for it, allowing him to hoist her up the bank.

He held her hand a moment longer than needed and again entrapped her gaze. "Wet and uncomfortable you'll be," René said, facing Gervais. "And not even a fish for your effort."

"Next time." Gervais grinned.

René jerked his head, beckoning Brigitte. "I would speak with you. Get your food."

She swallowed.

As Gervais stripped off his moccasins, socks, and trousers, spreading them over a branch, Brigitte set her spear on the ground beside his and turned her head to hide her blush. Clearing her throat softly, she hustled toward the group gathered around the pot of soup.

Quick glances about told her that René kept his eyes on her, aware of all she did. His attention struck her with fear. Perhaps he knew. She swallowed the lump in her throat, unsure how she'd manage to eat as she received a ladleful of stew. Another quick glance, and he jerked his chin to draw her away from the larger group.

She wandered behind him to a stand of fir trees apart from the voyageurs. She cupped her bowl in two hands and sat on the ground, as was their manner when they ate. She sipped the broth and chewed on a piece of stringy meat, hoping to appear unfazed.

René's shadow fell over her. "Marchal, if I am not mistaken. *Brigitte* Marchal." His voice, barely more than a whisper, pinned her to the ground. She was a fish caught on a spear with no hope of wriggling free. She looked up. His sharp eyes impaled her.

She lowered the bowl. Swallowed. The food stuck somewhere in her chest as she nodded.

"*Imbécile!*"

Brigitte cringed and stared at his legs as he shifted his weight back and forth. Her gaze crawled to the level of his hands on his hips, then to his face. She quickly looked away.

"What were you thinking? Why have you followed me? You must return to your home, to the convent."

She dashed a glance upward, but he wasn't looking at her. His chest rose and fell. His gaze swept about them. Then he focused on her again. A knot worked in his jaw. "I have no one to spare to take you back, but you *will* go."

"*Non.*" She shook her head. "I am going on. I am hired by the company."

"You cannot." He looked as though he wanted to shake her, but men did not shake one another. They wrestled. They slung their fists. Did he wish she were a man right now so he could beat her?

"I must." She set the bowl aside and pushed to her feet. Courage—nay, determination—burrowed deep in her soul. "I will not go back. I cannot. I will find my father, and if I do not, I will perhaps search for my mother's people or"—she shrugged—"or go wherever the river leads me. I will not be a burden."

A gust of breath rushed out of him. "You are already a burden."

"How? I have paddled as long as the rest. No one knows who I am except for you."

"We have traveled one day on a journey of weeks." He lifted his finger into the air and pointed it in her face. "One day!" His face reddened.

She stepped back, but her back stiffened. "One day or a hundred. It matters not. I will work as hard as the others."

"Tomorrow we portage the Long Sault. You know what that means?"

She gave the slightest nod.

"You will have to carry a pack. A pack which I doubt you can even lift."

There lay the crux of her problem.

"Show me. Show me how you will carry them." He marched several yards to a stack of bundles piled beneath the trees.

She stared at him, but he did not budge. He waited. She trudged toward him, stopping near a bundle of goods. Closing her eyes, she held her breath and lifted. The weight of it barely cleared the ground before it plunged back to the soil. She gasped as her face burned.

"In less than a day, I have discovered you. How long before these voyageurs do as well? And then what will you do? How can I protect you?"

"Protect me?"

"*Oui*. Protect you. You are one woman among many men." He needn't say more.

"I know the danger. That is why I am disguised."

He spat, then rubbed the back of his hand across his lips. "You are a fool."

"I would be a fool to stay within reach of Tristan Clarboux." She dared not cry, yet a hated prickling stung her eyes.

Blood drained from René's face. He leaned his fist against a tree trunk. "If you had only come to me, told me."

"Why? So you could laugh at my suggestion? So you could send me away before I had even begun?"

"I could have said you were the daughter of a *bourgeois* returning to her home in the Upper Country. You would have been protected, cared for. But *non*. You dreamed up this brainless notion, and to reveal you now would be to imperil you. What do I do with such a woman?"

"*Ikwe.*"

He straightened, riveting her with a stare once again. "What?"

"*Ikwe.* Woman."

His gaze narrowed. "You speak the native language?"

Her heart thumped. Much was lost in the abyss of time and childhood forgetfulness. Only bits of her mother's native language occasionally ran through her mind, as she had had no one to speak the words to.

She pointed at him. "*Inini.*" Man. She glanced at a voyageur filling his pipe. "*Asemaa.*" The word for tobacco floated from her tongue. She could hear her father saying it. Images of women bent over hides, scraping them, came into her memory. "Bear ... *makwa.* Beaver ... *amik.*"

"I know what you are trying to do, but we have a translator." His brows pinched.

"*Daga. Ningotaaj.* Please. I am afraid to go back, and to stay here, so near Tristan's reach."

He sighed. Pulling his fist from the tree trunk, he rubbed a hand over his face. "It is possible your skill could be useful."

"I know some words. The rest may return. I can mend. I can cook. I can tend the sick. I can set up camp. I can paddle." She wished she could think of something else. Something more substantial.

"Eat your soup," he said, his expression flat. He turned as if to leave her.

"*Nimaanendam.*" The word burst out of some lost region inside her. He stopped but didn't turn to her. "I am sorry—*nimaanendam.* But I will not go back to Montreal."

She watched as he stalked back to the others.

René stayed awake into the night. Sitting on his blanket, he listened to the rippling of the river as he chewed the stem of his pipe. Around him, men snored and snorted.

He spied Brigitte across the voyageurs' camp. She lay on her side, her back against a rock. The stillness of sleep did not lie upon her. She shifted.

She should not have come. How could he keep her disguise a secret? *Il m'est impossible de le faire.* It could not be done.

He should force her to stay behind. Perhaps someone near Pointe-Fortune would take her in and give her employment. The man she feared, Clarboux, he would not come here looking for her, surely. She was foolish to think so.

Where did she think to go? A Frenchwoman did not travel into the wilderness unless she was the wife of some *bourgeois* trader. Yet she was not a Frenchwoman. She was Métis. A mixed blood with a mother's clan somewhere to the west and a father whom she hoped might still be alive.

It was all too much. He tapped the dead ashes from his pipe onto the damp earth and tucked the pipe away, his sleep as far from him as ever.

Three hours later, having slept little, he strode through the camp to wake her. A few others began to rouse. He touched her shoulder with a toe. Startled, she bolted upright, her hand jerking to her sash. He stepped back when he saw the knife she kept there. Smart girl.

"Marchal."

She blinked, finally seeming to recognize him.

"You will continue to wear the disguise until it cannot be helped. Do not think of the packs. Take your personal supplies, and, I think, you will be able to help carry a canoe. When you get to the resting place, immediately gather wood or begin cooking the meal. The men will not bother you if you busy yourself on their behalf. When there is no cooking, find something to mend. It will do you good if you quickly learn to repair the boats. It must be done daily, and such work will keep you from being idle and falling under suspicion. You must be busy. I will tell your captain you are able to help with translation should the necessity arise. Sooner or later, you will stand out to him, so you must be useful."

She stared at him, unmoving.

"Do you understand all that I am saying?"

"*Oui.*"

"Good. You must be watchful. When the carrying begins, find your place with your *bateau* before someone else does and you are left with nothing to do."

At last, she nodded. She rose stiffly. "Thank you, monsieur."

"How far you will go, I cannot say. Perhaps you will be comfortable at home with the Indians."

A tiny frown touched her brow, but she only nodded again.

Throughout the morning, the girl hovered near the canoes, eating her cooked peas. The moment a trio of men neared, she leapt up and readied herself to join them. Taking her place in the middle of the boat with her own pack on her back, they hoisted the canoe and began a trot down the trail.

René nodded. If she took care, they might keep her secret hidden a while longer.

Brigitte kept keen watch on the trail lest she stumble over a rock or root as she jogged. Gervais was positioned just ahead of her, the canoe appearing light above him even as her shoulders ached. Long past winded, she tried to force her mind away from her body. Thankfully, the others seemed to be tiring, for their pace slowed. When she thought she could not go on a moment longer, the man in front called a rest.

They lowered the canoe, and she dropped to her haunches. Gervais did the same, twisting to face her.

"That was not so bad, eh, Bénédict? Not all the portages will be so long."

She panted for breath. "How far have we gone, do you think?"

Gervais shrugged. "Three, perhaps four miles." He pulled out his pipe but didn't light it.

She'd finally caught her breath when the *gouvernail* called them to pick up the canoe again and continue. By the time they finally reached the far end of the rapids and lowered the canoe, Brigitte could hardly walk. Had she any strength left, she would fan her hot face. Sweat ran down her back and sides. If only she might remove her cap, but her braid would fall free. She should have cut it off.

Her stomach rumbled with the hunger of a man and not a petite woman. Yet she would give up a meal for the chance to lie down and sleep. René's warnings haunted her, keeping her from giving in to the temptation. After catching her breath, Brigitte moved into the woods for personal relief and to find wood. There, she briefly pulled the cap off and fanned her face.

By the time she returned, the last *bateaux* had arrived. Men grunted and staggered as they dropped their packs. Many carried more than one. Others carried a pack while they shouldered the weight of a canoe.

I should thank God René discovered me. How would I ever have done it?

Perhaps the Almighty had, indeed, put His blessing on her journey.

That night, she slept hard and fast. When she awoke, her heart lay much lighter, and for the first time since her aunt's death—nay, since the night of the Clarboux's party—the wings of hope stirred within her.

CHAPTER 6

Dites-moi, dites-moi, ma belle, dites-moi sans mentir
Si vous êtes ici par force ou par plaisir

(Tell me, tell me, my pretty, tell me without lying
If you are here by force or for your own pleasure.)
                    —Blanche Comme La Neige (White as Snow)

More rapids followed. Some long, some short. The Carillon, Long Sault, and Chute au Blondeau marked only the beginning of Brigitte's river perils. With each new turbulence, her muscles burned against the stream, yet her endurance had increased. She hearkened to the commands of the *gouvernail* and drove her pole to the grunting chants of the singing crew as she trusted in the experience of those who'd done this many times before. When the currents rushing over the rocks and through narrow portals proved too tempestuous to drive against, they portaged around them. She kept as busy and invisible as possible.

She pressed on with the others, looking forward to each rest as it came. Again, the clamor of voyageurs disembarking. Again, halos of pipe smoke that kept the biting insects at bay. Again, blood flowing into Brigitte's tingling limbs. She had learned to accept the routine. At night, she slept among the others, yet apart, always with a rock or tree trunk to her back and a hand on her knife.

Gervaise had become a comrade of sorts, since her captain, Georges Munion, assigned them and two others the responsibility of daily patching small breaches in the canoe. A Métis man named Rupert taught them the proper way. Brigitte found it a pleasurable task. The silvery-white bark of the birch curved up the insides of each *bateau*, the seams tightly sewn with spruce fibers called *watap*, overlaid with layers of dark spruce gum.

A week into their journey, Rupert beckoned her, a sack in hand, toward a cluster of trees. "I will show you how to collect the *watap*. When there is time, we will soak the fibers."

Pulling a knife from his sash, he paused at a spruce sapling and burrowed into the soil until he'd exposed its roots. "We do not take it from the trunk, or the tree will die." With a small portion of the root in hand, he peeled away a supple layer, revealing the moist flesh beneath. "You see how we strip the fibers into long, thin pieces?"

Brigitte nodded.

"Here." He handed her the root, and she stripped off a section with her knife. He nodded. "*Bien*. Do some more."

She peeled until she had a small pile of stripped fibers. It was not so unlike whittling.

"Put it in the sack. There will be time after we reach Sault Ste. Marie to soak them. Then we can peel the soft layer inside from the outer layer. *Oui?*"

She lifted her gaze "*Oui*."

His eyes moved from the work she did to her face. She glanced down at the root in her hand, avoiding his penetrating gaze. He didn't speak as she turned the root over, peeling at what remained, but his intake of breath sent her nerves racing.

"Fill the bag as much as you can each time we stop."

"I will."

The Métis man sauntered toward the riverbank with a whistle. Brigitte breathed easily again. When she had filled the sack, she returned to the *bateau*, where the others prepared to continue on.

The men smelled of tobacco and grease, but she'd become accustomed. Her own body's stench was more bothersome. How she longed to get clean. She washed her face and neck when she could and tried to ignore the pastiness that clung to her skin. Gathering her pack, she positioned herself with two others to hoist the canoe.

Gervais joined them. He shook his head when he looked at her.

She frowned at his back. What was wrong with him?

They made camp later that evening on Calumet Island, ahead of the rapids. Tomorrow would come another portage, another overland trek by which her lack of strength and participation in carrying the burdensome packs would be obvious, and she might be discovered. There was nothing to be done about it. Perhaps, now, she'd come too far to be left behind. They would take her at least to some Indian settlement.

After her meal, she walked along the edge of the woods to get a better look at the *chute* they would pass around. Turning a bend, she halted at the sight of white crosses high on the bank. There must have been thirty, at least.

She shuddered, gazing from the crosses to the boiling cauldron roaring over the rocks. *"Mon Dieu."*

"Frightening, is it not?"

She jumped when the voice sounded behind her. She wiped the back of her hand across her brow to chase away a hum of mosquitoes. "Gervais, you should not sneak up that way."

"That is what the dead must be saying. You should listen to them."

She frowned at such an eerie thought.

"Perhaps you will meet the Wendigo."

"I do not believe in such things."

Gervais stepped beside her at the river's edge. *"Non?* That is up to you, but if you are wrong and his spirit still roams, seeking human flesh—"

"Stop it, Gervais."

"He will not rest, you know. He wanders to and fro, an outcast in the earth on account of the crimes he has committed. Crimes he continues to commit." His voice dropped deeper. "There are those of our brethren who have disappeared into the woods, never to be heard of again. All say it was the Wendigo."

"Gervais!" She punched his shoulder.

He grinned. "You sound frightened as a woman."

She turned away—too suddenly, she realized too late.

"Bénédict?" His voice lifted on the end of the word, ripened with suspicion.

She squatted and rinsed her hands in the current, splashing water on her face.

A sudden shove against her shoulder landed her in the dirt.

She glared at him. "*C'est quoi qu'tu fais?*"

He dropped to his knees and pushed her shoulder back, pinning her. "I will tell you what I am doing. I am finding out the truth."

She struggled against him, but he wrestled her down. He might be light, but he was sinewy, his muscles far more developed than her own. She wrenched from side to side, now and then upsetting but not unseating him. With clenched teeth, she clawed, but he held her wrists, slowly pushing them back against the dirt above her shoulders.

He laughed.

She spat at him, hitting him in the chest, but he ignored it. His gaze traveled up and down the length of her, his eyes narrowing. "*Bénédict.*" He loosened his hold and caught up her hand before she could strike him.

She ceased struggling. Panting, he clasped her hand, studied it, then stared at her again. "I knew it for certain when you bent to wash." He glanced over her again. "Your hips ..."

She yanked her hand free as he released her. Standing, he held out a hand, but she ignored it. Brigitte stepped back, putting space between them. What would he do with his discovery?

He crossed his arms. "Why are you disguised?"

"Why do you think?"

"Who are you really? The woman of some trapper?"

"It is none of your business."

His blue eyes narrowed. "Unless I make it so."

"And why should you?"

He shrugged. "It is useful information."

"I—"

"Not as useful as you think."

She wheeled around. René stood at the edge of the trees. "Marchal, if you are finished exploring, it would be wise for you to return. There are predators in the forest." He glared at Gervais, his eyes ferocious as the spirit of Wendigo itself.

Gervais lifted his chin. "I see now."

"You see nothing," she said. A glance at René silenced her from saying more.

"Come, Marchal."

Gervais followed as she hiked up the hill past René. "So that is your name."

"You may refer to her as Marchal. To know her Christian name would only jeopardize her safety among us."

"Then she does not belong to you?"

Brigitte halted and turned, as did René. She opened her mouth for a sharp denial, but René cut her off.

"*Oui,* she belongs to me, but she will remain in your boat, and you will see to it that her secret is kept and no one bothers her. Understood?"

Belong to René? The trader must be mad. She looked his way, but his features revealed nothing. Spinning about, she hurried to the camp. Her moccasins had gotten damp along the edge of the riverbank, so she sat down to remove them a few feet from where the voyageurs gathered together around a fire. They all focused upon a man who was regaling them with a tale.

"This is that very place," he said, his voice carrying an ominous note as Brigitte tugged off first one moccasin, then the other, and laid them on a boulder to dry.

Gervais dropped beside her on the ground. "What place is it you speak of?"

"The Legend of Cadieux."

"Will you tell it?"

"Gather round, children. For I, Jean Regolout, will tell it." He puffed on his pipe and stretched his legs to the fire. "In 1709, our story takes place. One hundred years ago. Jean Cadieux, a *coureur de bois*, came up this very river. To this same turbulence." Regolout glanced at the roiling river, and his voice dropped. "A brave man he was, a hero of his companions.

"The Iroquois came upon his party, but Cadieux was brave and loyal. 'Go!' he told the others. 'Hurry from this place, or surely you will not escape.' And they did. Our Cadieux stayed behind. He sacrificed himself to the weapons of the *sauvages*. He stood against them and died alone, here on Calumet, while his companions ran the Seven Chutes."

Regolout puffed long on his pipe, and Brigitte thought it the end. Such horror the man had suffered. Brigitte peered beyond them into the forest and shuddered.

"Remaining alone on the island, he suffered greatly from his injuries and exhaustion," said Regolout. "How many hours, how many days, we do not know. Bleeding his life out, starving, freezing. Such torments he endured to save his fellow voyageurs. When others came, they found him with a sheet of bark in his hand. On it, with his final breaths, he had written his death chant. It is forever called 'La Complainte Cadieux.'

> *"Petit rocher de la haute montagne, Je viens ici finir cette campagne! Ah! Doux echos, entendez mes soupirs, En languissant, je vais bientôt mourir!"*

Little stone of the high mountain, I come here to
finish this campaign. Ah! Sweet echoes, hear my sighs.
Languishing, soon will I die.

The words haunted Brigitte as several of the older voyageurs joined in the melancholy tune of the campaign's finish and languishing death.

The chant died away in swirls of tobacco smoke and the falling of night. The voyageurs' faces glowed in the firelight. No one talked. Even Gervais looked deep in thought. The water shone in the moonlight.

Brigitte shifted to peer over her shoulder. Behind her stood the woods, where she remembered the Wendigo and the crosses. René stood there, his shoulder pressed against a tree, his pipe in hand, very near her bedroll. His dark eyes watched her.

She rose and walked away from the others, stopping in front of René. "Why did you do it, say I belong to you?"

René looked over her shoulder, then his gaze dropped to hers. "What else could I do? I am responsible for you. If anyone else finds out, tell them you are my woman and that I will kill them if they touch you."

The violence of his suggestion, though spoken calmly, startled her. "But—"

"It is the best way. You might find you want to stay at one of the Indian encampments we pass. Perhaps you will find your mother's people. Otherwise, you may stay with us all the way to Fort William if that is your choice. I have been thinking …"

Moonlight glinted off his eyes, and she imagined glimpses of his soul. She sucked in her breath. "*Oui?* What have you been thinking?"

"You are good at figures. You can read, so you said."

She nodded.

"You may find employment with the traders, the *bourgeois* perhaps."

"You think so?"

He shrugged. "I cannot say with certainty. It is not a woman's way. Yet it is that, or you will have to stay with the Indians, or …"

"*Sinon?*" What else?

"Or else marry one of the voyageurs or traders."

She stiffened. "I intend to find my father."

"You might not, and you cannot remain safely alone."

"Some voyageur might prove no better than Tristan."

"That is a risk you will have to take eventually."

"No, it is not."

He frowned. "You are a selective woman. Perhaps you will later wish you were not. You may regret your decision not to find rescue in the convent, as one of them."

She pushed back her shoulders. "I doubt such a possibility, but I thank you for your suggestion, and for … for saying what you did to Gervais."

René tapped his pipe against the tree trunk. "He will spend too much time thinking about you now. His interest is not surprising, so you must expect it."

"I am not afraid of him."

"I did not say you should be afraid. Still, he may become foolish, besotted as young men are at times. It is up to you if you accept him or not."

She let out a huff. "Of course I will not accept him. Besides, you already told him I belong to you," she whispered with vehemence. If they had not stood in the shadowed moonlight, he might see her reddening face.

He gave her a small smile, his teeth white against the darkness.

She scowled. "I will watch myself. If I should have need of you, I will say so."

His smile fell away as clouds blocked out the moon, so she could no longer see his expression. "Let us hope you have no further need."

René pushed his pole against the churning current as the *gouvernail* shouted from the stern. He moved out of practiced habit while his thoughts remained full of his conversation with Brigitte.

How had he come into such a problem? How many others, like Gervais, wondered at a voyageur with such slightness of form and strength, whose voice sometimes gave her away? He ground his teeth. How many would take advantage of her?

Oui, he had done the right thing claiming she was his woman. Others would be interested, but they would proceed with caution. Perhaps he might yet get her to some safe haven if safe haven existed in the untamed territory of Upper Canada.

Hopefully, Gervais would help keep her secret safe. René had followed when she left the group, Gervais almost on her heels. He had come upon them just when Gervais shoved her off balance, then waited to intervene, watching to see what she might say or do to extricate herself.

How she had fought the young Gervais. Like a she-bear. He smiled at the memory. She in her oversized clothes. Where had she found them? How had she come to the North West Company so prepared? It had been a mercy when Gervais allowed her escape. Perhaps there was a hint of honor in him.

René had watched them pass the time together since they began their voyage. They seemed friends, or at least as much as friendship was possible. Gervais might remain a friend still, now his discovery was made, and become an asset in this difficult situation. Or he might become Brigitte's biggest problem.

Then again, Brigitte might find more than friendship in the lad. If he should ever see her in a dress—ah! René smiled, recalling the day he'd met her. She'd looked quite beautiful in a dress, simple though it had been. He had seen fine women in the streets of Montreal before. Brigitte was hardly one of them, but she was lovely. The braid that reached her waist must be quite something when it was freed. Now she kept it hidden beneath her cap, and good it was that she did. Her hair could be the undoing of young Gervais.

A twinge grabbed his shoulder. René rolled it twice and fell back to poling. She would have greater difficulties as the days continued to pass. She must have ... womanly needs. Had she prepared herself for such things? She'd thought of everything else. Why did such mysteries even come into his thoughts?

He breathed deep as he pressed the long pole into the river's silt. Behind him, the *milieux* did the same, forcing their *bateau* against the constant current.

It might be better if they all knew they traveled with a woman, like the times the *bourgeois* traders brought their wives along, and the voyageurs treated them like queens.

Too late for such a decision now. She must fend for herself, though nothing much could happen to her in the *bateau*.

Storm clouds moved across the sky, and thunder clapped overhead, pulling René's thoughts from Brigitte. They ought to stop and make shelter. René searched the shore. A cluster of islands broke the wide river ahead. They could stop early and make camp, then drive into Deep River on the morrow.

René pulled his *capote* tighter around his shoulders against the cold, misty rain. At the cook fire, Gervais held out his bowl, studying Brigitte while he waited for her to fill it. She cast the *engagé* a quick glance as she ladled corn mush into his dish. The young fool would reveal her to everyone.

René strolled over and took the ladle from her hand, scooping his own bowlful without a look her way. He handed the ladle to the next fellow, then followed her and took a spot on the opposite end of the log from where she sat. On another stump, Gervais took his meal, intermittently chewing and staring at her.

"Gervais, you should move if you have no control over your eyes."

The younger man dropped his glance sheepishly and shoved the remainder of his mush into his craw. With a nod at them, he rose and stalked away.

Brigitte kept her focus on her bowl. He knew her well enough now to recognize her embarrassment. She pulled her knees together and concentrated on the bowl of food atop them.

"Tomorrow we move on, rain or *non*."

She nodded.

"By nightfall, if we prevail, we will come upon a village of Métis. There, another Métis will join us, and we will trade for some fresh meat."

She swallowed hard. "Do you … will you make me stay there?"

"*Non*. Not if you do not wish it. You will not likely find your father there, so close still to Montreal."

She nodded, her shoulders relaxing a hint.

"Do you remember where your father most often wintered?"

She shook her head. "I remember him speaking of *d'en haut*."

"The upstairs country, *oui*. That is anyplace. The entire northwest."

"Ah." She frowned.

"Anyplace around Grand Portage or Fort William?"

She closed her eyes. "Saint …"

"Marie?"

"*Oui,* but another. Saint …"

"Croix?"

"Perhaps."

"How about rivers?"

"Only this one."

"Are you certain? Pigeon, perhaps? Rainy? Saint Louis?"

"*Oui!* Saint Louis."

"You are sure? It is a familiar enough name."

"I am sorry. I cannot say with certainty."

"For all we know, he went to Detroit, many leagues from here in another direction."

"He did speak of Detroit."

"Most do."

Her brow crumpled. "I am sorry, René. I did not intend to trouble you so."

"Sometimes things cannot be helped." He offered her a smile and felt strangely pleased when she returned it. "Do not look now, but your friend Gervais cannot keep himself distanced. Even now he wanders about, but his eyes come back to you. I am afraid you will be found out before long."

"What shall I do?"

"Do nothing. Perhaps in time, we will have a better plan. I am sorry that I offended you. I only mean it for your safety."

"I know. I am grateful, truly."

"Tomorrow, when we come to the village, stay where I can see you. There are sharper eyes there than those of your young friend."

"The Indians?"

He nodded. "They would not be surprised, but I would not want them to think wrong thoughts."

"Worse thoughts than those I might find among the voyageurs, you mean?" She blushed as quickly as she asked it.

"Not exactly what you may think. There are those of every nation, white or Indian, who would seek to trade their women."

"Trade?" She fiddled with her spoon. "I had forgotten."

"*Oui*. It is common enough. You will see that the women do much of the labor in the villages. They are valued for their strength and hard work, if not for much else."

She dropped her gaze and gave a slow nod. René scraped out the last of his porridge. "Have no fear, Marchal. I will not let anything happen to you. You may find that you enjoy our time in the village."

He rose to rinse his dish in the river. As he walked away, he caught the glance of Gervais straying yet again. Perhaps, once they came upon a destination where Brigitte chose to remain, the *engagé* would return to her. If Gervais were kind, perhaps she would have him. It would certainly solve René's problems. And yet, it didn't seem right to wish it. She hoped to find her father. After all she had left behind, satisfying her search would be the least René could allow her. No matter how futile the effort might prove.

CHAPTER 7

*"The cliff loomed tall and stained with the burned black
tobacco offerings the Natives shot from their bows.
There, in the shallows below, the new voyageurs were baptized,
I among them."*
— Journal of Etienne Marchal, Voyageur

Brigitte slid out from where she'd slept beneath the overturned canoe and sat up. A few feet away, along one side of her with his head beneath the shelter, lay the Métis man Rupert, and, on the other, her seat mate Pierre. Gervais slept just beyond.

The mist caressed her face in the wee hours of dawn. It had not stopped raining for two days. They had arrived in the village, and they ate and traded with the people, sleeping wherever they could find shelter.

She yawned. Rupert stirred, and she turned to see him glance at her from beneath hooded, dark eyes. She pushed back her damp blanket and rose to relieve herself. When she returned, several other voyageurs stirred about their encampment. Natives stepped in and out of small cabins and wigwams. Cooking smells, some she recognized such as meat and mush, others she didn't, floated on the mist and made her stomach growl.

Daylight crept over them, and Brigitte wandered into the main thoroughfare. A general cacophony of voices hummed throughout the village. Many spoke in the native tongue, enthralling her, even though she could understand only some of what was being said.

"Have you eaten your porridge?"

She jumped at the voice beside her. Gervais.

"Not yet."

"Come with me. There is a woman making *sagamité*. I will trade her some tobacco."

She followed him to a wigwam where Gervais dipped his head before going inside. She entered behind him. Smells assailed her, at once pungent and welcoming, teasing her memory. She recalled her mother stirring a kettle and calling to her, then tickling her toes when she did not rise to eat.

A dark-eyed woman with graying hair boiled hulled corn in a pot, tossing in bits of fish. *"Bendigen."* She waved them over and pointed at mats on the floor. *"Nimbakade?"* The woman pretended to spoon food into her mouth and nodded.

"Hungry, *oui. Eya'*," Brigitte said as she lowered herself to a woven mat.

The woman smiled, showing several missing teeth.

"You understood?" Gervais whispered, sitting beside her.

Brigitte shrugged. "She gestured. Her meaning was clear."

"Wiisini."

The woman served a scoop of the pale, soupy meal. Brigitte gave a grateful nod. "She says to eat."

"Merci." Gervais accepted a plate and joined her.

The *sagamité* lacked flavor but filled Brigitte as she and Gervais ate companionably. When they'd finished, he handed the woman a chunk of tobacco. Then he and Brigitte rose and bowed. The woman bobbed up and down, rattling off more words in Ojibwe that flew past Brigitte faster than she could collect them.

Gervais patted his stomach as they ducked out of the dwelling. "That wasn't too bad. Let us see what else we can find." He led the way, whistling.

Brigitte sighed in relief. It seemed that Gervais had decided not to make a spectacle of her with his awkward behavior any longer.

The mist had finally lifted, and she wandered beside him as he pulled out his pipe and ripped off a piece of tobacco with his teeth. He stuffed it into the bowl, stopping long enough to strike his flint and light it. A halo of smoke rose about their heads as he puffed and smiled at her, the stem of his pipe between his teeth.

"How long have you known René? You are young to have

become attached to such a man."

She rubbed her fingertips along the nape of her neck as she considered her answer. "I … he comes to Montreal now and again, as he did this year."

"I see. How did you meet him?"

"He would come to the nunnery on his visits—that is, the school where I attended."

"The nuns allowed you to go away with him?"

"I did not live with the nuns. Not when I met René. I lived with my aunt. We spoke together, several times. He … he gave gifts to the nuns." She remembered the day they'd met. Did the tiny babe left on the doorstep yet live? Her voice softened. "His heart seemed tender, yet strong."

Gervais was quiet, too quiet, compelling her to say more.

"And I was looking for a husband." She swallowed. How she definitely had *not* been looking for a husband.

"Why does he not want you with him? Why do you sleep alone?"

"René leads us. He has much responsibility. Too much to have me underfoot, adding to the list of his cares."

"It makes no sense. Jacques is our guide. If you were by René's side, he would have no need to worry about you day and night, as he must, eh?" Just ahead, a group of voyageurs traded trinkets. Gervais angled her away from them toward the edge of the village, where he rested his back against a tree and finished his smoke.

She folded her arms, determined to turn the conversation. "Why did you sign up with the North West Company? To seek your fortune, or for the adventure?"

"Both. A living is hard to find, and I haven't many trade skills. I am the oldest of my brothers, and it was getting difficult for my mother and father to feed all of us. Time I made my way."

He watched a bunch of youngsters scampering about, and Brigitte detected a twinge of homesickness in his voice. Facing her again, he raised a brow. "Perhaps I will find a woman to marry who will be like you. Someone unafraid of the wilderness."

Heat suffused her cheeks.

Gervais reached for her hand. "Are you truly his woman?"

She pulled it back. "Gervais—"

"Answer me."

She looked past him. The group of voyageurs who had been trading earlier walked by them, headed toward the shore. Brigitte stepped away from Gervais. "It is time to go." She caught up to the others, putting steps between her and his questions.

Near the landing, she caught sight of René. He glanced over her head, then back to her. "Ah! There you are. I thought I would have to come for you. We must make some adjustments."

Some men were reloading the boats. Stepping to her canoe, she realized her own belongings were not where she'd left them. Her heart quickened. In her usual place were other packs. Would René leave her behind after all?

He stepped beside her. "There is more space in this boat. Our two new passengers will do well here. We have moved your things to the front *canot*."

Two more passengers? And she would sit in René's canoe? She cast him a sharp glance, and he answered it with a flick of his eyes at Gervais's back. "It will work out better this way."

She'd grown accustomed to her place, but it did comfort her to know she would be closer to René. She strode to the other boat.

"*Que fais-tu?*" Gervais frowned upon his approach. "You are leaving?"

"There are new passengers, so I am moving to another *bateau*."

He eyed her with an acquiescing smile. "Farewell, Marchal. I will see you at the Pointe au Baptême."

She lifted her chin and followed René. "We are close to *la Pointe?*" she asked him.

"*Oui.* The place of the baptism."

"I must join the others being baptized?"

"All the new *engagés* must. The *hivernants* will make a ceremony."

His voice dropped lower. "I fear the time for exposure has come. I simply have not decided the best course to explain it."

As they reached the lead canoe, a Métis man and his wife walked by. A *woman*! A woman was to be their passenger?

Brigitte watched them move to her former position at the middle boat. She reached for René's arm, halting him with a hold on his shirt sleeve. He turned, and the flash of his eyes caused her to realize what she'd just done. She jerked her hand away. "Who are they?"

"He is a voyageur. She is both his wife and a very good interpreter."

The woman glanced their way and caught Brigitte's stare. The passenger gave a slow dip of her head, acknowledging Brigitte. Brigitte did the same, and the woman smiled.

The voyageurs began to board. In two hours, they would stop again for the ritual baptism of the new wintering voyageurs, making them officially *hommes du nord*—men of the north. Men … but not all.

René tucked his chin, darting one more glance at Brigitte before he stepped into his place at the front of the *canot*. As she stepped into his canoe, the pull to assist her forced him to hold himself in check. It would not do to draw attention, especially since others may have already seen her grab his shirt like a woman.

He must tell them at *la Pointe*. They would not accept one slight voyageur's rejection of the baptism. They would strip their chests bare and force her into the water if necessary.

Non. There was nothing else to be done. Soon the entire brigade would know, and they would look at her with new eyes, the way young Gervais already watched her. René expelled a breath as Jacques called out the charge to depart. Behind him, down the line of *bateaux*, the *chanteur* called out a tune as the brigade embarked.

They followed the curves of the shore, poling with a steady rhythm. Many times, René fought the urge to look behind to see how she fared in her new place in his *bateau*. Each time he denied himself. Each time he told himself it would not do. Not yet. Not until the others were told.

At last, two hours later, he saw it. A sandy piece of land tapered into the choppy waters that glinted in the sunlight. Beyond it, on the other side of the river, rose a dark cliff.

They neared the shore. Wind beat against René's shirt as he leapt out of the boat along with the others. Cold water lapped at his thighs as he and his crew gentled their long canoe onto the sandy beach. Boat by boat, the rest of the voyageurs followed.

Revelry broke out. Song, laughter, and excitement, both by the older voyageurs and the new *engagés*. Backslapping and jokes ensued. Pipes were lit. The *hivernants* harassed the pork-eaters who had never spent a winter in the upstairs country. The young men removed their sashes, stripped off their shirts, and either hopped up and down or dropped on their backsides into the sand to jerk off their moccasins.

René glanced at Brigitte. She stood round-eyed, her cheeks aflame. One of the voyageurs from René's *bateau*, a thick Scot named Alan, shoved her in the shoulder. "What are you waiting for? Afraid of getting wet? I'll help you."

He laid a broad hand on the back of her neck, and she cringed. René stepped forward. *"Attendez."*

"What? You want to help?" The Scot grunted. "Take his feet." He lurched and lifted Brigitte by the armpits. She thrashed.

"Stop!" René gripped Alan's arm.

The Scot scowled and set Brigitte on her feet. She wobbled, her eyes large.

René slapped Alan on the back. "First, I have something to say. My voyageurs!" His voice gained the attention of a dozen or more men. Their silence caught hold, spreading among the rest. They turned to listen, many of them half-naked. "Today you will become *hommes du nord*!"

A chorus of voices erupted in a cheer.

He raised his hands to quiet them. "All of our newcomers will become *hommes du nord*, except two."

Murmurs started as eyes turned to the wife of the Métis and searched the crowd for the second person to whom René referred.

"I have kept a secret, my friends. But before I tell you what it is, my secret comes with a staunch warning."

"He has a woman," a voice hawked from somewhere near the water's edge. René searched for the speaker, finally spotting Gervais's red hair. René scowled at him.

A clamor arose. Some eyes fell on Brigitte, the voyageur who'd just this morning been placed in René's canoe.

He quieted them again. "*Oui*. I, René Dufour, have a woman." He grinned, allowing them their conjecture. He took Brigitte's arm and pulled her close. With an upward sweep, he removed her cap. Her thick, black braid tumbled to her hips.

"Ah!" Men grinned and gaped. Many of them moved forward, staring at her with opened eyes.

Brigitte leaned toward René. "I will be baptized with the others."

He thought he had not heard right. He looked at her. "*Qu'avez-vous dit?*"

Her brown eyes turned to him. "I said I will be baptized with the others." She started away from him, toward the point where the *engagés* waited to enter the river.

Momentarily dumbfounded, René chased after his scattered wits. "My woman has earned the right to be baptized as a *woman* of the north!"

Some cheered. Others watched. Gervais ran to her side and leaned close, saying something. She shook her head and sat in the sand to pull off her moccasins.

The *engagés* entered the river in a line, their footsteps light, their arms clasped about themselves in the frigid water. Someone slipped and fell, dousing his head, and the rest guffawed. The captains of each canoe strode in to do the baptizing, René along with them. One-by-one, the *engagés* approached their *avant*, and water was sprinkled over head and shoulders while the captain pronounced each of them a man of the north.

As Brigitte approached, René reached for her hand and held it while he poured water from his palm over the shining crown of her head. She gasped when the cold trickle ran down her neck and into the folds of her shirt. It was the first time René had seen her without her coat or large overshirt, a fact that made him aware of how uncomfortable she must have been at times. Yet, he realized how desperately she'd needed the covering.

"I baptize you"— his voice faltered— "a woman of the north." He bent and kissed her head. It seemed the thing to do. He drew back, the brief brush of his lips on her crown strangely affecting.

Her eyes lit with surprise. He smiled and winked, causing a deep blush to flood up her neck and face.

How had anyone not known? Full lips parted and fine brows arched perfectly in her heart-shaped face. She was a beautiful woman. Barely a woman. A child really. She left his hands and stepped onto the shore to be swallowed by a gaggle of men, grinning and bowing and introducing themselves by name as though they'd never met. A slight smile lifted the corners of her lips.

René strode out of the water as most of the crew turned their attention to the captain, who opened the rum. When her group of new admirers finally thinned, and Brigitte's gaze found René again, he jerked his head for her to come along. She excused herself and came to his side. He led her up the shore. "Your work will be much easier now."

"But I will still pole and paddle."

"You may if you wish, but it is not warranted."

"I have been baptized. I must be a true *femme du nord*." She smiled.

He squinted in the sunlight. "A woman of the north, *oui*. Not everything will be so easy."

"You mean being with the men now that they know?"

He nodded. "Not all will have the strength to keep their distance with respect, especially if they are drunk." He glanced at a group of voyageurs filling their cups and tilting back their heads. "Do not wander off on your own. You must take me with you, even when you go to relieve yourself."

She gasped and flushed.

"You have nothing to fear from me." He grinned. "By the time we reach Fort William, you will have learned not to blush so easily."

She stepped back and folded her arms. "Ooh!"

He threw back his head and laughed, feeling free for the first time in days. As the sun warmed his face, he glanced at Brigitte in her oversized shirt. "Now you will not have to wear such a heavy coat when it is warm."

"I would learn not to blush if you would stop speaking so."

He chuckled again. "I think the more training I give you, the quicker you will adjust."

They came upon Rupert. He planted fists on his hips and grinned. "Now you are no longer hiding."

"*Non.*"

He rubbed his chin. "So, Bénédict ..." Dark eyes squinting, he rubbed his grizzly chin in study, then smiled.

"I am Brigitte."

He snapped his fingers. "Ah, Brigitte. *Oui.* I wondered. I tried to guess. For many miles, I asked myself if Bénédict might really be Marie, or Genevieve, or Anna. Many names came to me, but none seemed right. I had not thought of Brigitte." He bowed. "I am pleased to meet you, Brigitte."

Her cheeks flamed yet again. "You knew?"

"I sat behind you and watched you pick up your pole at Lachine. I knew that if you were not a woman, you were a very effeminate man." He smiled and dipped his head.

"You never said."

"You had plenty enough to worry about with your friend Gervais. I will leave you now and join the others. Congratulations on your baptism."

"*Merci.*"

The rest of the day was spent in frivolity. René kept Brigitte close to his side, enjoying the meal and relaxation with the others. But as the crew took part in their dancing, singing, and drinking, it would not do to leave her unguarded among them. Their tongues and morals loosened into ribald tales. René and the other two captains kept watch but allowed them to have their celebration. Gervais glanced their way a time or two but kept himself with the others, laughing at the jokes and drinking more than René considered wise. Ah, well, he would suffer for it tomorrow. As the day unwound and night fell, the men either settled down or passed out. Their heads would ache when they were awakened well before dawn, but they had needed the time to celebrate before the next leg of the voyage.

"Come." René beckoned Brigitte away from the fire where she sipped her coffee with Rupert and the two Métis.

She rose and followed him to the pile of packs beneath the trees at the edge of the forest. He reached for his bedroll. "Gather yours."

She hesitated, then pushed aside a pack to get to her own. She picked it up and followed him a few yards to where he had unrolled his blanket and indicated that she should do the same. She started to move off.

"No. Here, next to mine." She stared at his blanket on the ground.

"Now you will sleep next to me, or they will not believe you are my woman."

Her shoulders grew rigid, and then she sighed. "You are right, of course." She bit her lip and spread her blanket on the ground.

When she stepped back, René bent and drew it closer to his own. He gentled his tone. "Brigitte. We are friends, are we not?"

She nodded.

"*Bien*. Good. Then nothing can be wrong. Here." He plopped down on his bedding and patted her blanket. "Lie down."

After a moment's hesitation, she dropped to her knees and crawled beneath her blanket, turning on her side away from him. René scooted as close as he dared. "It is cold again tonight, don't you think so?" He laid his arm across her. "Do not be alarmed. We must be convincing."

She rustled but did not reply. He relaxed. His arm settled into the soft curve of her waist, just above her hip. He drew a short breath and forced his thoughts to the men snoring around their campfires, to the moon dipping in and out of the clouds above them, to the trickling sound of the river. Anywhere but to the warmth of her next to him. When her breathing deepened, he relaxed. His hand snaked the length of her arm and found her fingers clenched around the hilt of the knife in her sash.

He smiled into the night. "Sleep well, Marchal. Sleep well."

CHAPTER 8

When I must leave the great river
O bury me close to its wave
And let my canoe and my paddle
Be the only mark over my grave
– 'Mon Canoe d'écorce' ('My Bark Canoe') translated by
Frank Oliver Call

At last, they left the Ottawa River.

Running a small rapid, the voyageurs entered the Mattawa River leading west. The new river was narrow and rough, shot with rocks that kept them alert. It wound through thick forests and around islands, occasionally giving way to small lakes.

Through twists and turns, over numerous portages, beneath halos of tobacco smoke, men spoke often of reaching Lake Nipissing, leaving Brigitte to wonder what could be so different about that lake than the many others they'd passed through. Nevertheless, she kept her curiosity to herself as she grew even more efficient at patching and pitching tears in the bark of the craft and helping with the other tasks around their camp.

She obeyed René's request that she not leave the perimeter of the camp without him. Spending so much time in his proximity had allowed her to observe him better. The men respected him and heeded him most of the time. At times, he could be jovial. He sang like all the voyageurs, his voice deep and resonant. Now and again, he caught her gaze, his eyes glittering with reassurance, and he smiled beneath his beard as if friendship existed between them.

Gervais had rebuilt a friendship with her as well. In the evenings, he often joined her near the cook fire and chattered amiably. He seemed to have accepted that she must indeed be René's woman, an untruth she wished she didn't have to bear. She missed their camaraderie of the earlier days. She sat in a circle, across from him now, her mind wandering to those times as she scraped the remnants of her dinner into her mouth.

"And so I told him he was nothing but a pork-eater." Gervais finished another of his stories.

His wink and smile tugged a laugh from her. "I do not believe half your tales."

"Stick by my side, madam, and you will soon see they are all true."

She smirked, then rose to rinse her bowl in the river. Another voyageur stepped beside her at the water's edge. He smelled of rum, and he stood nearer than needed to rinse his dish. His elbow bumped her.

"So, you are his woman, eh?" He bent close and smelled her hair.

She leaned away.

"René has never taken a woman before." He brushed the braid on her back. She stood and attempted to move around him, but he blocked her path. "Perhaps you will tire of him."

"Enough." She looked past the brute to see Gervais ambling up. He gave the man a shove.

The fellow's bowl flew from his hand and clattered on the rocks. He glared at Gervais. "What is it to you, puppy?"

"Leave her alone."

"You have your own designs, no doubt." He pushed Gervais back.

Gervais punched the man's head. He stumbled. Gervais leapt on him, crashing him to the ground.

Brigitte jumped away, nearly tumbling into the water. "Gervais!" Where was René now when she had need of him? "*Arrêtez!* Stop!"

Her friend leaned back and slugged again. The man bucked and sent him flying onto the rocks. Blood spewed from Gervais's nose as the man heaved his weight atop him like a bear, spitting on Gervais.

Brigitte flung herself over the beast. He swatted her, but she pounded his back. "Stop! Leave him!"

"You do not have to fight for me." Gervais grunted and toppled them both.

Brigitte tumbled to the ground. The man rolled next to her and leered at her. Liquor and lust blurred his eyes. She would claw them out! But Gervais yanked him by the shirt collar as Brigitte was set on her feet. René stepped in front of her.

"*Quelle est la signification de ceci?* Why do you fight?"

The man glared at René. "We are voyageurs, are we not? Are we not men? What is it to you if we fight?"

"You fight over my woman." René's words ground out.

Never had Brigitte heard such menace in his voice. The tendons in his neck tightened. Even through his shirt, each muscle seemed more prominent, from his shoulders down to his hands clenched into fists.

She laid a hand on his arm. "I am unhurt."

He pulled her beside him. The muscles of his arms quivered.

"I fight for her." Gervais straightened. "*Oui*. I fight for her. I fight for both of you."

René didn't answer for a moment. He watched Gervais. He watched the man on the ground. Finally, his shoulders relaxed. "*Merci*. For looking out for her."

The other man spat, brushed a sleeve across his mouth, and stalked away. Brigitte wilted against René as her own tension melted away.

Gervais came forward. "Are you all right?"

She nodded. "*Merci*, Gervais. I thank you for your aid." She held out her hand, and he shook it, his hand lingering.

René cleared his throat and offered Gervais his hand as well. "I am pleased to have you watching out for her. You are good friends, and I will not impede that."

Gervais's eyes glinted as he seemed to consider René's remark. He shrugged. "My supper is cold." He walked away, leaving them alone.

René slipped his hand into Brigitte's and turned her away from the camp. The moon shone off the water. "I am sorry I was not here sooner."

"You did not know such a thing would happen."

"That does not matter. I should have protected you."

"René." She squeezed his hand. "You must not blame yourself. I alone am to blame. You told me not to go anywhere alone."

"Gervais cares for you."

She didn't know what to say. She didn't even want to think of the meaning behind his observation.

"You could come to care for him in return, could you not? If I did not stand in the way?"

"I ..."

"Please, it is all right. If he chooses you, and if you decide you would have him, you must tell him that we are not ... that you are not my woman."

His hand tightened over hers before he let go. Did he realize it? Releasing her hand, he took her by the shoulders and turned her to him. "He seems a good lad. I think you can trust him." René gave a small smile as he let go of her shoulders.

Trust Gervais? She trusted him as much as anyone. That was not a problem.

She blinked and glanced about for her bowl, still feeling the pressure of René's palms on her shoulders. There it was, where it had fallen during the scuffle. She bent to retrieve it while she pondered René's advice. Trusting Gervais wasn't so difficult, and yet ...

She straightened and glanced at René, waiting to walk with her to their camp. To marry Gervais and be free of René entirely? Such a thought left an empty space inside her. Her fingers curled into her palm where the sensation of his touch still lingered.

"*Et maintenant, mes voyageurs,* we throw away our poles!" Jacques bellowed the announcement as the crews halted above the Rapids des Perches the next day. He raised his pole to the sky. Brigitte, along with all the *engagés,* raised her own, almost in salute.

"Huzza! Huzza! Huzza!" The crews hollered, pumping their poles at the sky.

"Huzza!" Brigitte's voice joined the others. Then they pitched their poles onto the shore.

Gervais turned to her, his smile wide, his red cap in his hand. "And now we go downstream instead of up. Things will be easier, eh? We will speed toward the lakes."

She thought of the names the voyageurs had spoken around the campfire or as they pushed up the rivers. Nipissing. Huron. Superior. Brigitte sighed with relief to be rid of the fight against the current. "I hope you are right."

"Now we fly," Jacques called again. "Hup!"

Brigitte reached for her paddle, happy to be thinking of something other than what René had said to her last night. She'd slept fitfully, tossing with the idea of Gervais and herself. Together. Struggling with … with other feelings René had left her with.

"Attention!" René called to his crew. She glanced over the shoulders in front of her to find him watching her. He smiled, and her heart picked up its pace.

At that moment, the canoe bounced beneath them. The water churned. The boat rode high and fast. René's gaze turned to the rollicking current as he called out directions. Brigitte focused on the rhythm of the paddling, careful not to crash her own into the man's in front or behind her.

Never had she moved with such speed. The wind caught her cap. She reached up to pull it off, tucking it into her sash. Her heart quickened with the excitement and joy of the ride. As they emerged on the other side of the rapids, she cheered with the crew. Again, she caught René's gaze as he flashed a smile. Gervais nodded from his canoe. She laughed with him and the other men.

They paused for breath, drifting with the easier current, but an outcry caught up to them. Voices shouting, calling for help. Brigitte twisted in her seat. At the deep pool nearest the rapids' end, the second *bateau* had spilled.

René called to halt, but they didn't need to be told. Brigitte raised her paddle and joined with the others to push toward shore. The crewmen in the third *bateau* managed to grab some of the paddles and caps to prevent their floating away. Gervais led the way, wading to the middle of the river and back, lending a hand to the soaked, disheveled crewmen who gasped for breath. He snagged hold of packs that bounced along the riffles.

The voyageurs spent several hours righting the spilled boat, collecting its contents, and drying out the supplies and crew. Brigitte aided, spreading blankets and clothing to dry in the sun or by hastily built fires.

She hung a wet blanket onto a tree limb and glimpsed Gervais, now stripping out of his moccasins and leggings near one of the fires. On the other side stood René, speaking to Monsieur Munion. Gervais hung his moccasins on a stick and jammed the other end into the ground by the fire.

She smiled at his antics. He seemed determined to be heroic, both on the river and last night, protecting her. Perhaps René was right. Her gaze went between the men as she peered over the blanket. *Oui.* Gervais seemed a likely candidate if she were to wed.

She turned her focus to the task at hand. After they had rested for a while, the crew from the spilled boat repacked their damp gear. René and Jacques gathered their own crews together. Brigitte took her place with the rest. When the call to embark came, the *chanteur* started singing. She dug her paddle in time with the others but peered beneath her lashes at René. Her thoughts wandered again.

He sat at the bow, his shoulders rolling in time with the rest, his white shirt buffeting in the wind, his presence commanding them all. *What if I were really his woman?* Her breath caught, and she lost the rhythm of her stroke. She scrambled to adjust the motion of her paddling lest she strike the blade of the man in front of her.

I am foolish. René has put up with me, but he thinks me a girl fit for a boy such as Gervais, while he is a man.

She forced her thoughts back to Gervais. Perhaps God willed her to marry Gervais, and He had sent René to point out His choice. If, indeed, Gervais would have her.

She focused again on the song of the voyageur and dug deeper with her paddle. She must not think about it overmuch. By the time they reached Fort William, she might know.

During the final portage before Nipissing, she walked behind Gervais helping him and several others carry a canoe. He spoke to her over the thwart resting on his shoulder. "You should not do the work of men."

She smiled but didn't break her pace. "What would you have me do, Gervais? Run ahead with the *chaudière* and have your dinner waiting?"

"A pleasant thought."

She chuckled. "Ah, but you must only dream it."

They trotted over a winding height of land, then returned to the water and paddled into a beaver-dammed stream, following it through a succession of ponds and two more portages. After a final seven-mile portage, the vastness of Lake Nipissing opened before them. She pulled in her panting breath, exhausted and invigorated at once. They walked into the water's edge and settled the *bateau* gently in the choppy waves beside the two other boats.

"She is beautiful, is she not?" Gervais splashed beside her.

Brigitte gazed over the glinting bay edged by green forests. Far off islands broke up the horizon. "*Oui.* Beautiful." She had not seen such a large body of water since she was a child.

She turned back to shore, and Gervais took her arm, steadying her step on the pebbled bottom. Memories of vast expanses of water on her journey with Papa filled her mind. "It is the same with Huron and Superior, *oui*?"

"They are much larger, or so I am told." Gervais winked.

"Pray tomorrow the wind dies down." René set a pack down beside them. "The lake is big but shallow. The waves mean danger."

She nodded. She would pray hard for calm.

They launched into Nipissing before the next dawn, but when they stopped for a smoke, the *bateau* rocked on choppy waters, and wind gusted against the tall, curved ends of the *bateaux*, shoving them about so that the voyageurs had to continually right them. By afternoon, thick storm clouds blew in, and René called a halt. The men moved quickly to set up camp and cover the supplies. René shoved a hand through his hair as he watched the sky.

Brigitte and another voyageur stretched an oilcloth over their overturned canoe before she approached René. "You do not like having to wait."

"No. I do not."

Rain started to fall as Brigitte tied off her end of the oilcloth. She crawled under the canoe. Other voyageurs found a space beneath as well. When René followed her, she grinned at him.

"What are you smiling about?"

"Your impatience. As sister Agathe used to say, sometimes one must learn to wait." His brow quirked as he adjusted his bedding on the ground. She straightened her own as well. As they finally settled into place, the rain poured down, drumming against the bark of the canoe. The other men spoke among themselves. Brigitte turned on her side and tucked an arm beneath her head. She studied René.

"You are so driven, monsieur. How you managed to while away a winter in Montreal, I cannot imagine."

"I whiled it away rescuing young girls from undesirable suitors."

"More than one?" she teased.

"Ah, that it was so." His brow lifted, and she giggled.

The voyageur beside René snorted and rolled over.

She covered her mouth, hiding a giggle.

His gaze turned to her. "You think you are the only fair damsel in Montreal? Monsieur Clarboux has probably already found another."

She turned serious. "I can only hope." She rolled onto her back and looked at the smooth white birch curved above them.

"Incorrigible brat."

"*Non*. Truly, I do not wish him on any woman."

"Are you certain he did not harm you?" he whispered.

"I am certain, though not for lack of trying."

When she looked at René again, a flush had risen up his neck, befuddling her. He shrugged. "I must admit, I feel protective of you."

Now it was her turn to flush. She pushed a loose strand of hair off her overly-warm neck. "You will be relieved of your duty, eventually, though I thank you for it."

"Enough of your thanks." He rolled onto his back and tucked his arms under his head.

Propping on her elbow, she scooted closer and watched him as he closed his eyes. "I doubt I shall ever stop feeling grateful. My aunt would thank you. Sister Agathe …" A lump rose in Brigitte's throat as she thought of the kind woman who had tried so hard to help her find life's way. She blinked back tears at the assailing memories.

Brown eyes shot open, startling her. "You are homesick."

She rubbed her cheek to fight the sting in her eyes. "Only a little."

His arm snaked around her. Brigitte hesitated for a moment before laying her head upon his chest, allowing him to comfort her the way her father used to.

René tugged her close. She had no one, after all.

Except Gervais.

She would undoubtedly come to care for the young mongrel. How could she not? The way he looked at her—not with lust like the other curs René had been keeping his eyes on, but with true friendship and perhaps something deeper. It was idiotic of him to let Gervais go on in his agony. He should tell him Brigitte was free. Perhaps when they reached the fort. Then she could go off with him wherever she pleased.

His hand roamed up and down the length of her braid, stirring something within him. Like the touch of cold mist, his senses sharpened. He removed his arm, allowing her to settle in her own place. He'd be a fool to fall captive to her charms.

Sheets of rain droned on the bark and tarp over their heads, on the forest, on the rocky shore, and against the lake, drowning out the sounds of everyone not under the boat with them, even the snoring voyageur. He hazarded a glance at Brigitte and found her staring into the rain beyond the edges of the tarp.

Her eyes drew to his, as though beckoned. "How much longer?"

"What do you mean?"

"The journey."

He shrugged. "Many days, but it will go quickly for a while. The French River flows fast. It will have us shooting into Huron in no time. Paddling the lake shores will take longer, but nothing compared to the battle up the Ottawa."

"What is the fort like? I must have been there, but I do not remember it clearly."

How long the journey must have been for a child, and how strange the places she had encountered. What would she think of the fort now, returning as a woman reared in better society? "Fort William is a big fort. During the summer, thousands will come and live there. Traders, trappers, voyageurs, the natives. Your own family perhaps."

"I remember a place of many people gathered."

"Perhaps your father will be there." He wanted to offer her hope, though in truth, he felt none.

"Do you think so?"

"It is a possibility. Nearly everyone travels there from the upper country and around the lakes."

"Will you go to Grand Portage?"

"The British control it now, but yes, it is likely. They have not been able to enforce their hold on the country. I will then make my way around the head of the lake to my brother's post."

"You have not told me about your brother, except that you were both raised in Montreal."

René shrugged. "There is not much to tell. I taught him everything he knows, and now he has risen to the position of clerk with the company."

"How very good for him, even if you try to steal the credit."

"Truthfully, I steal no credit. Claude endured his apprenticeship well. He rose to clerk on his own merits. In fact, now he is impatient to become a partner."

"Then—truthfully—you taught him well."

René looked back to the rain, accepting the compliment. "I took Claude to the wilderness when he was just eighteen, like you. He had more ambition than sense." He sighed. "It was our mother's last wish that I look after him."

"Then you did not let her down."

"Claude is a man now." And even at twenty-five years old with an Indian wife and growing brood of mixed-blood children, René's promise to his mother hadn't changed.

"Then you are much older than he?"

"There are five years between us."

"Ah."

"What? Am I so old?"

"I do not know. How old are you?"

"I am quite young. Only thirty."

"Thirty." Her eyes widened.

"Horrified or surprised?"

She looked away and shrugged. "I am not sure."

"Not too old, I can assure you."

"Not too old for what?

For a girl. Now why had he thought that? "To out-paddle all these new *hommes du nord.* Your Gervais, for instance."

She looked away. "*My* Gervais?" Her voice was soft. "Why do you call him mine?"

He noted the tender tone of her words, adding certainty to his thoughts. "Is he not? He can be if you wish it."

She turned to face him. Her eyes, her nose, her mouth only inches away, so that her breath touched his face. "I do not know what I wish. Everything is new and unknown to me."

He gave what he hoped to be a comforting smile, despite the uptick of his heartbeat. "We will give it time. There are others to choose from, after all."

She pushed him.

He grinned. "It is true. Why do you shove me?"

"You are trying to be rid of me."

"Perhaps."

She shoved him again, and he grasped her waist. She giggled.

René's heart pounded, stirring his blood. He pulled away. "I have easier ways of ridding myself of such a pest." He turned over on his side, away from her. "All I have to do is go to sleep."

She harrumphed and pulled the corner of his blanket as she moved. Though he forced his breathing to calm, René did not sleep.

Brigitte dug deep with her paddle as the wind and waves bounced them along Nipissing's southern shore, only pausing now and again to rub away an ache. She captured a handful of water in her palm to drink and glanced to the clouds hanging heavy overhead. She had no sooner looked up when a fat drop smacked her cheek, followed by a pelting of others. Perhaps they would seek shelter among one of the many islands on their course.

An hour passed, and the wind buffeted harder. The waves

climbed to the gunwales. She peered once over her shoulder. A distance had grown between the three *bateaux*. She refocused on her task, shivering. Her hands were pink and shriveled from the damp, and it soaked through to her bones. Would they not stop? *Non*, the captains, Munion and Jacques, pushed them on. René pushed them on, anxious and driven.

A commotion broke out behind them, and René's crew paused stroking to look back.

The *gouvernail* in the stern barked a command to turn. Brigitte drove her paddle with the others back into the water to keep their own *bateau* from flailing against the swells as their craft swung about.

"What is it?" she asked the man in front of her.

A murmur broke out.

Brigitte strained to see what was happening ahead. René turned. His face registered horror before he plunged his own paddle in with urgency, joining the middlemen.

And then she saw it. One of the canoes had tipped. Her heart plunged to her stomach. Shouts and cries. Heads bobbing in the waves. Arms flailing. Packs floating away. *Mon Dieu!* The overturned canoe was half submerged. Wet hands slid off its sides, reaching up to grasp again. So many could not swim.

"Gervais!" Her voice was a terrified shriek in the battering wind. She half stood, fear for him and the others overpowering concern for herself, until the man next to her jerked her down.

"You will spill us as well."

She turned away from him. "Gervais!" she called again, barely holding to the seat.

The *bateau* rocked haphazardly in the waves. The men around her reached to gather packs and stretched out their paddles to aid the floundering men.

"Gervais!" The rain stung her eyelids, but she didn't care. She faced the wind and roiling whitecaps where the *bateau* had spilled. "Gervaise!"

"Pierre! Alan!"

"Georges, grab the paddle!"

"Jacques, hold! You will spill us all."

"*Gervais!*" Her chest burned.

Someone rose, gasping from the water beside her. "Rupert." She gulped his name and grabbed his forearm, drawing him to the side of the boat. "Hold on. I will help you." Rupert gripped the gunwale, panting, and she clenched her fingers tighter on his arm. "Where is Gervais?" Her throat strangled around her plea. Her eyes roamed from Rupert to René, who looked blankly back at her, then called out another order she made no sense of.

The chaos and clamor continued as the boats rounded up men and trade goods. The Métis man and woman sat in another canoe, shivering.

But not Gervais.

The setting sun broke through scattering clouds as they huddled around the fires. René and the other captains discussed a plan to search for Gervais and another missing voyageur. Hushed voices mixed with the sound of men chewing on their pemmican or spitting their tobacco grated on Brigitte's nerves. She strode away from them to the edge of the lake, her eyes searching for something she could not see.

Gervais.

Boots scuffed along the shore, and she turned, hugging her still-damp coat tight. René and several others stood around a *bateau*, ready to push it off.

She hurried to his side. "I will go too."

"It is too dangerous."

"The winds have calmed."

"It will be dark soon. I want you to stay here."

"Alone?"

His eyes glittered.

"I will go too."

She pushed past him, but he grabbed her arm, pulling her to him. "We will find him."

Tears filled her eyes, spilling over. She sniffed and shook her head.

"You must stay." A shadow stepped beside her. Rupert touched her shoulder, his touch soothing. "Rupert will stay with you while I am gone."

A sob escaped, hard as she tried to choke it inside. What if René joined Gervais in his watery grave? For certainly, that was where he was. What if René didn't come back?

René lowered his voice. "Stay with Rupert, Brigitte. *S'il vous plaît.*" He stroked her cheek with a finger, then cupped her chin in his palm.

She pulled her face away and wiped at the tears trickling over her cheeks. Grieving to do so, she nodded.

Rupert laid a hand upon her shoulder again, and she stepped away from René. She turned into Rupert's arms and sobbed.

He patted her back, but at the sound of the *bateau* whisking over sand and pebbles, she raised her head. Rupert released her, and she stepped to the shore as the men dipped their paddles and pushed away. Soon, René's *bateau* disappeared in the twilight.

No sound followed him. No song to mark the way he'd gone. No trail to promise her he hadn't vanished forever. After allowing her to watch for a quarter of an hour, Rupert drew Brigitte back to the fire. He left her there to collect boughs for her bed.

"I will do it." She took the boughs from him and laid them over the wet ground. She covered them with her blanket and sat.

"You must eat." He gave her some pemmican.

She shook her head. She could not eat.

Stars spangled the black sky. The lap of water against the grainy shore crawled over her anxious thoughts like shadows. They never should have kept to the lake. When the wind increased, René should have called a halt. He should have made them wait. Why didn't he make them wait?

Fear and anger co-mingled. She wanted to rail. She wanted to weep. She clenched and unclenched her hands instead, not even daring to pray.

At last, hours later, the soft *sploosh* of the paddles sounded moments before feet splashed into the water.

Brigitte flung back her blanket and rushed to meet them as they lifted the canoe safely ashore. She searched each face. René stared back at her, his eyes wide, then downcast. An ache laid hold of the back of her throat. She swallowed a wail. Stepping closer, she saw Gervais lying in the boat, his red hair like seaweed wrapped around his white face and throat.

She wanted to run away, pretend it hadn't happened. Pretend it was some other man lying there, and Gervais was in the camp somewhere, drying out his stockings. She crumbled, but René was there, catching her, holding her, kneeling on the damp ground with his arms wrapped around her.

CHAPTER 9

In our home I was the only daughter,
Yet they sent me to sea.
— Le Moulignier Amoureux (The Amorous Sailor)

Days moved on. Brigitte's soul remained haunted. Behind them lay the rushing, seventy-mile French River which had demanded so much attention she dared not think of other things. She dared not think of Gervais, but now, he was everywhere.

Lake Huron pressed before them. Miles and miles of ocean it must be, or so she imagined. Ocean like her father crossed as a boy. Water—endless water in her broken memory. Then mist fell over them, thick like snow. The voyageurs' songs carried across the water like the moan of gray ghosts as one *canot* and another appeared and disappeared again.

The haunting of Gervais's violent death began at Grondine, where the water groaned as it swelled over the rocks. It preyed upon her through the narrow channel called La Cloche where the waves rang like a bell, tolling for his lost youth. Now it buried her in mist and fog, draping her soul in mourning.

Wetness clung to her face. Mist mingled with silent tears. She barely noticed when René looked at her from the prow of the boat. Did he mourn the loss of Gervais and the other drowned man whom they'd pulled from the shallow Nipissing? Did he feel the same gaping hole as she?

He'd made them go on, though the wind told even an untried *engagé* like her that they should have waited. Shouldn't they? Rupert told her the waves were often so on those waters, and yet it had seemed too fierce.

Brigitte tucked her face against her arm as she paddled, wiping at the dampness. Better to feel anger—better to find a place to lay blame—than to feel the deep, torturing pain of losing Gervais. Had she loved him then? *Non*. Not as a woman loves a man.

Again, the following morning, fog moved like cream around them, but by midday, it rose. With shouts of joy, the voyageurs lifted their paddles to the sky and sang. Brigitte sucked in her breath, trying to forget, wanting the weight in her chest to lift like those paddles raised to the sky.

Mon Dieu, is Gervais in that better place, with Tante and Oncle? If he is, please tell him … tell him he was a fine man of the north. And the best of friends. Tell him that I thought so.

René filled a bowl with soup for Brigitte. She hadn't eaten much in the days since Gervais's death, so he tried to encourage her to keep up her strength. Her heart must have knitted to the *engagé* more than she cared to admit. Ah, such a travesty, but such things happened. Crosses marked many such losses on the voyageurs' journey. With time, she would heal.

He found her seated upon a smooth-washed log on the beach. "We will reach the Sault Ste. Marie tomorrow. Rupert has family there. Perhaps you will meet them."

She flicked her glance at him but said nothing. A small black book lay in her lap.

He lowered himself beside her. She scooted over. He frowned as he handed her the soup and watched until she took a bite. "Rupert is father of a large brood. Did he tell you?"

A longer look. She shook her head, her mouth full but not swallowing.

"Four or five children. I forget."

She swallowed hard. "I did not know."

"*Oui*. He is a family man."

"Perhaps that is why his heart is kind." She stirred her peas porridge, her voice thoughtful.

"You think it is?"

Brigitte nodded.

René studied her, wondering about her conclusions. She continued to stir. "Such things are important to you because you are a woman."

She stopped stirring. Her face paled, and she lifted her eyes to his. "You are not a ... a family man too, are you, René? I never asked. I did not know about Rupert, and you ... if you are—"

"*Non.*" He chuckled. "Do not misunderstand. We are all not harboring wives and children in the wilderness. Some are, *oui*, but not all."

Color returned to her face, more than before. She lowered her lashes. "I am sorry for misjudging you. And I am sorry for ... for blaming you."

"Blaming me?"

"For Gervais. I did. I blamed you."

So that was it. Deep brown eyes, glossy with tears, turned on him. He reached for her hand. "I am somewhat to be blamed, and I am sorry. More sorry than you know."

Her tears spilled over, jarring him. With his free hand, he stroked a thumb across her cheek.

She sniffed, pulling away.

"My mother used to tell me it was good to cry sometimes." He spoke as gently as he could.

"Did she?"

"When Claude and I were little boys, I hurt him. I didn't mean to, but I was bigger. I fell against him, and he hit his head and cried. When I called him a *bébé*, our mother told me that sometimes it is good to cry. It shows great feeling and can assuage the pain."

She blinked away the tears, and a smile touched her lips. "Do you ever cry now, René?"

When had he last cried? When their mother passed away. Then he and Claude had both cried. He'd not cried since. Likely, neither had Claude. "*Non.* Not lately. Not yet."

"Perhaps I will be done crying soon."

"Is it only for Gervais that you weep? You have lost much."

She nodded. "You are right. I am tired of losing people." Her voice grew stronger. "I was not in love with Gervais. I know it. Still, it is a shame that one so full of life …" She pushed the wetness from her eyes again.

"Will you forgive me, Brigitte?"

Her head bobbed, and again, the doe-like softness of her gaze met his. "If you will forgive me as well. You may have saved my life. It might have been I who died in the lake if you had not taken me into your canoe."

He tapped the small book on her lap. "You have a prayer book."

She brushed her fingers over the volume and sniffed. "I pray for him."

"His soul has flown where it would." René did not wish his words to sound harsh, but neither could he pull them in. "Release your pain, and shed your tears, but the time to pray for Gervais has gone. Pray now for those around you. Who knows if any of us will make it to our destinations." He squeezed her hand.

With her free hand, she clutched his arm, leaning into him. He raised his arm to pull her against him but checked himself. He must guard himself from comforting her overmuch. There would be someone else to do that eventually. He patted her shoulder and straightened as Rupert approached. "Ah, here is Rupert. Rupert. Come. Tell us about your family. How many children do you have now?"

The Métis smiled and squatted beside them. "I have one girl and three boys. Three!"

"And your daughter, how many years is she?" Brigitte asked, her voice nasally, but she wore a half-smile.

"She is old enough to worry over. She quickly approaches her fourteenth summer. I should stay home to warn away unruly voyageurs and the native men seeking to woo her already."

Brigitte's eyes rounded.

"You remind me of her, mademoiselle."

She flushed.

A moment later, the other Métis and his Ojibwe wife joined them. The woman lowered her short, round body to the ground and smiled, showing a gap between her front teeth. She turned to Brigitte and spoke rapidly in Ojibwe. René glanced at Brigitte. She looked at him and shook her head.

"*Aaniin ezhinikaazoyan?*" the woman said again, slowly. "What are you called?"

"Brigitte Marchal."

She nodded. "Your people live *Baawitigong*?"

"It is the name the *Anishinaabe* call Sault Ste. Marie," Rupert said.

Brigitte shook her head.

The woman smiled. "*Niin*—my name—Ojawa."

Her husband whistled several notes, then grinned.

"Bluebird," Rupert explained.

They chuckled. Brigitte smiled more fully, and René relaxed. She would eventually forget the pain of the past days. There would be a husband and children for her someday, for her heart must beat for such. He saw it in her eyes when Rupert told her of his family.

René would take her to a new place where all the sorrows would lie behind her, if he could keep her safe for the remainder of the voyage.

I remember. The sights, the sounds, even the smells harkened to Brigitte.

Broad and bustling, the village at Sault Ste. Marie spanned the St. Mary River. Just beyond the falls lay Lake Superior. Métis, natives, and Europeans—traders, trappers, voyageurs, and priests—populated the area.

She had once wandered through this village holding onto the

tails of Papa's sash as he spread wares on his trade blanket to barter for furs and food for their journey. Now and again, he'd wrap a muscled arm over her shoulders and say to those gathered around him, "This is my little one who goes to Montreal for her education. She will be a lady and not a *sauvage.*" She could almost hear his deep voice.

Never did he think I might return to the Upper Country without him, or that I would become a woman of the north.

She breathed deep and watched from outside the circle of those gathered as René prepared to barter among the natives. On the ground, he spread a thick blanket covered with beads, flints, nails, and other small wares, arranging them to their most appealing advantage. People gathered near. He talked quickly, convincingly, while Ojawa—Bluebird—repeated his words in a flurry of language, mostly Michif, the Métis mix of native and French. Brigitte grabbed hold of the words in her mind and practiced them silently.

Women prodded their men, and soon fresh meat and pemmican replaced the items René bartered from his blanket. When the trading was over, he gathered his items together. She stepped near, and his gaze rose.

"Watching you thus, I am reminded of my *père*. Things I had forgotten."

His brow lifted. "Oh? What things are those?"

She shrugged. "Your manner with them reminds me of his. Your voice even. How it appeals and entices them to the things you offer."

He tucked the rolled-up blanket under his arm and stood. "I shall consider it a compliment."

"I miss him."

"Come." He steered her toward the village. "Let us find something to eat, and you can tell me more about him."

They strode side by side down the street, farther into the town. Brigitte stepped closer to René as they passed three men going the other direction. They stared boldly at her as they passed. René's fingers wrapped her elbow.

"Competition has arrived."

"Competition?"

"It appears another brigade heads west. We will leave during the night, to remain ahead of them."

"Why must we?"

He glanced back at them. "The race is begun for the furs of the interior. Those who arrive earliest make the best trades."

Brigitte peered over her shoulder, and René followed her gaze. Sidelong glances from those of the other company fell their way. One man nudged his companion.

"See, they are thinking the same thing," René said. "Come." He led her around the corner up another street. "I know where we can find a good, hot meal. It is time you met Rupert's family."

They found their friend frolicking in the grass with a group of children outside a frame house not dissimilar to *Tante* Eunice's home in Montreal. Homesickness pricked Brigitte, even while she smiled at the antics of the voyageur and his children. One young boy hung from his papa's neck, but Rupert swung him around easily. He stopped when he saw René and Brigitte approach.

"See here, Victor. It is my good friend René Dufour and my new friend, Brigitte. Say hello." A chorus of small voices greeted them. Rupert slid the boy to the ground. "It will be hard to leave them in the morning."

René smiled at an older girl who watched him with her hands behind her back. "Perhaps they will not mind so much if I give them a sweet." He reached into his sack of wares and pulled out a package of maple sugar candies.

"Ooh!" A little boy clasped dimpled hands together and stepped closer. René offered him a candy.

"Don't eat it too quickly," Rupert warned.

"And here is a piece for your mama," René said, handing him another. "And for your brothers and sister." He held the package open.

"Except *le bébé*," said the little boy.

As he distributed the candy, a short woman with black, braided hair stepped out of the house. She wiped her hands on an apron before reaching to shake hands with René. Lines marked the corners of her eyes when she smiled.

"Brigitte, allow me to introduce Rupert's wife, Maemaengwahn."

"Hello."

"It is good to meet you," Maemaegwahn said.

"This is Brigitte Marchal, from Montreal."

Maemaegwahn looked at René, her eyebrows lifting. "You marry?"

René cleared his throat.

Rupert chuckled.

A blush rose up Brigitte's throat and cheeks.

"Mademoiselle Marchal looks for her father at the forts in the lake country," René said.

Rupert put his arm around his wife. "You know our friend René has determined not to have a wife he must leave for months on end, as he has seen me do to you, my dear."

That was why he had not married? Brigitte glanced at René, then away while while she considered Rupert's words, turning her gaze on the children who had finished their treats and returned to romping about.

Maemaegwahn laid a hand on her arm, drawing her attention. "You and René must eat with us."

"Now that is a most agreeable idea," René said.

After their meal, Brigitte and René left Rupert to be with his family for the remainder of the day. René accompanied Brigitte back to the camp on the edge of the village. Word had already spread of the other brigade.

"Rest while you can." René cautioned the crews. "We leave in a few hours."

True to his word, they left the village while the moon and stars still spangled the sky. Dawn seemed hours away. Jacques, René, and

Georges Munion urged quietness, but no one needed to be told. With only the softest grunts around her, the men hoisted packs, and Brigitte helped lift a canoe over her shoulders. They tread the portage in darkness on moccasin-covered feet.

Twice Brigitte tripped on roots or rocks, she couldn't tell which. Both were equally painful. She cringed and kept moving, staying behind René and keeping pace with the sure-footed men of her group. One by one, the bark *bateaux* slipped into the water, and the men boarded, pressing their paddles into the swirling river. This time, they moved without song, and only the far-off screech of an owl called at their passing.

For an hour, they paddled hard and fast, feeling the rhythm in silence. The river widened. The forested banks retreated as a bay spread open before them, allowing a greater view of stars and sky. A while longer, and the rush of water took on a new sound, a swell of wash against an endless shore.

And then the voyageurs sang.

The stars faded, and Brigitte grinned at her seatmate as she raised her voice with the others, exalting over having slipped away from the other brigade undetected. After several verses, the singing ended, and they drew the *bateaux* into a line near the shore, pulling out their clay pipes. The first hint of daylight filtered over them from the east. Water broke in gentle swells against the shore. Ahead of them spanned a vast nothing in the shadowy predawn.

She raised her chin and stared into the vacant distance, trying unsuccessfully to imagine the magnitude of Lake Superior stretching before them. Cold, deep, yet somehow majestic, it seemed the world's end. Yet another world—one where she had been born—lay beyond.

Brigitte bit the inside of her lip. For the second time in her life, she would travel these great and terrifying waters. A feat for any woman, to be sure. One she'd likely never accomplish again—if she even managed this time.

Halos of sweet smoke settled around her, bringing every sense to life. No one spoke. Some closed their eyes while they smoked, taking in what repose they could on their brief respite. René smiled, and she returned it. Without a word, she sensed his satisfaction. They had gotten a good start ahead of the other brigade.

Minutes later, they were off again, their song setting the pace as they raced for the northwestern Lake Superior trading posts, still hundreds of miles away.

Lusty voices rang out harmonies, carrying Brigitte's thoughts to Papa. Surely he must be alive. Tears sprang to her eyes, and she joined in the song. Better to sing of clever little birds.

No, no, Sir, I dare not,
because if my father knew I would be beaten!
But who is it that would tell him?
The birds of the woods!
The birds of the woods, do they speak?
They speak French, Latin also. They speak as they have learned.
When alas, the world is clever to teach the birds Latin.

The voyageurs' stories and tunes filled her head as they sang and paddled, paddled and sang.

Three days they pressed on, following the upward arch of the lake, but then high winds stopped them. For two days, they halted, waiting for calm. Brigitte mended her worn leggings and helped patch their *bateau*. Along with the woman called Bluebird, she cooked fish and elk meat they'd gotten in trade and stirred the pots of the pea porridge she had learned to call rubaboo. At night, she lay an arm's length from René and gazed upward.

"Are you asleep?"

She startled. Snores and grunts and the late hour had made her believe everyone was asleep. *"Non."*

"How far the stars stretch. I am ever amazed."

She glanced at René, who lay on his back with his hands tucked beneath his head. "God says they are without number."

"I believe it. I have tried to count them."

She grinned. "You have?"

"When I was a lad. Just when I would think I had worked out a pattern for counting, they would shift."

"God would not make it so easy."

"He enjoys keeping us guessing."

"Perhaps."

"I am certain He has a great laugh over it. And many other things."

That God had a sense of humor struck her oddly. "You should not say so."

He turned his head to face her. "Why not? You do not think God enjoys laughing now and again?"

"Not at us."

He grunted. "Why not? We laugh at one another."

"But He is God."

"Ah, you believe He is a sober judge then." He turned his gaze heavenward again. "God is bigger than that."

"What do you mean?"

"He is many things. Sober judge. Tender father. Humorous friend."

She stuck out her lip and pondered his words. "I think you go too far."

"To say He has a sense of humor or to say He is a friend?"

She wasn't certain God was her friend. He was distant, there beyond the stars, after all.

"You were taught by nuns, and yet you do not realize these attributes? I am a heathen, for the most part, and still I know these things."

"Who taught you?"

"The Heavens declare the glory of God."

She turned to face him. "*Oui*. But who taught you to value Him as a 'humorous friend?'"

René squinted in thought. "I remember a Bible story from

my youth, the nature of which led me to this belief. Perhaps you recall it. When the Christ walked the streets, hemmed in all around by the crowds, a woman with an issue of blood reached out and touched him and was healed.

"He said, 'Who is it that touched me?'" A deep-throated chuckle rumbled out of René. "The disciples were all puzzled by their master's question. 'There are people all about, and You ask us who touched you?' Such incredulity. Such shock."

"I still do not understand where the humor lies."

"You do not? Think. He was *the Christ*. The God of all in the form of man. The One who knows thoughts and intentions before they are uttered. Think you that He didn't know who touched him? But His disciples did not reason it themselves, and His question brought a confession from the woman. Her secret revealed, she was openly able to thank and glorify Him." René sighed. "Such a sense of humor in it all."

Brigitte shook her head. She still didn't quite see the point, but René continued to chuckle.

"Did He not make us in his image?"

"So I have been told."

"Look around you. Surely you must find humor in that."

She glanced at the sleeping forms of exhausted men. "In hard work and determination?"

René scratched his beard. "Not exactly what I meant."

"I know what you meant." She gave him a small smile. "I guess if we have a sense of humor, it must be because we are like Him."

His gaze settled on her and glittered. "You make an excellent point. There must be something of God in every man."

Her heart pricked. If man was made in God's image, was such a thing true? She could believe it in René's goodness and willingness to help her, in Rupert's quiet kindness, in her father's love, even in Gervais's friendship, but could there be anything of God in a man like Tristan Clarboux? She shuddered and huddled deeper into her blanket. If there was something of God in every man, then Tristan must be no man at all. Only devil.

"Are you chilled?" René's brows pinched. His arm snaked out from his blanket and tucked hers close.

"*Non*. I … it is nothing."

He continued tucking anyway. "The wind comes off the lake. You will not become rested if you are chilled."

The gentle rumble of his voice comforted her, and she studied his features yet again as he pushed the blanket's edges in. So much seriousness. So much care. "Thank you," she whispered.

His hand lay close to her elbow, and he patted her arm through the blanket.

She smiled and closed her eyes. If there was something of God in man, it was here, in this man who protected her.

CHAPTER 10

V'la l'bon vent
V'la joli vent
Go good wind, go pretty wind,
Go good wind, my beloved is calling,
Go good wind, go pretty wind,
Go good wind, my beloved awaits.
— V'la L'bon Vent, Voyageurs' Song

Voices roused Brigitte. René was no longer in his bed. She pushed her blanket aside and rose from beneath the boat's shelter to see him and Jacques with hands braced on hips and stances widened before a pair of men.

"You accuse us wrongly," one of the men said, his chin lifted so that it revealed a scar along his jaw.

"Do we?" René glanced at Jacques, then back to the two men facing them. "The bundles have been loosened, and you were awake before the others. Jacques saw you near them."

"It means nothing. You are mistaken." The man spat on the ground.

René stepped to one of the bundles and tugged at the loose ties.

Brigitte stepped closer, along with others, to see.

"See here how the fabric is loose." He reached inside and pulled out a bag of shot. Weighing it in his hand, his gaze narrowed on the two men.

Brigitte held her breath. Even from where she stood, she could see the bag was not full.

René handed the bag to Jacques. "What do you think, Jacques? Eight pounds? Ten at best?"

Jacques hefted the bag and nodded. He handed it back to René and curled his lip. "Not an ounce more."

René set the bag onto the bundle and looked at the men again. "Empty your pockets."

"We will not." The scarred man pushed his shoulders back. The other, a short, barrel-chested man, curled his hands into fists at his side.

"Must we assist you?" René gave a quick glance around him, and several more voyageurs drew into a close circle, ready to aid their leader.

Jacques took a long step nearer the men. "Do you think it will go well for you if we must use force?"

The men stared back. Tension filled the air. Then the shorter man loosened his fists. He glanced at the scarred man, who remained stiff. Not waiting any longer, the shorter man took a step away and reached into his coat pocket, withdrawing a small drawstring bag. From beneath the coat, in another satchel, he exposed a pair of stolen knives.

The scarred man let out a gusty breath. He pulled a pouch of the missing shot from his pocket. From another pocket, he withdrew a small sack of what appeared to be trade beads. Jacques stepped forward and snatched the things away.

René said to another voyageur, "Search their belongings." He turned his gaze back to the thieves as he spoke loud enough for all to hear. "Your fine will increase for each item found, to be taken from your own supplies when we reach the fort."

One of the men swore. René stepped toward him, standing nose-to-nose. "You think you deserve more than the others? You have carried more? Paddled harder than the rest? That which you agreed to be paid when you signed your contracts is no longer enough? And what of your fellows? Should they lack so you may have more?"

René turned to the crowd gathering around. His gaze swung past her. "These men will perform the least favored tasks for the rest of the voyage." He paused, his voice thick with warning. "We will see whether their future behavior warrants further punishment once we reach Fort William."

The thieves curled their lips and glared at the pronouncement but no longer argued. Brigitte was happy they hadn't come to blows.

Despite the turmoil, the brigade was soon on its way. They set off in a cold rain surrounded by fog. At noontime, the sun re-emerged. Along the shore, enormous rock faces jutted upward, resembling blocks of cast iron. Near them, the water lapped brown and murky from the previous rains, but the water away from shore was green and clear, despite a light wind that frequently changed directions, batting it about.

The *bateaux* traveled three abreast. Rupert and the other two Métis paddled several rods away from Brigitte's canoe. The husband of Bluebird murmured to seemingly no one. A man behind him leaned forward and tapped his shoulder, handing him something. Brigitte squinted. A penny piece glinted in the sun.

The Métis raised the penny with more murmuring and dropped it over the side. Another voyageur handed him a bit of tobacco, then some flint steel and punk. He dropped it all over the side.

Brigitte turned to her seatmate, François. "What are they doing?" She dipped her head toward those in the other *bateau*.

"Conjuring."

"Conjuring?"

"*Oui*. To ask the spirits for help."

"The voyageurs believe in such?"

François shrugged. "We must gain a fair wind somehow."

She frowned and watched the ceremony continue. "They should pray to the true God."

"A god is a god."

"You are not a Christian to say so."

He grunted.

"You are all full of nonsense!" The fellow behind her yelled. "Put away your mysticism, and paddle. We will leave you behind."

The craft lurched beneath her. The *milieux* dug their paddles with greater vigor. A murmuring of voices rose like a deep hum as they strengthened their pace. The crew in the other boat ceased their conjuring and leapt to the chase.

Tendrils of hair escaped from Brigitte's braid and whipped across her face. She smiled, forgetting the conjuring. With her own paddle, she pulled, stretching her limbs to the task.

Neck-and-neck they raced. She glanced back. Behind them, Jacques's *bateau* picked up speed but remained farther behind than René's and Georges Munion's, the two that had begun the challenge. The minutes passed. For surely a quarter of an hour, they kept their speed. Every muscle in Brigitte's arms and torso burned. Only the song and barks of the captains, along with the continual spurring on by one another, kept her and the others at their paces.

"To *le point!*" From the other boat, Munion pointed to a forested tip above an outcropping of rock reaching out toward them on the horizon. As one, both boats found another burst of speed, and, with another backward glance, she saw the third canoe closing in from behind.

Minutes later, René's canoe reached its destination by a mere half-stroke ahead of the other boat.

Brigitte and the rest of the voyageurs fell off paddling, their chests heaving, sweat dripping from their brows, streaming down their backs, and lining the armpits of their shirts. Rank they smelled too. Sighs and laughter surrounded her. Some of the men slurped water from their palms.

Brigitte gasped for breath and hoped for the weather to warm so she might bathe soon. Her woman's time had come upon her for the second time since leaving Montreal. How she wished to be clean again.

The boats hugged the rugged coast, but those seated on the right kept their paddles extended so as not to allow the fragile crafts to bump against the rocks. She was glad to be on the left of her seatmate so that her arms might lie limply over the paddle on her lap.

Smoke wove above her head as the crew lit their pipes. Brigitte dug in her sack for pemmican.

"*Il fait du vent*. See how the wind blows?"

Brigitte hooked a finger around a strand of hair sweeping across her lips and tucked it behind her ear. She squinted into the sunlight glinting off the waves. A few gray clouds puffed toward them on the horizon. Someone grunted. Brigitte frowned. Had their superstitious practices brought the wind around to push them toward Fort William? *Non*. She did not believe it.

The boats lolled on the waves, dipping and bobbing, the wind prodding at them. Whatever the reason for the wind, they would speed west now. The *avant* in each canoe called out, René with them. He swept her with a gaze that renewed her strength, as one-by-one, the boats struck out away from the rocks.

Snores and grunts assured Brigitte that the voyageurs slept. Clouds skidded across the moon, opening and closing the world to shadows and light. Beside her, René lay in repose, his eyes closed, his breathing deep but silent. She took the moment, as she had many times before, to study the man.

How much she owed him. He had remained constant to her protection and guidance, taking responsibility for her though he had no reason. He could have taken advantage of her naivety and innocence, of their forced companionship, but he did not.

Inching farther from René, she pushed out of her blanket and rose, shivering. The brisk Canadian spring nights still stole her breath, but she must bathe.

She gathered her necessities and crept away on a cushion of pine needles toward the lake. Water lapped against the shore, breaking the stillness and covering any sound she might make. She hastened over rocks and driftwood, moving farther from the camp into the moonlit darkness.

She looked ahead and behind, hoping none of the men might have roused as she left and worrying about the stories taunting the edges of her mind. Surely the Hungry Heron, who devoured the unwary, must be asleep on his perch somewhere. Maybe not so, the *Inini-Wudjoo*—the Great Giant. She'd tried not to listen to the tales the voyageurs told around their fires. Even so, now they stirred her fear.

Was she any better than those whose superstitions allowed them to conjure a fair wind? Nevertheless, her breath came faster as she hurried to her task.

When at last she felt she'd gone far enough from the camp, she stooped behind a pile of driftwood to disrobe. Gooseflesh jumped up her spine and down her arms and legs. Her shoulders trembled as she tiptoed into the tide. The water wrapped around her toes, turning them to ice. It stole her breath as she dropped to her knees, skinning them on stones beneath the surface as she let the water wash around her waist. Her teeth chattered, and her whole body shook as she rushed through the process.

Chilled though she was, she longed to plunge her head beneath the water. But then she would be blue with cold, and perhaps a hungry fish would pull her down. Dread raced through her. Crazy notions, terrifying thoughts of what lay beneath the dark surface of the water. She dipped once, twice. Water like icicles flowed down her hair between her shoulder blades. She bit her tongue to keep from crying out as she rushed out of the water, quivering almost violently.

She tugged her clothes back over her wet skin. Sand clung to her as she forced the shirt over her head and cinched her trousers. Oh, for a dress.

Bundling her things together again, Brigitte stumbled back toward camp. She burrowed under her blanket, tucking it close. Wet hair clung to her neck, making her shudder. She longed to move closer to René, to collect his warmth, but she didn't dare.

Instead, she pressed her eyes closed and clenched her teeth, willing herself to warmth.

René listened to the chatter of her teeth, felt her moving behind him, and it almost made him moan aloud. Ah, the girl. What she'd done to him.

Some sense had woken him. He'd not heard her, but once she'd gone, he awoke. His blood had roared warning, fearing some mishap, and he leapt quietly from his blanket to find her. The snores of the others remained unchanged as he stepped hastily through the camp, looking for her.

He'd lingered on the edge of the forest, waiting to see if she would return from the woods, but she did not. After several minutes, with nerves taut as a beaver spring trap, he'd bypassed the *bateaux* and sleeping men and followed the shore instead. As the moon appeared from behind a silver-lined cloud, he'd spotted her moving over rocks and sand, around logs washed smooth but heavy with water. He could not imagine why she went so far, so he'd followed. Then she'd disappeared behind a twisted mass of driftwood. He'd waited, expecting her to reappear in a moment, so he could see her safely back to camp.

But when she did … René swallowed hard at the recollection, almost gasping now just as he had then. He'd looked away and back again. Much as he had tried, her maidenly image would not leave but seemed to push and pull at him, tugging him to gaze. He'd seen her as she rushed back out of the water, hiding behind the driftwood again. Even now, the memory made his heart beat wildly. She'd been a silhouette in the distance. That was all. Still, her womanhood had been revealed in the moonlight.

He'd cursed himself. *Fool. She only wished to bathe.* He should have let her be. She'd had reason to leave him sleep. Did not Bluebird go alone into the woods without her husband's aid? And

René was no husband. He was nothing to her. Now he had invaded her deepest privacy.

Movement behind the driftwood had assured him she must be dressing again. Knowing she was safe, he'd returned to the camp before she could discover him. Before she knew he saw her.

He had barely managed enough time to lie still beneath his blanket and calm his rapid breathing before she returned. He kept his back to her but sensed her hurry to cocoon herself inside her blanket.

The chattering continued. She must be half frozen. His muscles tightened with concern. Slowly, he turned, and she stilled, her eyes wide upon him when he looked at her.

"You are cold?"

"I will be all right."

He moved closer anyway and draped his blanket over her.

"René—"

"Shh. It is all right. Go to sleep."

She tucked her head low, and he boldly laid his arm across her, her trembling easing. Soon she fell asleep, but each time he closed his eyes, he remembered her there in the moonlight. Not a girl, but a woman who now lay warm and soft in his arms.

CHAPTER 11

And it floated on the river
Like a yellow leaf in Autumn,
Like a yellow water-lily.

— Longfellow, Hiawatha

Clouds masked the heavens, and the wind rose again the next day. Beneath the boiling sky came waves in tall rollers that lifted the canoes like leaves caught in the wind. Brigitte's *bateau* teetered at each crest, then hurtled downward, as though into an abyss. With each descent—each crash that pummeled the bark beneath Brigitte's feet—terror raced through her. Her stomach rose to her throat. She paddled as furiously as the others, struggling to climb again. No song rose now, only shouts and cries. They were all afraid, yet courageously so.

Beside her, François reached for a handful of corn and tossed it into the angry depths.

Sweat ran down her temples, mingling with the drizzle. "We have no time for your spells."

He might have heard but for a sudden surge breaking over the stern. The man tilted precariously, upsetting the contents of the kettle beneath his feet.

Brigitte reached for his sleeve, letting her paddle flounder. The boat lurched. Men reached out their paddles to steady it as yet another wave rocked them like a twig caught in its maelstrom.

"Bail!" The order came from the steersman as he tossed a sponge forward. Brigitte grabbed it. She dipped and squeezed, dipped and squeezed, as the water coming in kept pace with what she dispensed. The drizzle turned to rain and fell in earnest. The fury of a storm lay upon them. Still they rode on. Still she bailed with the sponge.

Mon Dieu, save us!

Beside her, François made the sign of the cross.

Why did no one call for a halt? Did demons drive them on?

Up the mountainous crests, shooting down them again, they paddled like demons themselves.. At last, they rounded a point into a shallow bay where the wind weakened. She raised her head. René's chest heaved. He, too, was drenched to the skin, his dark hair dripping. "Now we beach!" he called breathlessly.

Brigitte's heartbeat thumped against her wet clothes as she took calming breaths. The men rested and allowed the breakers to carry them toward shore.

"Everyone is with us? *Bien.*" René cast them an anxious smile, the wind buffeting him.

The man behind her patted her shoulder. She turned, and he chuckled, relief smoothing his brow. She let out an airy laugh and faced forward again as the canoe drifted close to shore.

Brigitte leapt into the wash with the others. She wobbled ashore on weak legs as the men lifted the canoes free from danger.

Thunder rumbled low and rolling. Lightning emblazoned the sky, turning back the curtain of gloom. Brigitte hurried with the rest to cover the packs and turn the boats. The crew sought shelter beneath a canopy of trees, and soon, a fire blazed beneath the edge of the forest, hissing at the rain.

"Are you all right?"

René's voice, behind her ear, startled her. She turned, nodding. "I am fine."

He had stripped off his wet shirt, but his gaze was steady. He unnerved her as much as the storm. "You are a brave one, Brigitte." The corner of his mouth lifted, hinting at a smile.

"No braver than you or the others." Why did he look at her so? They'd faced other storms, even Gervais's death. She frowned. "Why did we not stop sooner, seeing the danger?"

He opened her pack and pulled out her blanket. She stared, wondering at his gesture as he placed it around her damp shoulders.

"I don't want you to catch your death before we get to Fort William. Tomorrow we enter the Baie du Tonnerre."

"The Bay of Thunder? Have we not endured thunder enough?" As though to emphasize her words, the sky cracked again, sending vibrations through the ground. She jumped closer to his side.

René laughed. "It is just the name. We cross to reach the Kaministiquia. There, at its mouth, we reach the fort." His eyes lingered on her. "Your journey is nearly at an end, mademoiselle."

At an end? It didn't seem such a thing would ever be. "I—I do not quite know what to think. We have been traveling so long."

Would she find Papa there? What if he was not? She would have to stay at the fort until she knew what had become of him. What would it be like to live as a stranger in an unfamiliar place full of trappers and Indians? The notion of finding her mother's people—more strangers—now felt foreign. Had she been a fool to come after all?

"What if … what if my papa is not to be found, and there is nothing for me to do? How will I find my place?"

His brow furrowed, but he rubbed it smooth. "Do not fret. You will have your pick of men to marry."

The heat of anger flashed through her. "And if I do not wish to marry one of them?"

He slipped his arm across her shoulders and turned her away from the others. "Lower your voice. Do you want to make yourself vulnerable now? I know you are nervous after what happened in Montreal, but you might change your mind. All men are not like Clarboux. There will likely be someone who pleases you." He shook his head. "As it is, we are jumping to conclusions. Did I not tell you that you will find employment while you await word of your father?"

"I am sorry, René. There is just so much I cannot imagine." She lowered her head to hide the flush creeping over her skin. She'd trusted him so far, and he'd not let her down. She would have to trust him still. She sighed and found the strength to look at him again. "Tell me more about Fort William."

He straightened and released her. "Coffee first." Rain pummeled the branches over them, drowning other conversations as he poured some muddy-looking beverage into a cup for each of them. "It is a colorful fort, full of song and dance and trade. Indians camped all about. Trappers bringing in their furs. Hundreds of people coming and going. Much food and drink and joviality. Sometimes too much drink," he added with a note of chagrin.

"And there are other women there as well?"

"Métis and natives, *oui*. No French. Englishmen, Scots, but no European women." He took a sip of his coffee and winked at her over his cup. "You will find your place while you wait for news of your *père*. Perhaps he will even be there with all the others who go to *rendezvous*."

At last, after finishing their coffee, the rain stopped. They cooked their evening rubaboo and made their beds on branches of soft pine shaken off and laid over the wet ground.

In the morning, no one needed rousing. A spirit of joviality hung about the camp. It increased as the voyageurs reloaded the *canots* and pushed off to Fort William. Songs echoed over the bright blue water as they rounded Thunder Cape. They paused for a *pipée* once they edged into the mouth of the bay, and the exuberance on each of the voyageurs' faces worked to push away Brigitte's concerns.

The bay stretched calm before them. Such a pleasant sight after yesterday's storm. As the voyageurs sang, Brigitte turned her face to the sun's warmth. They would arrive at their destination warm and dry after all.

Across the bay, they paddled. A shore that seemed miles away gradually grew into sharper focus.

"The River Kaministiquia!"

The voyageurs cheered. As one, they raised their paddles into the air, shouting for joy, then plunged them into the depths again. The shore came to meet them, and the river opened its mouth but resisted their entry. René called a halt, and they made a landing at a broad island.

Jokes and laughter accompanied general bathing. The older voyageurs leapt into the water's edge and made quick ablutions in the stream, stripping to the waist and braiding their long hair. Brigitte flushed, and Rupert spoke beside her. "We are vain in our appearance, though it may surprise you. We ready ourselves for our grand arrival." He smiled and strolled off whistling.

René stepped beside her. "Perhaps, up the shore, you will find some privacy away from these smelly ones." Laughter lay beneath his words, but when she looked at him, softness filled his eyes. "Come, I'll show you."

They walked away from the others, appearing every bit like a man and his woman. It was much too late for such thoughts to bother Brigitte. For a thousand miles, the others had believed her to be his. She would likely never regain her reputation, no matter when René left her or how either of them explained that he was merely her protector. *Non*, it would not be believed.

When they'd walked several hundred rods, René pointed to a group of trees around a small point. "I will remain here. Do not worry. I will busy myself." He jerked on his bundle.

Brigitte nodded and left him there, certain she could trust him. Well … fairly certain.

She continued on alone, walking up to a tiny lagoon with two points shouldering out on either side of her. Still, she didn't completely disrobe. The risk was too great. Removing her moccasins and leggings, her uncle's long shirt hung almost to her knees like a dress. She pushed up the sleeves and lifted the hem as she waded in to her calves.

The sun melted into the bare skin of her arms. She glanced back but saw no sign of René anywhere. Then she heard him singing, his voice coming from somewhere distant through the trees along the shore. Contentment, like the clean water lapping around her legs, washed over her. His voice was deep as the lake but warm and mellow.

Stepping into the water, her toes sank into the sandy bottom. The water she sluiced over her face and arms wasn't as icy as the last time. She flipped her head forward and dipped, scrubbing the sweat from her scalp and the dirt from her tresses. She wrung it out, twisting it on top of her head to still the dribbles from wetting her shirt too badly.

When she finished washing, she went back to the trees to dress. She dried her hair with the damp shirt and exchanged it for another, then she plaited a fresh braid.

René's singing had stopped. She stepped out of the woods to return to him, but a movement on the water halted her. Shielding her eyes against the glare, she peered again. A song carried from across the glinting bay. Another brigade cut across the watery expanse toward them.

She hurried up the shore, dodging brush and driftwood. "René!"

"I am here," he called.

She pushed back a branch and found him standing in the sand. He wore a clean, white shirt with a rainbow sash. His black hair shone in the sun and was tied back with a bright braid of ribbon—black, red, and green. He smiled, his teeth white against his tan face and dark eyes.

She paused for only a moment—a bit taken back by the look of him, so cleaned up and his beard trimmed. So handsome.

Brigitte sputtered then found her voice. "There … there are *bateaux*—several of them—coming this way."

He frowned and stepped past her to look, to turn his ear. Their song grew louder, more distinct. He lifted his satchel. "Come, we must hurry. We cannot let them pass us."

She ran behind him, light-footed in her moccasins. As they reached the others, René called out the orders. "To the boats! Another brigade approaches."

Brigitte glanced at the voyageurs as they received the news. All were bedecked in fresh clothes and colorful sashes of red, green, and blue, some outfits even frilled out in feathers and beads.

"It must be the one we slipped away from all those miles ago at Sault Ste. Marie," François said. "They have caught us."

He emptied his pipe into the wash, and the voyageurs set the boats afloat. They grabbed their paddles and plunged on.

"*Dépêche-toi!* Hurry."

"We must not let them pass."

"They have spotted us."

"Will they stop?"

"They might, but they will likely try to pass us on the river."

"Paddle. Harder." René barked the order over his shoulder.

Brigitte glanced back at their pursuers. She made out the shapes of faces and saw splashes of color in the hats and sashes in the *bateaux* as the other brigade closed distance.

"Don't look at them," said François. "Pull."

The boats surged as every man found new strength. Competitiveness, like sweat, oozed from their pores, its energy filling Brigitte. Exciting her.

"We cannot let them arrive first."

The imperative cut through the waves before her, and she followed it.

The chorus of the competition clashed with their own like a dissonant echo, but René's brigade maintained its lead and finally opened a distance between them, rounding a bend in the river so the other *bateaux* dropped out of sight.

Brigitte leaned toward François. "Will they not pause to make ready as we have done?"

He grunted. "They would rather catch us."

The *chanteur* changed the song to a tune with a different tempo as they surged up the river's throat, pressing hard against the flow. The sun crested the tall pines hemming the water in on both sides. Brigitte's heart pattered with delight as she listened to the rhythm of the paddles stroking the rushing water.

Her arms shuddered, exhausted. René looked back, catching her eye. He winked playfully and turned away. She tucked her chin and smiled as she bent to scoop a handful of cold water.

Another cheer rose up. She jerked her head to see around the broad shoulders in front of her. The voyageurs clamored brighter in song as the pickets of Fort William came into view.

CHAPTER 12

"Goods of every kind: corn, flour, pork, and tools arrived
from Montreal and Mackinac, and for their exchange,
furs. Thousands of bales from the wintering posts. Business
abounded, as did feasting, dancing, drinking, gambling,
and fighting. Here I met Waasnodae, and determined to
marry her."
—Journal of Etienne Marchal, Voyageur

She glanced side to side at the sea of camps outside the pickets as she followed René into the fort, soaking in the grandness of the place around her. Agents, workers, *bourgeois* clerks, and gentlemen partners roved past her, in and out its gates and buildings. All forms of busyness, like a small city, surrounded her. Buildings, almost a dozen of them, stood neatly around the square. To think such a place existed so far from Montreal and the rest of the world.

"There is the Great Hall." René leaned close and nodded toward a tall, windowed building. "The partners, superior clerks, and some of the apprentice clerks and agents take their meals there." He pointed at one corner of the building. "The wintering partners are housed in the North West House on the corner of the Great Hall."

He directed her attention to the other buildings around the square. "Those are the merchandise and provision stores. We have quality retail shops for partners and clerks as well. Over there are the equipment shops for outfitting the *engagés*. See, there is a warehouse holding stores for the outfitting of posts in the interior." He put his hands on his hips and nodded at another white building. "The superior agents occupy the twelve bedrooms in the Bell House."

She stepped a few feet away from him and continued her study of the compound while René stopped to speak to men he seemed to know, then he took her hand and led her back. "That is all the tour I can give you right now. I must return you to the camp of the *hivernants* and look for my brother Claude. The Indians arrive as well. We must trade for the best of their furs ahead of those from the other brigade." She glanced at him, and he smiled. "It is something of a contest."

Outside the fort again, they wove westward between the river bank and the pickets, and here too, Brigitte's gaze was captivated by the numbers of people gathering. "Only the winterers camp on this side. To the east is the camp of the *mangeurs de lard*. They will make the return trip to Montreal in a few days." René took long strides as he spoke, leaving her to keep up.

The wintering camp was larger than she'd grown used to during their travels. Many other *hivernants* had settled there, setting up canvas tents. She spotted faces she recognized from their crew. "There is Bluebird."

"I will leave you in her company," René said.

Bluebird knelt in front of a steaming kettle doing her laundry as they approached. "Our camp is better than those filthy pork-eaters', eh?" She curled her nose toward the east where the other camp lay.

Brigitte glanced over Bluebird's head to where tents were arranged like a small city around campfires where people cooked, smoked, and talked. Some, like Bluebird, did their wash. Tarps covered supplies. Stacks of firewood were covered with pine boughs, protected from possible rains. Over other smoking fires, meat dried on sticks driven into the ground. Brigitte had not been to the other camp.

Bluebird withdrew a shirt from the kettle and wrung it before hanging it over a small teepee of bare sticks. She dried her hands on her apron. "A careless bunch," Bluebird added.

"I have not been to their camp," Brigitte said.

"All the better for you." Bluebird gave a brisk nod.

"I leave Brigitte with you and your husband," René said. "I

must attend to business."

"*Mino*. Good." Bluebird smiled so that the gap between her teeth showed. "I expect you."

René turned Brigitte aside. "It is the first time I leave you, but you will be all right with Bluebird. Everyone is busy now."

Brigitte raised her chin. "I am not afraid."

"Good." He smiled and squeezed her shoulder. The caress was comforting and his gaze warm.

He sighed as his hand dropped away. "I will see you again as soon as I can." With a sharp nod, he left. Brigitte stared after him.

Bluebird grasped her sleeve and tugged. "Come. We go visit."

Brigitte pulled in a breath and turned to follow. They made their way through the camp to the farthest edges and down a wooded trail. Soon they came upon another camp, very different from the voyageurs'. a few small houses, mostly *wiigiwaams*, were scattered about among the trees.

"Métis," Bluebird said. "Ojibwe." She pointed as she explained. Winding among the *wiigiwaams*, Bluebird dipped her head and led Brigitte behind the robe flap covering a birchbark lodge.

It took a moment for her eyes to adjust to the dim interior, where a small, smoky fire burned in the center. Cloying odors of hides, oiled bodies, and herbs swam over her. Two women sat cross-legged on piles of robes. The older one sewed while the other cut meat into a kettle simmering over the fire. Beyond them, a girl of about six played with a naked toddler.

Bluebird pointed to a blanket on a pile of robes. "*Daga*."

Brigitte tucked her legs and lowered herself to the blanket. The old woman gestured at her and murmured toothlessly.

"The *nookomis* says you should take off your men's clothes."

Brigitte jerked back as the grandmother gestured with greater urging. The woman held up the garment she stitched. A skirt of blue calico bedecked with red ribbon. Brigitte glanced around the room again. The child had slipped behind her and stroked her long braid. She leaned over and grinned at Brigitte, and Brigitte could not help but smile in return. The grandmother continued making circles with her hands.

She wanted Brigitte to change now? Brigitte looked to Bluebird. *"Maintenant?"*

Bluebird nodded.

Brigitte slipped out of her uncle's trousers and took the skirt from the old woman. The soft cotton slipped like smooth cream around her waist. Small, colorful beads dangled at the bottom, dancing just below her knees.

The younger woman rattled on and pointed at the stew pot without looking up from her work. The little girl offered Brigitte a pair of blood-red leggings. Brigitte took them, bowed her head in thanks, and put them on.

The old woman handed a soft, white shirt to Bluebird, followed by a belt trimmed in bright blue beads woven together to look like flowers. Brigitte removed her uncle's shirt and slipped the new one over her head. Bluebird wrapped the belt around her waist. The little girl giggled.

The younger woman's eyes shone as she plopped more meat into the pot.

"Why do you do this?" Brigitte whispered.

Bluebird patted her hand. "You need not look like a man any longer. Rupert and my husband have purchased it. It is a gift." Brigitte didn't know what to say, but blinking away the wetness in her eyes seemed thanks enough. Bluebird's lips bowed. "Come. René will be pleased with his woman."

Brigitte's heart tripped. She would like him to be pleased with her.

Thanking the women in the lodge and smiling at the little girl, Brigitte and Bluebird left. They returned to the encampment of the *hivernants* where they found Rupert and Bluebird's husband cooking the rubaboo.

Rupert's mustache thinned as a smile stretched over his face when he saw them. He walked in a circle about Brigitte. "Ah… and so you look like the little mademoiselle I imagined when I first saw you. Very lovely indeed."

She blushed. "*Merci* for your kindness, Rupert. You should not have spent your wages on me, but I am grateful, nonetheless."

He squeezed her hand. "You are like my own daughter."

The back of her eyelids stung. Not since her uncle had anyone spoken to her so. A carousal of distant laughter interrupted her memory, and she blinked her eyes dry. "I hear a celebration."

Rupert nodded. "It is revelry at Jean-Marie Boucher's house. He runs a canteen for the voyageurs. There they drink their watered-down rum and hope to purchase something better for their supper than peas and fat. They are not privileged to eat inside the fort with the *bourgeois*. Come along. We shall see why they laugh and shout. Perhaps it is a good tale."

"I leave you with Rupert," Bluebird said.

Brigitte threw her arms about Bluebird. As they parted, she patted Brigitte on the arm.

"Will I see you tomorrow?"

Bluebird shrugged. "It is probable. I will be here and there. Not far." She turned to her husband who still bent over the rubaboo.

Brigitte put her arm through Rupert's. They soon came upon the noise and mayhem of Boucher's, a long log house with a window and a door on each end. A massive pair of moose antlers hung above each door.

Light spilled out through the windows, and campfires lit the area. Men stood about, swilling their drink. As the first door burst open and two men stepped out, the smell of roasted meat followed them.

"You are hungry?" Rupert asked.

"*Non*. I am fine. Save your money."

"A wise woman. These"—he waved at the crowd— "not so wise. As you know, we are all forbidden by the company to go into debt, so the men must pay for their luxuries with their cash advances. The money they earn *from* the company returns *to* the company. It is quite profitable—"

"For the company."

He laughed. "Precisely."

Rupert patted her hand and took her inside the canteen. Chairs crowded around a scattering of tables. A man served rum from a short bar on one end of the room and took orders for food while another man shouldered past them bearing a trencher of meat heaped high over potatoes and smothered in gravy. The aroma tugged at Brigitte's nostrils, and she eyed the plate as he passed. Though she wasn't hungry, she hadn't seen a meal consisting of more than peas and fat in many weeks.

Rupert nudged her. "I insist you allow me to purchase us each a stick of dry beef. We would not want to insult our host," he said with a grin.

He made the purchase while Brigitte watched a group of voyageurs playing at cards and drinking from tin tankards.

A man with a bandaged hand set his tankard down and belched. "And so, someone may find where she has gone and become very rich."

Another shrugged. "She has likely entered the convent of the Grey Nuns. No one will ever see her again."

"Or she followed the old woman to the grave," said a man in a dirty red cap.

A thin man leaned forward and crossed his elbows on the table. "She was robbed and murdered, no doubt. Her body dumped into the river."

The storyteller with the bandage gave a nod. "Likely you are right. Just the same, when a rich man like Clarboux offers a reward, all possibilities should be considered."

Brigitte's chest tightened.

"No soft woman from Montreal would come to the west."

"*Non*, indeed you are right."

"But what if someone has spirited her away?"

"Someone? Surely you mean some*thing*. A devil perhaps. Ach!"

The man in the red cap waved off the nonsense they spoke of. "Women go missing every day. What is this one to any of us?"

"Montreal is hundreds of miles away. So is this reward of which you speak. Better to return with furs and sure profit than a full imagination and an empty purse." The thin man threw his head back with a tankard to his lips. Liquid dribbled down his chin, into his beard.

The others murmured while Brigitte stood rigid with fear, kept on her feet by Rupert's support.

His gentle tug finally woke her from her paralyzed stupor. She shifted her gaze only to see the black, menacing eyes of an Indian boring through her from across the noisy, crowded room.

René set down his coffee cup. The brew did little to relax him as Claude pushed out a harsh breath.

"I cannot believe it. You! They chose you, and you do not even *want* such a promotion," Claude said, disgruntled.

Dust moats swam on morning sunbeams flooding over the dining hall. Forks and knives clattered as more than a dozen men broke their fast on eggs and cakes and side pork. René's gaze swiveled back to Claude, whose face had reddened with a scowl even though he'd managed to keep his voice low.

His face looked more like their mother's. Not quite as dark as René's, but with the same blue eyes. His hair, a shade lighter as well, was combed back and tied in a neat queue. Youthful manhood lay upon his shoulders and drew the gazes of the two native kitchen maids who cleared some of the empty platters from the long table.

René laid aside his napkin. "You have only been seven years with the company."

"Seven years. *Oui. Seven.* A lifetime of slavery. How many more must I spend wintering with the natives before another such promotion is given? I could be passed over entirely. I begin to think the others are right. It doesn't matter how hard we toil. Our efforts are not as well rewarded as our connections." He glowered across the table at René. "Last year, I exceeded the returns on my adventure. I am no longer in debt to the agents."

"I?"

"We. Of course, I meant *we*. You and I."

"Be that as it may, there is nothing to be done about it."

Despite Claude's success, what he said was true. René lacked connections. For that reason, he had never allowed himself to wish for a partnership as nearly every other clerk did. Partnership was the product of a treasured hen held out in promise by the company, but one that seldom offered to lay a golden egg. René had been as surprised as anyone when it turned out the fabled egg lay in his basket. Just this hour he had received the news.

Claude harrumphed. "I do not understand. How did they choose you?"

"Apparently, my few youthful years serving on shipboard have proved fateful. Captain Fortenay's wife, it turns out, is cousin to McGillivray himself. I was told that the subject of the wintering partners arose at a dinner party, and my old captain off-handedly mentioned a youth who'd once shown great promise"—he paused to quirk a brow at Claude—"but who'd gone off to become one of the Nor'westers. One could call it a grand twist of fate."

René swirled the remaining coffee in his cup and set it down. "It would have been folly to refuse." Claude chewed like he meant to kill his pork a second time. René pushed back his plate and folded his arms. "Really, Claude, what is so very different? I will travel more, but I will still supervise your district. I will winter at the inland forts, just as before. There must be some comfort in that. Believe me, I was as surprised as you to hear, but when you are ready, I myself will be allowed to cast a vote for your own promotion."

"When I am ready." Claude clamped his lips.

René smiled. "Cheer up, little brother. I am happy to see you."

He sighed and shook his head. "It just comes so unexpectedly." One corner of his lips tweaked up. "I am glad to see you as well. Did you stay up late last night for the dancing?"

"Was there dancing?"

"Ah, yes, but there are never enough women."

"Which reminds me, how is your wife? Will I find a new *bébé* in her cradleboard on my next visit?

"Naturally. It was a cold winter, was it not?" Claude smiled more generously, the expression reminding René of his mother's sweetness.

"I suppose you hope it will be a boy."

"That would be welcome indeed. Unfortunately, to get him, his mother must first grow fat."

René picked up his cup again, frowning at the dredges. "That is how it is done, I suppose." He began to weary of Claude's callous talk. It was time he found Brigitte. How had she fared last night with Bluebird and Rupert? He shouldn't worry so here at the fort where there was some civilization. She was a grown woman, able to take care of herself now.

A grown woman, certainly.

"I must be off," he said, pushing back his chair.

Claude rose as well. "What now? Taking up your new duties already?"

René picked up his cap. "Old duties, actually. I have a charge I must see to."

"And what charge is that?"

Claude would have to know sooner or later, and Brigitte would expect René to tell his brother. "I brought a young woman from Montreal who is looking for her family. She is to find employment."

Claude gasped. "You return with one surprise after another. I thought such days for you had passed, but *non*. You have finally taken a woman."

René scowled. "I did not say she was that, nor is she. She is young. A Nor'wester's daughter left in Montreal with her relation.

Now they have passed, and she comes to find her father."

Claude rose, and they strolled out of the building. René scanned the courtyard, gazing past the people milling about.

"Who is this father of hers? Someone I know?"

"A trader named Marchal. Have you heard of him?"

Claude shook his head. "You think he might be here?"

"He might. Do me a kindness, will you? Keep your ears open for a man by such a name. Ask those you know. It would be a service to her—and to me—if he were discovered." René felt Claude's study as they walked toward the gate. "Think no more of it than that."

"All right." Speculation laced his brother's tone.

"There is one thing you should know." René kept his voice low lest others hear him in passing. "She was in danger in Montreal. I agreed to bring her along on that account. Don't make more of it than that."

They passed through the gates and neared the riverbank where he spotted Georges Munion eating his morning porridge. "Georges." The broad-shouldered man stood and shook René's outstretched hand. "How fare you this morn?"

The man belched then smiled. "Well enough."

"Have you seen Brigitte?"

"Your woman is at the camp with the others."

Claude seared René with another glance, but he ignored it. Walking further up the bank, they came closer to the camp, and René's step caught as he recognized Brigitte. Where had she come by a dress? The shirt that hung over it, belted at her waist, accentuated her petite, womanly shape—a shape he knew better than he ought.

She looked up from the pot she stirred and smiled. Claude elbowed him.

René struggled to find words. "There you are."

"Where else would I be?" Her eyes shone. She looked happier than he had seen her in a long while as her gaze settled on Claude. *"Bonjour."*

"*Bonjour.*" Claude stepped forward. "I am René's brother, Claude."

"Ah." She blushed, and her eyelashes swept her cheeks in a flutter. "How good it is to meet you." She held out her hand.

He smiled at René before bowing over her hand, sweeping his tall hat across his waist. He'd certainly not lost his charm during his time spent wintering at his wilderness post. In fact, he seemed to be quite practiced.

René cleared his throat. "Claude, allow me to introduce Mademoiselle Marchal, lately from Montreal."

"I understand my brother has carried you safely across the lakes to us here in Upper Canada."

"*Oui.*"

"It was little work. She is an admirable voyageur, like her father. She was even sprinkled at the *Pointe au Baptême.*" He pressed his lips into a smile he hoped Claude would perceive as that of a proud big brother and nothing more.

"You do not say. Well, she is a courageous *petit oiseau.*" Claude's gaze swept the "little bird" from her toes to her braid.

Irritation pinched René, but he quashed it. After all, women— even native—were largely outnumbered. Every man noticed when one as pretty and young as Brigitte graced their presence. His brother was no different, and Claude's wife was many miles away.

René stepped in front of Claude. "I thought you'd like to come with me, and we will speak to someone about work for you—that is, if you are willing to stay."

Her lips fell into a line. "I … I suppose I must."

Her hesitation bothered him. But what else would she do? And where else might she expect to cross paths with her father again, if he lived? "*Oui.* It is likely best. You should have no trouble. You are qualified for many kinds of work."

As they turned to head back to the fort, Claude fell into step on the other side of her. "And what might that be?"

"I can cook and serve, of course. I used to keep the gardens at the nunnery."

"The nunnery?" Claude's voice rang with surprise.

"*Oui*. I lived there for a time."

They approached the gates, but Claude halted Brigitte with a light touch on her shoulder. "You mean you have been schooled?"

She nodded.

"She has likely had more of books than I," René said, realizing it must be true.

"An educated female, here at Fort William. Well, I should say she is qualified for work. She might find something suitable for her skills, something with advancement."

"It does not matter, as long as it will help me find my papa," she said.

They moved on, and Claude winked at René over her head.

Brigitte finished scrubbing all the tables in the Great Hall. Dropping a rag into a pail of water, she wiped her hands on her apron then hefted the bucket with a sigh. René and Claude had departed to their own business and left her alone with her new employment.

René has seen to my transport, my safety, and my employment. I have a roof over my head and plenty to eat. I am free from Tristan and the past. Soon, I will make new friends and adjust to my new life. I must not act a fool over his departure. Besides, there remained plenty of time before he departed. It was not as though he was already gone.

"Dump that pail, and put on a clean apron. The men will be in for dinner by the time you have the tables set."

Brigitte turned and curtsied to the heavy-boned woman who supervised the kitchen and serving staff. Dinner time. Already. They had barely finished cleaning the room and washing all the dishes from the morning.

"You will serve the tables."

Brigitte nodded before hauling the bucket to the back door and dumping it. Returning inside, she retrieved a new apron. She tied it on and wound her braid at her nape before her next round of duties began.

The evening grew long and wearisome as she hastened in and out of the hall with platters of pork, venison, and lamb seasoned with wild onions and sides of greens. Ah! It was a pleasure to serve gentlemen. How differently they behaved from the voyageurs. She recalled last night's visions of the men eating at Boucher's house. Drunk and slovenly they were compared to these fine men. It almost seemed as though she had returned from the wilderness and was back in Montreal.

At last, René came in and caught her gaze from his place among a crowded table. He gave her only the slightest nod and a small smile, but it was enough to warm her. She dipped her head and set down two baskets of bread. When she looked again, it was Claude who watched her, and—it happened so quickly, but she was certain he winked.

CHAPTER 13

*"Every partner must winter two years out of three,
managing a post."*

—North West Company Rules

B rigitte stood on the edge of the square, wearing her new clothes. Fires and torchlight cast pool and shadow, and a group of musicians—fiddlers, a man with a mouth harp, and another with a mandolin—filled the open space with joyful strains. Other women from the encampments, as well as most of those employed within, joined in the revelry of the dancing.

In only a matter of days, the voyageurs' sojourn at the fort would end, and they would return to their long toils. Until then, *bourgeois* partners, traders, and even the voyageurs were allowed to enter the gates for the festivities. Brigitte supposed some of the men might act as depraved as Tristan at her first dance, but it was hard to imagine anyone assaulting her as he had.

As others danced, Bluebird stood beside Brigitte, offering a matronly protection of sorts, sending away those who leered and introducing Brigitte to those whom she knew and believed trustworthy. Brigitte had her share of dances, and none of her partners seemed to mind her clumsiness for they had their own way of spinning her about the square that embodied less finesse than zeal.

Well into the evening, René approached along with Claude. "So, you are having a good time, *non?*"

"Good but for your absence. I should scold you, René. You have stayed away from the festivity most of the evening. I cannot stay up all night waiting for you to join us. I must rise to serve breakfast in a few hours. Eat, eat, eat. That is all men do."

He chuckled at her reprimand. "In a few days, you will be

wishing for a night of revelry to break your boredom."

"There are other things men do," Claude said with a grin.

The music started again. Several voyageurs strode in Brigitte's direction, so she stepped closer to the brothers. Claude leaned toward his brother. "René, will you not spare her from being thrown about the square by these uncivilized clods?"

"She said she was having a good time."

"If you will not rescue her, then allow me." He held out his arm.

Brigitte glanced at René, but as he stepped back and did not intervene, she took Claude's arm and allowed him to lead her. Claude was graceful in the dance, even with the rough ground beneath their feet. Like Tristan, he seemed at home with the steps, yet he did not grasp her nor did his hands rove. His feet led her across the square with only the most gentlemanly touch of his hand at her waist. He was much gentler than the last fellow, who had indeed flung her about.

He smiled at her. "You dance quite naturally."

"It is you, *monsieur*, who make it seem so."

"How very kind. It is something I seldom get to practice, as you must imagine. My life in the wilderness is harsh at times and much less than civilized."

"How did you come to learn the steps?"

"Our mother taught us in what she considered to be more refined arts. She wanted both her sons to become gentlemen."

So René knew the steps too. "René has mentioned your mother. She must have loved you both very much."

"*Oui*. Mothers are like that."

"I—I would not know."

"Oh?"

"*Non*. I have no mother, you see. She died when I was a *bébé*. I lived with her people for a while, and then my papa took me away."

"That's right. You are hoping to find him. Have you discovered any trace of him yet?"

She shook her head.

He drew her closer, but his touch remained gentle. "Do not fear. I am sure we will discover his whereabouts, eventually. Might he have gone to the mountains in the west or farther north?"

She shrugged. "It is possible."

"Since the Americans have passed their laws against the *Canadiens* trapping inside their borders, many traders have gone to the far west, although there are those of us who are not particularly alarmed at the Americans' demands." His lips curved into a smile identical to René's.

"Is that where your post is, beyond the American lines?"

"Precisely." He turned her about, their feet matching in rhythm. "The Americans are slow in establishing their posts. We have removed from Grand Portage, though merely in name. The company still supports a small trade there, but nothing like when my brother first came to this country. Then Grand Portage was as lively as the fort you see about you."

"It must be lonely living so far away in the cold of winter." The gleam in his eye spoke warmly, yet it didn't frighten her like Tristan's had. "I did not mean—"

He tilted back his head and laughed. "You did not mean you hoped to find a husband. I know this, but I cannot help being charmed."

She turned her face away, thankful that the warmth she felt could be blamed on the dancing.

The song ended, but Claude danced with her twice more. Brigitte saw Bluebird dancing with her husband, but not once did she see René among the dancers. And not once did he ask her for a turn.

The following morning, her limbs dragged as she served breakfast in the Great Hall. How wonderful it would be to climb onto her mattress and curl beneath her blankets again, yet her new duties demanded she spend another day serving and cleaning. Later, when the traders and voyageurs left, then she might find time to sew a new dress or attend with those who worked in the garden. Perhaps she might spend more of her days out of doors, gathering on her cheeks the warmth of the sun and the cool wind off the lake.

How surprising that the long, dangerous voyage—barely finished—should cause her longing.

She checked a grin as the men around the table pushed their untied hair out of bleary eyes. Several smothered yawns as they thanked her when she poured them their tea. She filled cups again and listened casually as they conversed.

"I will send my men out in the morning. We haven't many weeks to see that the shipment gets to the agents in Montreal."

"Europe never tires of her beaver hats."

"And for that, we are grateful."

"Hear, hear."

Forks clattered. The aroma of sausage caused Brigitte's stomach to growl.

"I pray there are no mishaps. My load is heavy and must make it back by August."

"Will it be shipped through Lewis?"

"*Non*. Clarboux."

Brigitte sloshed tea across the gentleman's plate "*Je suis vraiment désolée, monsieur*. I will get you another."

He frowned at her as she reached for his plate. "Never mind. It matters not."

She curtsied, but her hand trembled as she poured the next cup.

"The agent assures me that if my boats arrive in time, I will get a better price from Clarboux than I did last year from Lewis."

The other fellow grunted. Brigitte took a deep breath, but her heart thumped in her ears. Would she never be able to forget the vileness of Tristan Clarboux, though he was more than a thousand miles away?

Relief flooded her when the men finished their meal and took their leave. She was alone in the room, sweeping the wide floorboards, when someone cleared his throat. She looked up to see René watching her. He looked like the other clerks in his coat, cravat, and hat.

He stepped forward with a smile. "You look suited to your new life."

She rested on the handle of her broom. "As do you."

He plucked off his hat and glanced down at his clothing. When he looked up again, chagrin etched his face in a half-smile. "It is a necessary evil. Not nearly so comfortable."

"If you had been dressed half so fine the day we met, I might not have accused you of leaving *le nourrisson* on the doorstep."

"Ah, but I believe you would have." His grin broadened, and he turned his hat in his hands. Even at thirty, his smile made him youthful.

She chuckled. "Perhaps I would."

"So determined you were to put me in my place." He stepped closer.

"I am embarrassed by it. Please, you must not speak of it."

"Do not be embarrassed. You are to be commended for your compassion."

"Ah … well, I thank you. Did I ever tell you that I named the babe for you?"

His shoulders straightened with surprise. "*Non.* Why would you do that?"

"I thought it a good thing to do, to remember you by, for your generosity to the nuns." She lowered her chin to her knuckles atop the broom handle. "It was a girl."

"Pah!" His laugh eased her. "You gave a girl such a name?"

"Renée is good for a girl, and I think of you as her patron. Someday, I will write to Sister Agathe and ask if she lived. For now, I have not the courage, but someday I shall, and if she is alive, I will send her a letter and tell her all about you."

"So she can have fanciful notions." He shook his head. "Never mind. I come to you with news."

Brigitte straightened. "What news?"

"There is a voyageur who came into the company store, an older fellow, well beyond my years. I thought to ask him if he'd ever met Monsieur Marchal, and he had. He remembered him well."

"Papa is alive?" Her grip tightened on the broom.

"I do not want to stir false hopes, Brigitte. I have not come to do that." He stepped closer again and caressed her shoulder. "The fellow last saw your father several years ago, at Grand Portage. He has not seen him or heard of him since."

Her excitement slid away, and she let her shoulders slump. René dropped his hand, stealing away his comforting touch.

"I am sorry there is not more."

"It is all right." She lifted her chin and took a breath. "I have not heard from him longer than that. Three times, Papa returned to Montreal bringing me gifts with his stories and songs, always telling me I looked more like my beautiful *mère* every time. The last time was before I turned sixteen. To know he was seen by this man several years ago gives me hope that he is alive at least. Perhaps I will find him yet." She frowned as an idea crept over her, and she could not silence it. "René … how far away is Grand Portage?"

"It is not so very far. Hardly a day's journey."

She clutched his coat sleeve briefly before pulling her hand away. "I want to go."

René was already shaking his head. "There is no reason—"

"But if it is possible my father should be somewhere near—"

"It is unlikely. The fort is not what it used to be. That is why we are here."

"Will you go there on your way to … to wherever you must travel?"

"*Oui*, but—"

"It matters not how uncivilized. No one else here has heard of my papa. I must go elsewhere if I am to continue my search."

"You have a new life here."

She turned and gazed out the high window that looked above the picket. In the distance, smoke from the voyageurs' fires curled into the sky. "I have employment, but I have yet to figure out whether or not I have a life. My heart pricks me." She pressed a fist to her breast, but she could not settle the disquiet inside. "I am not sure this is where I am meant to be."

"There you are, René." Claude entered the room.

She turned to face René, holding onto the broom like a lifeline and silently pleading with him to help her cause once again.

Claude's gaze bounced between them. "I am ... interrupting something important?"

René sighed. "*Non. Non,* you are not."

"But—"

He held up his hand. "What do you need, Claude?"

Claude looked between them again. "I need signatures from you, for my adventure."

"I will come."

Brigitte stepped forward and touched René arm. *"S'il vous plaît.* Think about my request."

He sighed. "I will think about it, but I doubt it will be to your avail, so please, do not hold false hopes." He turned and strode from the room.

Claude hastened outside after René and hurried down the steps of the Great Hall beside him. "What is it the little bird asks of you now?"

René could hear the amusement in Claude's voice. A quick glance as he veered toward the provision stores revealed an impish twist on his brother's lips. "She wishes for me to take her to Le Grand Portage. It is impossible, of course. She is where she should be, able to work, to hope for a reunion with her *père,* to find a husband who will care for her."

"Why does she want to go to *le portage* then?"

"Her father was seen there some seasons ago, but she has no understanding of such things. He is most likely dead. You know it as well as I."

Claude clasped his hands behind his back and stuck out his lip as they strolled. "Certainly. But you have already given her a thousand miles of hope. Will you steal it back now, when the place she seeks is so near?"

René glared at him. "And what will she do once she is there?"

"Whatever she does here. Cook. Clean. Marry if you insist."

"Marry a *sauvage*? That is all who remain at Grand Portage."

"Why not? She has enough of the savage in her."

René ground his teeth. "Forgive me if I forget."

Claude laughed. "You are quite taken with her."

René turned on him. "I am quite *put out* with her."

Claude held up his hands and stepped back. "I am wrong. Forgive me. Why not bring her along? The thought of her pleading will plague you if you do not. She will be no less happy than she is here, wondering."

René growled, but Claude's words sank in as they entered the supply store. There would be nothing for her at Grand Portage, even less once the Americans arrived, as they would someday. He could not picture her married to one of her mother's people, even being half Ojibwe herself. She'd been raised in Montreal and was no longer accustomed to the ways of her Indian relation.

Yet, to refuse to bend to her wish sat hard with him as well.

René fumed. It was bad enough he must argue with Brigitte, but that he should waste his time arguing with his own brother over her cause was as much as he could bear.

"Forget about it. Show me what I must sign."

CHAPTER 14

One Sunday night you see,
My friend François and me,
We went off for a walk to find some company.
A visit we did pay, to old bonhomme Gauthier.
I'll tell you just what happened next, but
En Français!

— Youpe! Youpe! Sur La Rivière

Brigitte wrapped her work dress, apron, and voyageur's clothing in her pack, choosing to don the blue dress Rupert had bought her. There was no need for disguise anymore, not even while traveling. Everyone knew she was a woman now. If not René's woman. How they must wonder, but they would not wonder when they saw her leaving with him again.

She secured her bundle and left a note on her cot for her employer. Leaving the Great Hall behind her, she crept out and watched René pace the length of the waiting North canoes, just as he had in Lachine. The only difference was that more Indians prepared to accompany him than before.

When he turned his back and occupied himself speaking to a group of traders, she crept down the river toward him and placed her belongings in a tight space in the middle of one of the *canots*. Once it was secure, she stood beside the boat with her arms crossed over her middle, bracing herself to face him.

It wasn't long before he picked up his head and saw her standing thus. He drew up short, then took quick strides to her. "What are you doing?"

"I am going with you."

Thunder darkened his brow. "I told you, you cannot."

"Why not? I will not take much room, and you said it was less than a day's journey. You will be rid of me before nightfall, just as you wish. I will pay you if I must."

"*Oui*. You will."

"Fine then."

"That did not mean I grant my permission."

"I am not looking for you to grant it. I will go."

"Brigitte."

"René."

A bark of laughter deflated her. Over René's shoulder, she glimpsed Claude from the group gathered around the boats. "You sound like an old, married couple." He strode toward her. "You can ride with me, Brigitte. I will see you safely to Le Grand Portage."

"*Merci, monsieur*." She lifted her chin, challenging René to deny his brother.

"But you must always call me Claude."

"*Merci*, Claude."

She stared at René until at last he harrumphed and turned away, shouting orders as voyageurs hustled out of his path.

Her shoulders slumped in relief. What if he had stood his ground? Her chest ached. *He truly wants to be rid of me.*

She squeezed her eyes shut for a moment as the pain of that truth battled with relief that Claude had intervened, then she moved her things into Claude's craft. This time, however, she was not given a paddle.

Several minutes later, their brigade of four North canoes embarked. Claude steered the last boat, in which he'd settled her in front of him. He whistled a tune that kept time with the water swishing off their prow and the dipping of their paddles.

She glanced over her shoulder. "Do you sing?"

Claude gave her a grin and broke into a chorus of "Alouette." The rest of the crew joined in.

As the song finished, she looked back at him again. "Your voice sounds much like René's when he is not angry."

Claude chuckled. "His anger will not last long. By this evening, he will be sorry he was harsh."

"Even if he is not, I would not change my mind."

"Your will is strong. I understand. Mine is as well."

He likely told her the truth. After all, he'd convinced his elder brother to bring him into the wilderness when he was just eighteen, as she had.

"Tell me about your post."

"It is a small fort at the head of the lake with the river nearby. There are Indians everywhere, of course."

"Of course."

"They do most of the trapping and hunting. We purchase their furs and food."

She turned, and Claude grinned. "And what will René do?"

"René will do what he does best. Look after everything. Now his oversight will go beyond me." He glanced at her, then past her. "He will travel while the weather holds, never staying too long as he supervises a broad region of traders. He will endeavor to please the Indians and his clerks, but not *too* much. He will govern. He will trade. He will be noticed for his efforts on every front. When snow falls and the lakes freeze over, he will winter at an inland post."

She frowned. "You will not see much of each other then."

"Not as much as in the past, *non*. René's ship has come in, as they say …" His voice drifted off, and he gazed over the expanse of lake as he paddled. "You will see him from time to time, too, perhaps." He cast a quick wink at her.

"Please, you must not think I mean anything to him. We only pretended for my safety."

His paddle faltered. *"Vous avez feint?* You pretended?"

René had not told him? She cringed over the need to explain and looked across the water toward the other boat. Then she turned in the tight space to face him better. "We pretended I was his"—she licked her lips and whispered— "I was his woman, so I would be left alone."

His burst of laughter startled her. He tossed back his head, disturbing the rhythm of his stroke.

She peeked at the Indian man seated ahead of her. His stroke remained unchanged, though he must surely have heard. Refocusing on Claude, she leaned toward him. "Please, monsieur. You must not laugh."

"Of course not." His shoulders moved with greater vigor as he paddled harder. "I wasn't laughing at you, you understand. It is such a story. You see, my brother has vowed never to take a woman—a wife, I mean. Not as long as he works for the North West Company. Someday, perhaps, he will retire and buy a farm. Then he may wish for a woman to warm his old bones and children to call him papa. Then again …"

She was too embarrassed to reply. She faced forward, wishing she was given a paddle to use with the others.

"I, on the other hand, do not intend to wait until I am old to enjoy such warmth and companionship."

She cleared her throat. "You, you intend to marry then?"

When he did not answer, she glanced back at him. His gaze was most unsettling. Finally, he smiled. "*Oui*. Of course."

Brigitte shrank inside, and her nails bit into her palms.

"You, I doubt, will ever need to pretend again."

"Please—"

He laughed again, then broke into a robust song. Soon his voice was joined by others in the boat along with the crews from the other canoes.

When the sun hung low above the trees, softening the daylight and pinking the western sky, they slid into a bay. Narrow pickets and a roofline silhouetted the shore above the tall, reedy grass. Brigitte squinted into the sunset and shaded her eyes. The water lay calm and blue, flowing gently off the line of paddles that brought the shore close.

Then all was busy again as they slid along the dock and steadied the boats for disembarking. She waited for the rocking to settle as the men climbed out, then looked up from her seat to see Claude offering his hand. He tugged her to her feet, smiling the Dufour smile that made him seem so familiar. Holding her hand a moment longer as she gained her legs, he released her as René approached.

On the open grounds outside the fort, the now familiar sight of birch-bark *wiigiwaams* edged the forest, and native families milled about, cooking their evening meals. Brigitte's stomach growled at the sight of meat hung to dry and the familiar heady scent of herbs and fish simmering over low fires. Men sat cross-legged in the evening breeze, sharpening their knives and sharing talk.

A strange familiarity plucked a string inside Brigitte as they crossed the grounds. Not the familiarity of the general sights and smells, but something more.

Here, the voyageurs, as well as the *bourgeois,* were welcome inside the mostly deconstructed fort, and Brigitte remained between the brothers as they entered. René was right. It was a smaller post. A handful of old buildings dotted a barren square where grass grew along the edges of old foundations.

"What happened here?" she asked, looking at the empty spaces.

René followed her gaze. "There used to be eighteen buildings. When the partners agreed to move their headquarters to the Kaministiquia, they took them there. You saw some of them. Sturdy cedar and spruce split with whipsaws were deemed too valuable for their work's sake to leave behind for the Americans to eventually occupy."

An ember of recognition stirred to life in Brigitte. They walked toward a graying building where a thin stream of smoke issued from a mud-daubed chimney. "Still, someone remains?"

Claude cleared his throat, drawing her attention. "You will find we are guests of a lone usurper. He occupies the place until such time as the Americans drive him off."

"As we do at the head of the lake," René added. The brothers exchanged a grin. "Here, the Indians coming down the Pigeon River route can find quick payment for their hides."

Claude opened the door, and the three of them stepped inside the small trade shop. Brigitte wandered about the room while René and Claude spoke to the trader. Eventually, she stopped and gazed out a small, smudged window to where a handful of young boys played lacrosse in a clearing.

She drew in a sharp breath, her heart pattering faster. *I remember this place. I have been here.*

A sudden gulf opened in her memory. She could see the long-gone buildings—the storehouses and shops that stood along the wood line, the countinghouse to the right, just out of sight, and the big mess hall—their door frames and windows painted Spanish brown. Farm animals scurried out of the way as men hastened about with their bundles of furs, going about their business of buying and selling, of fighting, drinking, and laughing as they had at Fort William.

She had stood in this spot before, as a small child, watching other children play, wishing she might join them. She had eaten and played around the fires of her mother's family somewhere in the woods away from here. It seemed a long journey with her father to find this place, and they had yet to cross the lakes to Montreal. Had it been so far from where she'd lived to here?

Brigitte spun about, anxious to tell René what she remembered, but he was busy with the trader and Claude discussing the upcoming season.

Excitement overcame her trepidation, so she slipped from the room back out to the fading day. She took slow steps along the pathways, exploring the grounds.

Looking at the sites, she could almost hear the noisy rollick of the past. How she'd gawked then. She remembered now. *Oui,* this place had been part of her for a brief time.

Finally, she'd come home, or very near.

Real voices—not imagined—called her attention. She strolled down the path to the side of a building where she saw an Ojibwe woman serving her family around a fire near a lodge. The woman glanced at her. Brigitte gave a short nod and smiled. The woman called to her, but Brigitte hesitated. She glanced back at the store. The woman picked up what looked like fry bread and gestured for Brigitte to join them. Brigitte walked closer. She accepted a piece of fry bread and a handful of blueberries.

"*Miigwech,*" Brigitte said, thanking the woman.

The woman scolded a child and nodded at Brigitte. "I see you with the white men," she said to Brigitte in Ojibwe.

Brigitte thought carefully through the words, putting them together to understand the language she once knew well. She nodded.

"*Aandi ezhaayan?*"

Where was she going? How was Brigitte to answer? She had finally reached the place she'd intended, but—even now—she wondered if it would be as easy to settle as she hoped.

She pointed around the fort, but her gaze drifted beyond the gates.

The woman said something Brigitte didn't understand, then walked to a lodge down the path, leaving Brigitte to nibble on her bread in the company of the Indian family who ignored her.

She was about to thank them again and head back to the store, where René must wonder at her absence, when the woman called out from the lodge. The woman marched back toward Brigitte and rattled away in the Ojibwe faster than Brigitte could comprehend. She didn't know what the woman wanted, but a tall, young man followed her.

Worker. Traders. Hunt. Beaver. A barrage of words flew at Brigitte, but she ceased to hear them. She recognized the man—the same man whose black-eyed stare had bored into her outside Jean-Marie Boucher's canteen at Fort William, the unfriendly nature of it striking deep inside her.

CHAPTER 15

"During the whole month of July, the natives (seeing us weakened no doubt by these outfits) manifested their hostile intentions so openly that we were obliged to be constantly on our guard."

— Gabriel Franchère,
A Narrative of a Voyage to the
Northwest Coast of America 1811—1814.

She froze beneath the Indian's stare. What if he knew of the reward offered by Clarboux? He could have heard the talk of it in Boucher's canteen the same as she. His suspicions were written in the hardness of his eyes.

She could not stay at Grand Portage. Not now. Surely René would understand. She was foolish to think she might find Papa here. He had probably not been here for a long time.

She sucked in her breath and batted her eyes against threatening tears. Nevertheless, fear choked out a sob as she hurried back to find her rescuer. Oh, that he would rescue her again.

She burst through the door of the store. René jumped to his feet, knocking a ledger from the counter. His black brows bent together. "What is it? What is wrong?"

Her glance darted between René, the trader, and Claude, whose brow also furrowed. Both brothers came to her.

"I cannot stay," she whispered as the tears leaked out.

René grasped her shoulders and pulled her aside. "What happened?" His voice was gentle. "Where did you go? Did someone—"

She shook her head. *"Non, non.* It is just ..." She gulped, unable to look him in the eye.

"Quoi? Tell me."

"I am sorry, René. You were right. I was wrong. There is nothing for me here. My papa will not come to this place like he did in years past. I realize it now. I remember it all so well. But it is not the same." Her voice broke. She took several breaths, pushing down the unsettledness inside her over the Indian. René would tell her she had nothing to fear. Tristan was far away. Men had shown much interest in her these past months. Not like this, but still, he might not understand.

He sighed and released her shoulders.

Claude appeared next to him. "She must come to *le fond du lac*. I will give her tasks to busy her while she awaits word of her *père*."

Did he truly mean it?

René rubbed the back of his neck. "It would be better for her to return to Fort William."

"How? When? She would have to remain here alone until someone returned. She has no chaperone, no guide. She might as well be with someone she knows inside the St. Louis fort at *le fond du lac*. There she will be protected, have shelter."

"And what about—"

Claude gripped René's forearm and leaned forward. "All can be arranged."

The uncertainty written on René's face revealed his doubts. Nevertheless, her hopes lifted. "If … if I can be of use …"

Hesitation flickered in his eyes, but René nodded. "Claude can arrange work for you in the post. He has plenty to do, especially now, with the Americans trying to establish a new Fond du Lac depot up the river."

Claude took her hand and squeezed it gently. He offered a smile. "You must not remain here if you are not certain. My brother has brought you this far. Who knows but that your lot does not lie with us a while longer?"

As her gaze sought René's, she trembled to know he was not angry with her.

"*Oui*." René conceded. "Who knows?" But he did not sound

so sure.

Claude finally released her hand, and René beckoned her to follow.

"René." Her voice trembled. He paused, then opened his arms, and she rushed into his embrace. "I am sorry. If I had realized—"

"Shhh." His hand stroked the braid lying against her back. "It is all right, Brigitte." His voice rumbled low and tender. "You will be safe. I will see to it."

Did his lips touch her hair? She jerked back and wiped her eyes on the insides of her wrists. Such a burden she was. She must get hold of herself.

With only a glimpse at the softness in his gaze, she nodded. "I am ready now." She sniffed. "Thank you."

A small smile played on the edges of Claude's lips as she brushed past them both, walking out of the store.

They left the following dawn. Two other Frenchmen, a Scot, and a dozen Indians accompanied them. To Brigitte's horror, one of them was the native man who seemed to always watch her, his expression blank, yet intent. His dark gaze seemed to seek her out, take her in, and sift her. She felt the heaviness of it, even when she wasn't looking.

The shore of the lake led them on, rocky and wild. Gusty waves slashed at tall crags. Wind swept their craft across the swells, and danger lay always with them, but she thought little of it. Danger seemed elsewhere now, in the mystery of the man accompanying them.

He was taller than most of the others, and she thought him Métis also. Perhaps that was why he stared—he recognized her heritage. But why such cold intensity in his gaze? *He wishes to get the reward.*

She squashed the thought.

That evening, their party camped on a rocky beach where a river rushed into the big lake. There, the dark thoughts returned, creeping into her dreams.

They camped again the next night, but on the third day, a ghostly arm of land appeared on the horizon, barely discernible.

"*Le fond du lac!*" the Frenchmen cried out.

The Indians whooped and hollered, and the Scot joined them. Claude and another man lit into song. Soon the others joined.

Her own heart lifted on the strains until—in looking around the happy crew—her eyes caught those of the Indian. She looked away, the song dying on her lips before it began.

An hour later, the imposing, rugged coast swept in to meet the broad head of the bay, where flat and gentle land spread out in varying shades of green. They followed a long arm of land that eventually opened for passage.

The fleet paddled into a smaller bay. A muddy river met them, spilling silt into their path. They turned northwestward and drove along the reedy coast. Ahead, on the forested shore, spirals of smoke leaked above the treetops. As they approached, the rhythm of drums and singing reached them. Around the bend, tall pickets appeared. Beyond, a much wider river stretched its maw into the bay. The boats surged ahead before heading to the shore, the energy of the men like a rushing current.

"Is this it then?" She twisted to peer at Claude.

He smiled at her, satisfaction in the generous bow of his lips. "It is Superior Bay, and this is the river of St. Louis. *Oui*. This is it. The post was built by Monsieur Cadotte while you and I yet crawled about the floor in our *couches*."

She laughed. "Now you have made me imagine things I should not."

"René tells me you are familiar with the care of *bébés*."

"I am."

"There are several little ones whose mothers live at the fort. You will enjoy them, no doubt." He pushed harder with his paddle. "Unless you are happy to be free of such things."

"*Non*. I am glad to be with children. I admire their innocence. They are so truly helpless and dependent, not unlike I have been."

"*Bien*. You will find yourself at peace at Fort St. Louis, I am sure."

Ease spread like wings inside her, fluttering, landing softly in her heart. Already this place felt different, livelier than lonely Grand Portage. She would ignore the Indian and stay clear of him until he left. Until then, she would find work with Claude's guidance. Then, perhaps, René would not be sorry for helping her.

Her gaze drifted to him in another canoe. He'd risen to stand at the prow, a broad smile on his face. How wildly handsome he looked with his dark hair blowing free in the wind. How virile and intense with his chin raised.

Claude's words came back to her. *My brother has vowed to never take a woman—a wife.*

Why was it so? She had not been well acquainted with a great many men in her life, not until the recent months, yet how plain it was that René was a man who would make a fine husband and father. He had pitied the abandoned babe at the convent and was benevolent in memory of his dear mother. He had charmed Rupert's children. Had given Brigitte shelter and protection under the guise of their pretended relationship.

Had I indeed been his woman ... had she indeed been his woman, how might have he behaved? As it was, he barely allowed her to leave his sight. She smiled at the thought of how comfortable she had become in his presence under even the nearest and most private of circumstances. Even when he was angry with her, he was patient.

Brigitte tossed her head and glimpsed him again, as loose strands of hair blew across her eyes. A man of such compassion and strength should have a wife and children. He should have a home to return to, as Rupert did. He was not too old, even if she had made him think so. If he had been too old, the voyageurs would not have believed their story. She almost believed it herself.

The bowman gave a shout, calling her attention forward again. The voyageurs lifted their paddles to come ashore. There was a new burst of activity as they disembarked and boats were lifted. Once on shore, René came to stand beside her as he called the crews together. "We will thank the Almighty." The men removed their caps. René bowed his head and led them in a prayer of thanksgiving for dangers safely passed and the welcome rest at hand. Her heart swelled at his speech, and she peeked at him as he prayed.

René, you are a fine man, indeed.

The boats were soon unloaded. As René and Claude directed the workers with the wares, René kept a stern eye on all that transpired.

He shifted his gaze to Brigitte standing a few feet away. Her concentration on the activities about them absorbed her completely. What must Fort St. Louis look like to her? Did she see only a primitive palisade with posts twenty feet high, sharpened at both ends and driven into the ground? Or did she sense safety behind its double-ribbed gates and grim, two-storied log tower that formed a bastion at one corner, bristling with port holes for musketry?

The scent of her hair swept over him, and he pulled his gaze away. As he did, an Indian passed by with a sack of corn on his shoulders. His dark eyes regarded Brigitte too, as though her scent had caught and held him as it had René.

René frowned. He looked at her again. This time she blinked at him. Closing the space between them, he laid a hand on her shoulder and turned her aside. He smoothed his brow. "Come, I will see you settled." He took her arm and steered her away from the commotion. "I see you are aware that someone notices you."

She nodded.

He bent his head toward hers as they walked. "He joined us with the others at Grand Portage. Did he speak to you there?"

"*Non.*"

"But you saw him."

"*Oui.*"

"When you came back to the storehouse at Grand Portage that day …"

"It was because of him." Her voice trembled.

Things were clearer now. The man had frightened her with his black looks.

"He was at Fort William also."

René stopped short and turned to her. He squeezed her arm, not letting go. "I am sure it is nothing. Nevertheless, I will see to him. He will not trouble you further."

She exhaled, and her arm relaxed. "*Merci*, René. I should have told you. I did not want you to think me foolish."

"In the future, should anything upset you when I am away, you must tell Claude. He will not doubt you, and he will look to your well-being."

"*Merci*," she said again, her breath a vapor of pure relief.

For the first time, he dared admit that he was glad he'd brought her from Fort William, and again from Grand Portage. Here, she would remain safe under his brother's watchful eye while he was away. Here, he would see her again.

He escorted her into the fort and past the canoe yard. Later, she would find her way about the shed, warehouse, and longhouses that combined stores, magazines, and workshops. For now, he meant to see her settled in one of the white, heavy-timbered dwellings where she would live until another voyageur like Gervais married her. The idea soured him a little, but such could not be helped unless her father turned up sooner rather than later.

They crossed the courtyard where the Indians brought their game and peltry for trade. "Here we are." He led her up a path between the warehouse and store to the home he shared with Claude. He pushed open the door and stepped into an open room with a fireplace on one end. A little boy scampered off, calling for his mama. Down a hall to the left of the main room, he pushed open another door and stepped aside. "You will have my room, as I no longer will have need of it."

Brigitte's eyes were wide as she glanced around the simple room. René cleared his throat. *"Excusez-moi."* He moved past her and gathered the remnant of his belongings, some clothing hanging on a peg and a leather wallet of papers, bound with a cord, sitting beside a candle on a bedside table. "There. Now you will feel more at home." He glanced at a small trunk sitting against the far wall. "I will have Claude send the remainder to the storehouse."

"But ..." She turned luminescent brown eyes on him. "I do not want to displace you."

"You do nothing of the kind. I will hardly be here, and you must be comfortable now that you are out of the wilds. Claude and Mina will see to anything else you need."

"Mina?"

A child giggled in the hall, and Claude's wife called after it. Soon, Brigitte would be quite at ease here with them. Claude must have spoken to her of his family during the voyage down the lake.

The child burst into the room, and right behind him, his mother grabbed him up and held him against her. He pushed his head back, laughing still. The woman tickled, but as she lifted her gaze to them, her expression sobered. She set the child down, and he pressed against her skirts.

"Ah, Mina. Brigitte, this is Mina. Mina ... this is Brigitte Marchal. As Claude has probably told you, she will be staying here." He searched his limited Lakota vocabulary. *"Ee ay ... Hay nah' kink tay."*

Brigitte dipped her head. *"Bonjour,* Mina."

Mina looked her over with upraised chin. *"Hau."* With a quick glance at René, she turned and left the room, taking the squirming child with her.

René regarded Brigitte again whose gaze had followed Claude's wife. "Well ... I leave you to get acquainted. I must go to the warehouse now and see to the unpacking of the supplies."

Brigitte faced him. Her brow knitted. He tucked his papers with the clothing and laid a gentle hand on her shoulder. "You are tired. Rest. And worry for nothing."

She sat on the bed and nodded. "Thank you, René."

He smiled and closed the door as he left. Mina met him at the end of the hall. Questions rolled off her tongue in her native Sioux, and René did his best to understand, but his Lakota was limited, and he mixed it with French.

"As I said, her name is Brigitte. She will stay here for a while. Claude will explain it further. She is eager to help with the children." The same brown-eyed toddler anchored himself to René's leg, staring up at him.

René patted the child on the head while the woman rattled off more words in Sioux. René shrugged and smiled. He patted the child again and disengaged himself. "You must talk to Claude. Good day."

The woman turned silent as René departed. He met Claude on the pathway between his home and the storehouse.

"You have found a nest for our little bird at last," Claude said.

"*Oui.* She seems quite comfortable. I believe she will sleep now."

Claude pursed his lips. "And you explained to Mina?"

"As best I could. I did not have the benefit of an interpreter." René gave Claude half a grin. "You are worried about the fires in your home?"

"*Non.* Not … that."

René raised a brow.

"Never mind. Let us see if Mina has remembered my appetite, shall we?"

"You go home and greet her. I have other business to attend to."

"All right." They grasped forearms. "Tonight then. For the festivities."

René departed, determined that he would know more about the Indian who'd accompanied them from Grand Portage. His interest in Brigitte niggled at René, and he would know she was safe before he left her.

He stopped a man exiting the warehouse. "Do you know where the man called Bemidii has gone? The one who traveled with us from *le portage?*" The man shook his head and moved on. Once inside, René inquired of several others who'd been part of the brigade. Finally, the apprentice clerk, Henri, raised his head from his work. "Do you look for Bemidii? He lives in the village. He has probably headed there."

"Merci." René nodded and spun about. *Our mysterious friend has come home as well.*

The Ojibwe village lay through the woods beyond the rear gates. René followed the heavily wooded trail that wound away from the fort to an encampment half a mile away. Even before he reached it, he smelled meat on spits and heard the singing and drums of a celebration.

As he stepped into the encampment, women smiled and dipped their heads. Young men stood tall but moved aside as he strode among them.

René approached the nearest young man. "Bemidii?"

The man pointed to a lodge farther off. Two children dodged across René's path as he approached the *wiigiwaam*. Before he reached it, the broad-shouldered Indian stepped outside. He saw René and stiffened.

"Bemidii."

The man acknowledged René with a jerk of his head.

"I would speak to you apart."

He nodded again before stepping back inside the lodge. René followed.

No one else was within. Bemidii pointed to a couch of furs along the wall, and René seated himself. Bemidii bent back out the doorway and called for something. As he took a seat facing René, a pretty girl brought them food and drink.

"You are here to know of my interest in the woman who came with you and the other Dufour."

René gave a short nod, hoping his surprise didn't show. "You have followed her from Kaministiquia."

Bemidii drank from a gourd, then handed it to René. René accepted and swallowed. A cool, herbal tea slid down his throat. He handed back the gourd. "I would know why."

"I come to my home, here."

"But you *are* interested in her. Your interest is peculiar."

"She is not *Anishinaabe*."

"Only in part. Her father is French."

He nodded. His eyelid twitched. "I have heard she looks for this father."

Now they were getting somewhere. The man's curiosity about Brigitte likely stemmed from something he hoped to gain. "*Oui.* What is that to you?"

"I have heard his name spoken." Bemidii offered meat to René. René shook his head and laced his fingers together. Bemidii set the food aside and leveled his gaze at René. "Is she frightened?"

René's fingers tightened as anger boiled through him. "She wonders why you look at her without friendliness."

The Indian lifted a shoulder and dropped it, his nonchalance only fueling René's impatience. "I mean her no harm. I would only know more about her."

"Where did you hear of her father?"

"It is not important." The Indian's gaze remained stoic. René returned Bemidii's stare as the moments passed. Finally, the Indian's posture relaxed, if only slightly. "At Boucher's store, I discovered she looked for him. That is also where I first saw her. She was not with you or the other *bourgeois* trader then. She was with the Métis."

"You have some knowledge of her father, and now you hope to gain something with your use of it."

"I have no need of gain."

"Then what is your interest in either her or her father? Do you know where he can be found?"

The man folded his arms tight across his chest. "If I do, I will tell her."

"Why not tell me now? You know I am trying to help her."

"I have not said I know where he is."

The man exasperated René. "If that is the case, then you must leave her alone. Stay away from her. Stop watching her." With that, René left the lodge.

Dissatisfaction weighed hard upon him. He halted and turned to find Bemidii close behind him. Controlling his voice, René said, "You will not remain employed by the North West Company unless I have your word."

Bemidii's face hardened. He dipped his head in something less than acquiescence. René frowned and turned away. Tomorrow he must leave Fort St. Louis, and he must leave Brigitte, less than certain her safety was secured.

CHAPTER 16

Come, my love, a dancing, so far into the night.
Our feet will trip so lightly! We'll forget that time's a flight.
— Come a Dancing (Voyageur's Paddling Song, 1725)

Brigitte woke early the next day, refreshed from her journey and anxious to begin a new life. First, however, she must hurry to find René. She didn't want to miss telling him farewell. She found him busy with his preparations, as always, already loading his *canot*, but when he saw her coming toward him, he stopped his work and met her.

A smile that didn't quite reach his eyes touched his lips. "I am to leave you at last," he said, a bit of levity lifting his voice.

Brigitte schooled her features, not wishing to appear distressed at his leaving, though suddenly, she felt his imminent distancing. She quirked a brow. "And I am to be free of your fathering."

Now a true smile stretched from the corners of his eyes. "I am not so old as that."

Her breath stole away. "*Non.*"

They stood silently for a moment, their gazes locked, before the awkwardness of parting took hold. She cleared her throat and turned her face to survey the horizon, but he took her hand and squeezed her fingers lightly. Her eyes caught his gaze once again.

"About the Indian, the man who upset you, his name is Bemidii. He lives in a village nearby. He has been warned. Remember, you must tell Claude if you have any need or cause for worry." He leaned forward and kissed her on the forehead, his breath brushing her cheek. "Be well, Brigitte. I hope you will find happiness here."

She nodded.

"Perhaps next time I see you, you will have found your *père*."

She took a sharp breath, pushing away her threatening

emotions. "I promise to do as you say."

He chuckled, and she relaxed at the sound. He stepped back. "I doubt it."

She swallowed. "*Au revoir*, René."

"*Au revoir.* I will see you again."

She nodded as he climbed into his North Canoe.

Brigitte stood on the shore and watched his small party leave. She pulled in a long, deep breath of lake air and closed her eyes. Their voyageurs' song wove through her, putting her there with them, feeling the movement of the *bateau* gliding along beneath her. She opened her eyes and waved. René lifted his hand in salute.

"I will miss you, René," she said, but only the wind heard. She gnawed her lip as the song grew faint. The *bateau* slipped out of sight around the bend, whisking up the mouth of the St. Louis.

She stared into the distance, seeing nothing but the river, until her body grew cold. Brigitte wrapped her arms around her middle and the wind—surely it was the wind—made her eyes water.

More tears slipped free. *He is gone. Mon Dieu, protect him. Bring him safely back.* Pulling in a shaky breath, Brigitte turned. In front of her lay the fort, drawing her toward it. Claude stood outside the gates, watching. She pressed her eyelids closed and then blinked them dry before leaving the riverbank.

Claude smiled at her as she approached. "My brother must begin his first sojourn as a wintering partner while I must remain here. It will not be so bad now. I feel there will be much pleasure in having you here among us."

His words cheered her. "You are kind to say so."

"You will assist me in the storehouse. There is always much to do with sorting goods and supplies. There are tedious amounts of bookwork, and you are educated. Perhaps you might even have a hand in helping me with them."

She clutched her hands over her chest. "Truly? I may at last be useful?"

"Certainly. Had you any doubt? Come, we will begin today."

Brigitte followed him to the storehouse where he put her to work measuring out small sacks of corn and meal and recording their weights and number in the book. The distraction helped her to corral her thoughts of René's departure.

In the afternoon, the two small children from Claude's house burst in along with the domestic woman who brought him his meal. The little ones ran about while the woman chattered and scolded after them.

Brigitte smiled. "May I?" She pointed to the sack of maple sugar candy she'd seen lying on a corner shelf.

Claude grinned. "Go ahead. But if you spoil them, you will have to pay the price."

She gave them each a piece of candy, which they crammed into their mouths, quieting until it was gone. Then they begged for more.

"*Non, non*. That is all." Offering them a smile in place of more sweets, she returned to her work.

Their mother soon called to the children, and they left the building. Brigitte watched them leave with longing. A pang of homesickness for the orphans at the nunnery ran through her. "I am glad I will see them again at your house."

Claude glanced up from his books. He tapped his pen before returning to his work. "*Oui*. I'm certain you shall have your fill of them. They are always underfoot."

"I see your *domestique* is expecting. Where is her husband?"

Claude paused again, but this time he didn't look at her. "He is employed with the company."

"I see." She nodded, and—finished with her task— closed the book. "I tried speaking with her at the house, but we could not understand each other."

"She is Sioux, so I am not surprised."

Brigitte picked up a feather duster and swept along the shelves. "I wondered." She moved past Claude, who continued scratching away with his goose-feather pen. "I suppose in time we will come to understand one another."

"That is always a possibility." He closed his ledger and cleared his throat. Turning in his chair, he clasped his hands together. "Brigitte, are you certain that nothing lies between you and René? Nothing of an amorous nature?"

She faltered with the duster, then moved it swiftly over the next shelf. "You embarrass me, Claude. I told you there was nothing."

"Good." He stood. "I think we should call our work done today. The Scot is still here, and he has informed me that his bagpipes need use. Tonight we shall enjoy the remnant of summer. We shall eat and drink and dance. I expect you to show me you haven't forgotten the steps since we left Fort William."

"*Très bien.*" She turned away, hiding a smile. She and Claude walked about the room and blew out the tallow candles. He latched the door behind them before walking her home.

"I must admit, I have enjoyed my work today," Brigitte said as they entered the house. "I am glad I came. Thank you for helping me."

He moved to a chair by the fire and bent to pull off his boots. "I was more than happy to do so."

She smiled as Mina came into the room. The Sioux woman jabbered to Claude, casting only a glance at Brigitte. Brigitte turned to go to the room she'd been given.

"Brigitte."

She looked back.

"Do not retire just yet. Remember, tonight we celebrate with a revelry to begin the new season."

A revelry. Always, it seemed, these traders and voyageurs found reason to celebrate. She nodded and left him to speak to his *domestique*.

Later that evening, a party began in the fort's courtyard. Claude released a cask of rum, and singing broke out as the Scot's bagpipes trilled and mourned. The gates stood open to the bay, where a campfire burned.

Brigitte walked with Claude. He introduced her to all they met. Soon they found themselves outside the fort, where the sounds of revelry fell away, and the moon cast silvery reflections on water that lapped against the sand. Brigitte lifted her shoulders and took a deep breath. Stars filled the sky with sparkling effervescence, and the inky blackness of Lake Superior yawned fathomless, like gazing into eternity.

She shuddered. The nights that stretched behind her—memories of crossing through Superior's sea—clamored. Terrifying tales of giants and spirits, ghosts of men lost, like her friend Gervais, crept out on the water washing on the shore. The toes of her moccasins pressed into the beach as she strolled beyond the perimeter of the hunters' fires. Claude walked beside her, keeping fear away.

He sighed. "Summer will not last. Even tonight, I am surprised at the balm. *Supérieur* is not usually so generous with her warmth."

"I do not mind. Seasons must come."

"You are not the sort of girl I remember from my youth in Montreal. You intrigue me, if you do not mind my saying so."

She wrapped her arms around her waist, restraining the unsettling feelings his comment caused. Thankfully, the darkness hid her blush. "I think I have always been meant for this country. When my father took me to Montreal, I cried. Not at first, of course. It was a grand adventure. But when he left me there and went away, I felt as lost as I could be. My *tante* Eunice was good to me, and I loved her very much. Still, nothing compared to when my papa would come to see me. Every time, I begged him to take me back with him. Of course, he had other hopes for me."

"Why did you not marry? Surely someone must have—"

She laid a hand on his arm, stopping his words. "I have no joy in remembering my prospects there."

His hand fell over hers, pulling her arm through his. "Then I will not speak of it again."

They stood in the dark, and a strangeness—surprising, but not unwelcome—swept over her. René leapt into her thoughts, but then Claude guided her toward the fort. "Come. We must return to the feasting and dancing. I am the *bourgeois* here, and I must not let them miss me." They strolled back without speaking, passing inside the gates where the festivities continued.

He left her side then, and Brigitte contented herself walking among the Indian families and voyageurs, the workers, the hunters, and all who swelled the ranks of their small society. At last, fatigue from the long day claimed her. She slipped away toward the white house next to the storehouse.

Bemidii stepped from the shadows before her. Her breath stopped. René had expected the man to leave her alone, but he had been wrong, or else René only said those things to assuage her fears.

The light of the fires glittered in Bemidii's black eyes, pouring heat into her.

She turned to run, but he grabbed her arm and clamped a hand over her mouth. He pulled her into the shadows.

"Do not fight." He hissed into her ear as he wrapped one arm around her shoulders. She pushed against him and stomped on his foot, but his arm coiled viselike around her. The hand over her mouth pressed tighter, threatening to suffocate. "Stop."

She struggled more, but his hold seemed to grow stronger as her strength drained away until she fell limp, supported by his grip around her shoulders. Fear clamped her throat shut.

"I wish to speak to you. Do not cry out, and I will release you."

Her body tensed. Everything within her screamed to break free and flee the moment his grip loosened, but he held fast.

"No harm shall come to you. You must listen."

His grip relaxed only slightly, and Brigitte tore free, putting several steps between them before she spun about, stepping back against the house.

He held up his hands, palms turned outward. "You are Marchal's daughter."

Her thoughts tumbled, catapulting into darkness as thick as

night over the lake. She felt around to gather them in, but confusion tripped her. Was it not the reward he sought after all?

"I am not wrong?"

She gave a hesitant shake of her head, her heart still hammering in her throat. She angled toward him, stepping away from the house. "You know him?"

He gave the slightest nod.

A breath gushed out of her. "Papa ..."

"I can show you where he is, but you must come with me."

As they stood between the buildings, the dancing fires, singers, and the clamor of the fort lay a hundred yards distant. She looked for Claude, then again into the duskiness of Bemidii's beckoning gaze.

He flicked his fingers. "Come."

She checked for Claude once more, then turned to Bemidii, who had walked toward the back of the buildings and was about to disappear into the night. She sucked in her breath. *"Mon Dieu,* protect me."

CHAPTER 17

Listen to the wind, it talks.
Listen to the silence, it speaks.
Listen to your heart, it knows.
　　　　　　　　　—Native American Proverb

Brigitte kept behind Bemidii along the dark trail through the woods. Now and then, he paused to wait for her. As the forest thickened between her and the fort, dread clawed its way into her.

What had she done? She was at his mercy. If he intended to turn her over for reward, or if he had some other design in mind, she could do nothing about it now. Her rash decision might lead her to Papa or to her own undoing.

I will only know the truth by following.

Blinking into the darkness, she concentrated on her footing and not being swallowed by the forest. They soon entered into a quiet Indian encampment of bark-covered *wiigiwaams*. A few fires burned low. Through the dimness, Brigitte spied tools neatly organized beside the homes, and several hides stretched to dry. The scent of smoke and herbs teased her nostrils. A surge of childhood memories leapt at her.

The place was so like the village of her mother's people. She wondered for a moment if it was the very one. But, *non*. That village bordered a jumping river on one side and a hilly meadow on the other. In other ways, however, this one felt the same.

He halted. "My village."

She glanced about the encampment. A baby's cry came from inside one of the lodges and was hushed. She looked at him and swallowed.

Bemidii pulled back the flap on the nearest lodge and spoke to someone inside. Then he dropped the flap and continued on the path ahead. "Come." He held out his hand, and she paused. Should she turn back now, run into the forest the way she'd come? He gestured with his hand, waiting but not forcing her.

"Is he not here?"

"*Non.*"

"You are lying to me."

"I do not lie, but if you will not come, you will not find him." He held out his hand.

She stared at it, trembling, but with a breath, she laid her hand in his calloused one. Her heart raced as his fingers wrapped around hers. He guided her through the village then back into the woods. Above her head, the trees opened to reveal the night sky. The Big Dipper tilted to her right. Did they walk in a circle? She cocked her head at the gentle rush of water, and a moment later, the forest broke open. They'd come to the lake again, but so far along the shore, the fort was out of sight and sound.

She pulled her hand free. "Where are you taking me? You tell me you know something of my father, but you do not say what. You frighten me with dark looks and ask my name, but you do not tell me how you know these things. You take me away in the night, and I am to follow you without knowing what is to become of me. Will you kill me or turn me over to the hands of … of someone else?"

He stepped closer to her so that she could see his frown deepen in the faint moonlight. "Did I not tell you no harm would come to you?"

"*Oui,* you told me, but why should I believe you? I know you are Bemidii, but that is all. Who is Bemidii that I should care or listen to him?" Her shoulders shook, but she lifted her chin, bracing herself.

"Who is Bemidii? He is the one you must trust if you want your answer. I take you with me by night while no Dufour interferes. I tell you no harm will befall you. If you do not trust Bemidii, go now. Follow this shore back to the fort. You will find your way."

He turned, and, from the rushes along the water's edge, pulled out a small canoe. With gentle hands, he settled it in the water and waited.

Brigitte pushed her shoulders back and walked past him, her moccasins dampening in the wet sand. She settled in the boat, and then he shoved off. Without going far from shore, he paddled them deeper into the night along the edge of the bay, farther from the fort and Claude's home. She shivered.

"You are cold. I should have thought to bring you a blanket."

His comment encouraged her.

As they glided over the dark water, her thoughts turned to Claude. Would he worry for her? Likely not. He would think her asleep in the room that had been René's. Again, she prayed.

The shoreline grew marshier, and Bemidii pushed away from it, paddling them across the bay. The moonlight outlined the long arm of land they'd passed upon her arrival with the voyageurs. He skirted along it, making hardly a sound. As the ride grew long, she rubbed her arms and turned her gaze to the moon making its slow walk across the sky. It was better to focus on the light in the heavens than on the unknown darkness around her. Finally, Bemidii paddled toward shore again, and she dropped her gaze to the blackness, wondering what lay beyond.

The canoe's bottom brushed softly against reeds, and Bemidii jumped out, drawing the craft ashore and steadying it for her. She alighted from the *canot* and stood by as he brought it up on the beach. Then she followed him a hundred paces across the wooded spit to the lakeside. Water brushed the sand in whispers as the faintest cast of eastern light lent ghostliness to the skyline. Dawn would soon be upon them.

"We will wait."

She turned to study him. "Wait for what?"

"We must have the light now."

She trudged up an incline into the grass and dropped onto the ground beneath a tall pine. Her gaze leveled on the distant horizon and the pinking of the sky until a deep weariness claimed her, and her lids drooped closed.

She fought the jostling that woke her. Peeling her eyelids open against the daylight, her body ached with stiffness. Where was the camp? Had they left her behind? Her bleary vision was slow to focus.

Bemidii rose from where he squatted beside her. "We must go now."

Reality righted itself like a canoe having been harried by the wind. She pushed to her feet, stretching the ache from her legs as she followed.

She scowled. "I am hungry."

Reaching inside the bag hanging at his hip, Bemidii offered her a piece of pemmican. "It is not much farther. Come."

Doubts assailed her, but she chewed the pemmican and continued trudging behind him through the shadowy woods.

They stepped into a small clearing and halted. She looked past him at the scene before her. Gooseflesh raised on her arms.

Mounds of earth, unnatural to the land, filled the space. Totems, upside down, ranged among them. A graveyard. Over some of the graves stood spirit houses, small house-like structures with windows facing west. She remembered seeing something like them before, long ago. She stopped walking and looked closer. Offerings lay on the graves. Beads, *opwaaganag*, pipes, flint, feathers. She spied a little bell, arrowheads, and bunches of sticks tied together in shapes and bundles.

Prickles ran up her spine, and she stepped back. *Papa.*

Bemidii took her arm, and they circled the edge of the burial ground. She breathed easier when they came to the other side. Papa was not there. The Indians would not have it so. She should have realized. Then they were back in the woods again, striding through tall pines. They arrived at a hidden bay.

There, Bemidii stood still, and she stepped beside him. Sunlight crested the treetops. Bulrushes, sedges, and cattails encompassed the bay, brown and heavy with clay. Sumac and ivy sprouted out of the sand, and on the edge of the forest stood a small wooden cross. She gasped and stared.

"He has the white man's marker."

She turned to Bemidii, and his eyes were softer than she'd ever seen, answering her unspoken question.

"Papa."

Weariness fell over her as the world spun. She crumpled to her knees and clutched at the ache in her chest. Her chin trembled as tears blurred her eyes, then poured out. "Papa." She finally had an answer, but she didn't want to know. All this time, she didn't want to know what the cross told her must be true. Papa was gone from the world.

She crawled across the ground to his grave and stretched her hands over it. She squeezed the sand in her fists as the pain enlarged, and quiet sobs shook her. Her fingers trembled over the shape of the cross.

Many minutes later, as the ache in her chest eased, she turned and saw Bemidii waiting as stoically as ever, his arms over his chest, sadness in his eyes she hadn't expected. He dropped his gaze and walked to the water's edge where he lowered himself to the ground, facing away from her. She turned to Papa's grave and wept some more.

When, at last, her tears had dried up, a hand lay upon her shoulder. She looked up. Bemidii held out a small gourd filled with water. She took it and drank, then wiped the back of her hand across her mouth, across her eyes. When she extended the gourd, he took it and moved away again.

With the sun now high in the sky, her stomach growled, yet she felt no desire to fill it. It had been many years since she'd last seen her father. When had he died? How?

Bemidii sat cross-legged in the sand and ferns beneath a tall pine. His eyes were closed, but his arms braced across his chest told her he did not sleep.

"How did my father die?"

"He fell through the ice."

She gulped. The horror of it brought fresh tears.

"Hunters found his body many days after his spirit had flown. They were going to leave it, but a white man among them said he must be buried. It was near here, so this is the place they laid him. I was told later, and I came to see."

"You?" She frowned. "When did this happen?"

"Five winters past. I remember it well. It was my third year as a hunter for the North West Company. I did well. Killed many deer, caught many beaver."

She closed her eyes. Beaver, deer. What did those things matter to her? Her hopes had crashed around her, and now she had no more dreams. She would rather she did not know the truth about her father. She would rather carry her false hope into the future, thinking that someday she might find him.

"The shadows of the sun grow short. You must go back. The trader will be angry with me for taking you."

She looked up, swiping again at the endless flow of tears. "It doesn't matter," she whispered.

He held out his hand. "It matters."

She gazed at his hand, steady before her. Laying her own in it, she allowed him to pull her to her feet. This time she didn't mind his hand holding onto hers. He led her back to the canoe. He was silent as they climbed inside.

He offered her more of the pemmican. "You should keep up your strength."

She took it and nibbled but tasted nothing. Silently, he paddled her across the bay. They stopped before reaching the fort and banked the canoe. Then she followed him down the path that wound deep into the woods by way of Bemidii's village. She didn't think to ask him why but decided it was to slip her in unnoticed, lest he feel Claude's wrath, for certainly now she must be missed.

At the village, he stopped near a cook fire outside a lodge. A woman handed Brigitte a bowl of stew.

The pemmican had awakened her appetite, so she took a bite of stew and chewed it slowly, swallowing hard and looking to her strange guide. "Thank you for taking me to see my father. I am sorry for fearing you, for being ..." She dropped her head.

When she lifted her gaze, he nodded. "Think not of it, *Aamoo*."

"What?" She felt the blood drain from her face.

His brows twitched as some emotion she couldn't quite fathom flitted over Bemidii's face. He lowered his gaze, but his hand fisted against his side.

"Bee?"

He shrugged and looked back at her. "You go here and there seeking your answer like a bee seeks nectar."

Her thoughts misted together, then slowly cleared. *"Aamoo.* I have not heard it since I was a little girl. My father sometimes called me little bee."

Bemidii gestured at the woman who'd given Brigitte the stew, calling her over. "This is my mother. She is called Keeheezkoni."

The woman arched a brow at Brigitte, watching her carefully. Brigitte nodded. *"Boozhoo."*

Keeheezkoni smiled in return.

"Finish eating, and I will take you to the fort."

A boy strolled past them then, nearly as tall as Bemidii, and Bemidii reached out and gave him a light shove. When the boy's head spun toward him, Bemidii grinned. The boy grinned back before turning to Keeheezkoni for his own bowl of stew. Bemidii's smile lingered as he glanced toward Brigitte, before dropping his gaze back to his food. His behavior surprised her, almost made her forget the stern looks of the past.

After they finished eating, Brigitte wiped her hands on the grass and followed him through the forest. By light of day, it was a clear, well-traveled path. She could surely have followed it back herself. "I can find the fort myself. I will explain to *Monsieur* Dufour. He will not be angry."

Bemidii shook his head. "He will not understand. His brother, the other Dufour, said I must not watch you or bother you."

"I will explain."

"If you choose, but it will go better for me if I return you whole." She stumbled over a root, and he looked back at her. A slight smile, like before, edged his lips, and this time a tingling ran up her back, as her memories sparked. "Do not fall. You will not be believed if you return injured."

Moments later, they broke from the edge of the forest. Beyond a stretch of open ground stood the rear gates of the fort. Brigitte's breath quickened, though not from exertion. The memory niggled, calling Bemidii's smile back to her thoughts. The quirk of it, lifting on one side ... just so ... Her heart pounded harder. Brigitte reached for him, touching his shirt. She drew back when he turned, his eyes widening in question. "Bemidii—"

"I know nothing more of your father's death."

She shook her head. "*Non.* It is not that. It is something else. Something I saw when I tripped on the root. Something in you."

His mouth fell into a flat line. "What is it?"

"Why ... Why did you take me to my father's grave? You could have told me anytime. It was nothing to you. He was nothing to you ... was he?" Something squeezed around her chest, tightening her breath.

The fort faded away as Bemidii's eyes looked steadily into hers. Something familiar and warm leapt out of them.

She gasped.

"*Aamoo.*" His face crumpled. "I was seven summers when you were born. Six when my father left my mother to take another wife."

Brigitte covered her mouth. She wanted to touch him but could not. Could such a thing truly be?

"He called you Bee. I heard him, and I was jealous of you, jealous of the woman he took instead of Keeheezkoni, my mother. But as you grew, I could not hold onto my jealousy forever. He took you away to your mother's people in another village far from here. He returned from time to time with the other canoe men. When he did, he remembered I was his son. He took me hunting. Taught me how to catch the beaver. He did not return to my mother's lodge, as I wished, but he taught me.

"Some summers he went far across the lake to the place called Montreal. One year, he came to a great carrying place called Grande Portage, and I was there. I was only a boy, thirteen or fourteen summers, but I had trapped beaver, and I was proud of the pelts I had gotten. The men in my village let me go with them, and I brought them in for trade. I found our father there, and you were with him. I wanted to stay with him, but he was taking you away. I remember your face as you watched the many things going on in that place, little sister. I felt compassion for you." His hand covered his chest. He rubbed the spot over his heart.

A new sting bit the backs of Brigitte's eyelids, but instead of crying, she smiled. "I have cried enough today." A small laugh escaped her, weariness coming with it. She never dreamed she had a brother. She didn't recall aunts or cousins among her mother's people, even though there had likely been a relation. But a brother!

She looked into his eyes again. They didn't seem so dark now. Her father's spirit lived in his features, in the strength of his jaw, his brow, his height. Her father had been taller than most voyageurs, taller than Claude or René. Her brother was the same.

"Our father …" She swallowed hard. "Our father never told me."

"He sometimes called me Benjamin, but Keeheezkoni would not allow it. I am Bemidii. And I am Marchal."

Brigitte's fears evaporated. Her loneliness fled. His arms went around her, and she laid her head against her brother's chest.

CHAPTER 18

"For the netting of snowshoes, making nets from twine,
sewing and mending clothes, and washing, the women
were paid from the stores an equitable sum of trade goods:
3 Kettles, 15 pounds rice, 25 pounds flour, 1 pound trade
beads, 4 knives, 1 two-point blanket, 6 combs."

—NW Company Store Ledger of
Claude Dufour, Fur Trader

Brigitte pushed away a loose strand of hair and drew her shawl tighter around her shoulders as she hurried up the path from Keeheezkoni's lodge to the fort. Autumn's brisk fingers trailed shivers up her neck, reminding her that soon, the pinch of winter would confine her to the storehouse listing figures in a ledger, or to the hearth mending and washing and patching clothes. Her walks to the Indian village in the woods would necessarily become less frequent.

The days since learning she had a brother had flown by. Bemidii's mother had warmed to her. Perhaps she felt pity for her son's orphaned sister. Keeheezkoni had another husband now, and Bemidii had a brother about sixteen summers and a sister, Shenia, who was several years younger than Brigitte. Shenia seemed keenly interested in Brigitte, but when Brigitte spoke to her, she turned away, aloof, and pretended not to hear.

Brigitte smiled, thinking of her growing friendship with Bemidii. At times, he teased her, at others, he ignored her, for she was just a woman. Yet he behaved at ease around her now, after having discovered their close relation.

Claude had been shocked by the news. He refused to believe it, said the Indian must be tricking her for some reason. However, in time, he too saw Bemidii spoke the truth. Claude treated him with mild respect, but Brigitte thought Bemidii held Claude at a distance. Now that Bemidii had gone to hunt and trap for the company, she would not see him again for a while.

She slipped inside the back door of the house, shivering as she shook off the shawl and hung it on a peg. She passed by the back bedrooms on her way to the fireplace in the main room. Mina sat across the room, netting a pair of snowshoes for the coming winter.

Brigitte pushed up her sleeves and knelt by the hearth, absorbing the warmth. The aroma of simmering meat rose from a pot hanging on a tripod over the fire. She inhaled and looked at Mina. "It smells wonderful."

Mina passed her the smallest glance as her hands concentrated on her work.

Brigitte picked up a spoon to stir the broth. Mina set aside her work and hurried to her side, slapping Brigitte's hand away and yammering something unintelligible in Sioux, grabbing the spoon and shaking it.

Brigitte relinquished the task with a sigh. There was no understanding the woman. She refused to speak to Brigitte unless it was with a biting tongue, and Brigitte's small overtures of friendship were met with narrowed, suspicious glances. Such a woman! Mina's behavior was unacceptable, but Claude only smiled and shrugged if Brigitte complained. She rose and backed from the hearth while Mina continued to scold and scowl.

The back door slammed. A moment later, Claude came into the room. "What is the yelling about? I could hear it outside."

Brigitte sighed. "I am afraid I upset her."

One of the little ones ran to Claude and grabbed him about the legs. He patted the child on the head and frowned at Mina, addressing her in a spattering of Sioux.

Mina rattled off a string of words, and the way her glance continued to slice into Brigitte, she feared what the woman was telling him. Probably that he was a fool to allow such an ignorant woman a place in his house. Brigitte would have apologized if she knew what to apologize for.

Then she heard René's name. Claude's face reddened, and his words grew stern. Brigitte inched away, skirting around them to leave the room.

Mina shouted, and Claude shouted back. Then she grabbed the child and barreled past Brigitte, knocking into her and storming down the passage. Brigitte backed into a corner of the room. Claude looked her way only briefly, his fingers clenching at his sides. Then he followed Mina, marching up the narrow stairs that led to the attic room where she slept with her children.

Their argument continued upstairs.

Brigitte let out a sigh. Such a quandary her presence had created. Did the woman think Brigitte was trying to take her place? Perhaps that was the reason for Mina's sharp attitude toward her. She might fear losing her position as a *domestique* now with Brigitte's arrival.

At last, silence settled over the house.

Brigitte went to her room to gather the tanned leather and sinew she'd saved for stitching a new pair of moccasins and returned near the hearth. Before settling into a chair, she gave a surreptitious glance down the hall and bent to stir the stew. *Humph*. What Mina didn't know would prevent them from eating a burned supper.

Brigitte inhaled the aroma of the stew before setting aside the spoon. Taking up her leather and tools, she considered Mina. Claude had told her little of the woman. Beyond learning that her husband was employed by the company, there was little Brigitte had gleaned. She should have asked René to tell her more before he left. Perhaps he could have offered some insight to help her smooth the way between them.

Brigitte punched the awl through the leather with a soft pop.

Claude did say that Mina's clan lived somewhere down the St. Louis River. Perhaps Mina would visit them sometime during the winter, or mayhap her husband would return and take her away. Brigitte sighed. How long could she endure living with such an unwelcoming woman? Yet …

She glanced at the pot simmering over a bed of coals, then back to her work. How fortunate for Mina that she had employment in Claude's home during the terrible Lake Superior winters. Claude was probably loath to send her and her little ones off to survive the harshness of the forest outside the fort as long as she could stay to mend and cook and clean.

Sometime later, as Brigitte finished punching holes through the leather and picked up her needle and lacing, Mina marched down the stairs again, a little girl clinging to her dress. She scooped stew onto a trencher and pulled the little girl onto her lap to feed her.

Claude followed some minutes later. He gave Brigitte a nod and retrieved a trencher of stew for himself. After he'd taken it to the table, Brigitte set aside her work and dished her own trencher. She carried it to the table in the center of the room and took her seat. They all ate together in silence. Then Claude left the house, and Brigitte resumed her work on the moccasins.

When the light grew dim, and after jabbing herself with her needle a fourth time, Brigitte gave up her lacing. Frustrated at the little she'd accomplished, and with Mina casting her smug looks, she decided to return to the storeroom. Perhaps Claude had need of her and could explain Mina's irritability.

Brigitte petted the head of one of Mina's little ones as she reached for her shawl. The girl gazed up at her with big, sober eyes. Ah, Brigitte would love to pick her up and cuddle her, but she had incurred enough of Mina's disfavor for the time being. At first, she'd been allowed to play with the children, to hold them, feed them, sing to them, bathe and dress them. Lately, though, Mina chased her off, just as she had from her task by the fire. Her children had become off-limits.

Brigitte stepped outside and squinted against the lake wind chilling the air. A peek toward the open front gates showed a glimpse of whitecaps churning up the bay. How dreadful it would be to ride in the *bateau* now. Hopefully, René was safe and dry, wherever he was. She breathed a prayer for him and thought of the day they'd stopped at the church of St. Anne's to beseech a blessing for their journey. It seemed so, so long ago. Much longer than a handful of weeks.

She stepped through the door into the storehouse, and Claude glanced up from his books with a smile. "The little bird has flown in from the cold."

Oui, *the cold of Mina's companionship.* "I must ruffle my feathers," she said, joining him in his jest.

"Perhaps we will see frost tonight." He turned to the inventory of a shelf loaded with wares, then stepped back to the ledger again.

The front door opened with a bang. Brigitte turned to look as three Indians stepped inside. She didn't recognize them, but Claude pushed back his shoulders and smiled in welcome, as though they were familiar. She moved to the corner behind him, attempting to remain obscure while they spoke to one another.

They settled a bundle of furs on the counter, and Claude made them an exchange of goods—some flint, a trap, a small bag of lead—then he poured them each a tin cup of rum. They guzzled down the drink and left some minutes later.

Shortly after they left, the door opened again. This time Mina strolled in, her chin lifted and her eyes searching until they found Claude. Brigitte turned her back to measure out pouches of lead. She jumped when Mina began shouting in Sioux.

Claude hissed something in reply, his words broken.

Brigitte peeked over her shoulder and cringed as Mina picked up a copper pot and flung it. More fiery words shot off her tongue.

"*Assez!* Enough!" Claude took Mina's arm.

Brigitte fidgeted with the drawstrings on the lead pouches as he walked Mina outside. A sharp gust of air swam around the room in their wake. Mina's shrill voice resonated through the door. Brigitte stilled, unable to concentrate on her task.

What was the matter with the woman? No domestic should treat her employer so rudely. She acted more like a fishwife.

Shaking her head, she tightened the drawstring on the last

pouch. Perhaps Claude owed her husband some favor and put up with her for that reason. If the opportunity presented itself, she would ask him.

Brigitte moved to the counter and withdrew a book to record the weights of the pouches.

Finally, when silence settled around the room, Claude stepped back inside. His glance flicked sheepishly at her. He shrugged. "She had a complaint."

"I see. Is it settled?"

He nodded, going back to his ledger of hides taken. His fingers twitched as he laid back the pages, and his pen fell to the floor.

She pulled in a breath. "I am surprised you let her treat you so."

He retrieved the pen and shrugged. "We have known each other a long time. I've come to care about her welfare."

For the flicker of a moment, Brigitte wondered just how much Claude cared. "And you promised something to her husband?"

He paused. "You could say so. One needs to take great care in relation to the natives."

Brigitte nodded. After all, how could one not care? Hadn't the woman's children endeared themselves to her?

She continued her work of shelving the lead pouches. How unfortunate that Mina's foul mood had followed her from the house to the store. Now it seemed she would consume Claude's good spirits too. Brigitte sighed. Perhaps things would be better tomorrow.

Night fell fully. A shiver ran through Brigitte as the wind rattled the door. The fire had burned down to cinders in the clay fireplace. At last, Claude picked up a candle, its light casting shadows on the wall, drawing Brigitte's attention.

"We should retire now. Morning comes soon enough."

Claude held the door, and she made her way outside. Cold rain spit from the night sky, falling like ice against her face. Brigitte scurried to the house ahead of him and rushed inside. She shuddered, unwilling to remove her shawl as she trod through the dark. She stopped in the middle of the main room. Only small embers glowed in the hearth, barely giving heat, where normally a warm flame would be casting its light and their supper would be waiting.

"*Qu'est-ce qui se passe?* What is the matter? Why is the house dark?" Claude moved past her. "Mina?" He stooped to stir the coals and added wood. He tipped two candles to light their wicks and set them on a rough-hewn table near the hearth. Stillness lay over the rest of the house.

Brigitte's stomach growled, but looking to the stew pot behind Claude, she found it empty. Remnants of congealed grease covered the bottom. "Where has she gone?"

He frowned and went out the front door, slamming it in his wake.

Brigitte sighed, picking up one of the candles and going in search of something for their meal. She pulled her shawl tighter as she lifted the latch to a wooden door on the windowless side of the room leading to the cold storage. Thankfully, Bemidii's younger brother had earlier given her a small duck which she had cleaned and wrapped in cloth, hoping to prepare it tomorrow. As soon as the fire grew, she would spit and cook it. She raised the candle, casting light along the shelf in the dark, chilly room until she saw the clothbound duck. She clutched it and hurried out, closing the door with a shiver.

As she turned around, Claude returned. Mina was not with him. "It seems she has decided to stay in her *wiigiwaam* tonight."

Brigitte frowned and set the duck on the table. "She will be all right?"

"She will be fine."

"And the little ones?"

Claude gave a slow nod, staring at the fire.

She hesitated, wanting to ask more, but clearly the situation bothered him more than he admitted. He would do something for Mina if she would let him. Brigitte could do nothing.

She removed her shawl, rubbing her arms against the chill in the room. "I will cook us some food. I have duck, and I will make *galette* as well, so there will be something when she returns in the morning."

"I do not expect she will return." He turned his gaze to her.

"*Non?*" Her word was a whisper.

"*Non.*"

"I am sorry, Claude." She stepped closer. "I fear I angered her today. She likely thought I meant to take her work. She has gone because of me, has she not?"

A nerve twitched in his eyelid. His eyes, already so very dark in the firelight, seemed to deepen in intensity and shine with some thought he did not share.

Her guilt sharpened at having driven away his *domestique*. "I am sorry," she whispered again.

"It is not your fault. *Oui*, she left because she thought you meant to take her place, but it is nothing you did. I explained to her that René left you in our care. In *my* care. She is a woman of some vanity. She thinks, perhaps, you cannot do the job she has done."

Brigitte rankled. "She is going to have a *bébé*. How can she continue to clean and do the work here with another little one to care for? Surely her husband would have her return to her people, to be cared for until he is able to return to her himself."

He nodded. "*Oui* … certainly he would." He leaned an arm against the stone above the hearth. "I think we must let Mina decide what she wishes to do. Stay or go."

Wind rattled the window pane.

"But the little ones …"

Claude stepped closer and settled his hands on her shoulders. "They will be fine, Brigitte. Mina's lodge is warm. She has wood for a fire and many hides to sleep upon. If tomorrow she changes her mind, we will open our door to her, eh?"

She nodded, blinking away the moisture in her eyes. He

squeezed her shoulders again but did not drop his hands. He stood so close she felt his breath upon her forehead. His touch became a caress.

She inhaled and stepped to a shelf where she pulled down a large bowl and a sack of flour, then returned to the work table. "I will have our dinner ready *un rien de temps.*"

Claude said nothing, but she felt his gaze as she worked the flour into the *galette* and spitted the duck. Her pulse jumped, and her throat thickened.

As Claude watched, she chattered on about nothing at all—the stores, Bemidii, the duck, the rain turning to hail pelting the one small window pane in the room. All the while, he sat silently in a straight-back chair by the fire, a few feet away.

At last, the duck was cooked, and Brigitte's face was hot from kneeling by the hearth. She sat back on her haunches and wiped a forearm across her brow. Claude caught her hand. She startled. He drew it close and held it.

"Brigitte."

"*Oui?*" Her voice croaked. How his features reminded her of René's. He held her gaze so that she hardly knew he raised her knuckles to his mouth until his lips brushed gently on her fingers. She pulled in a breath.

He dropped from the chair to his knees beside her. "Do not be afraid. I long to have you for my wife."

She tugged her hand free and gripped it with the other. "I—"

He lifted her chin and leaned close. Brigitte scooted back from the hearth and jumped to her feet. "Claude."

"You do not deny that you have feelings for me."

Her lips worked to form an answer as her heart pounded. Feelings? They burst through her, but she could not be sure what they meant. Claude had often complimented her, looked out for her, and even flirted with her. Perhaps she had flirted too. *René would wish it.*

Non. She shook her head, her dizzy head.

"René does not expect you to remain alone. He will not be surprised." Claude stood but did not move closer.

He read her mind, and yet … she smoothed her hands over her apron.

"I will not hurt you. I would never come to you without your agreement."

"Come to me?"

"*Oui.*" His lips drew up in a gentle smile.

"Are you speaking of marriage or …" She swallowed.

He shrugged. His mouth twitched. "It is *à la façon du pays*, in the custom of the country."

"The custom." Brigitte muttered the words, a frown pulling at her brow and her heart, slowing its erratic rhythm. She razed him with a look. "I would never do so."

"Brigitte."

"*Non.* You must be a fool if you think I would do such a thing."

He studied her and crossed his arms. "All right. Settle, my dove. There is no need to rage."

She sucked in her breath. At least he had heeded her reason.

"If it pleases you, we will seek out the medicine woman from the village."

"But she is not a Christian."

"You must understand." He stepped nearer now. "There is no priest. Surely God will allow for it if we seek assistance from your brother's people."

Would He? Brigitte recalled the medicine woman who performed spiritual ceremonies using sweetgrass, cedar, and tobacco offered with prayers to the spirit world. Dare Brigitte stand before a medicine woman and be joined in the holy union of matrimony? What else had she expected upon coming to this country?

There had been many diverse prayers while she passed through the storms on the voyage from Montreal, especially during the tempest just before arriving at Fort William. The voyageur who offered corn to the wind and waves in supplication of some spirit had nearly swamped and drowned them all.

Had God approved then? Some others in her canoe thought not. They'd reprimanded the man for his superstition.

She thought of the incense the priests used. Was it really so different?

Her brain argued that it was not. Her heart cried differently. She clenched her gown. What else was she to do? The father she had longed to find lay dead, and she could not expect to live off Claude's charity indefinitely. *Not if he does not willingly keep me in his employ.* Her future hung by a precarious thread. She wished she could go to Bemidii and ask him what to do, but it might be many days or even weeks before he returned with the hunters. "Claude, I ..." She slid her hand to her throat.

He stirred warmth and excitement in her, but could she love him?

He took a step closer. So like René, he gazed at her across the brief distance between them, waiting for her answer. His eyes kindled a blaze.

She blinked, and in that instant, she stood in the forest mixing peas and fat in a pot while René remained poised nearby, encouraging her silently for her industry. A moment later, she stood upon the lakeshore in the night, mourning Gervais while René's arms comforted her. With great sorrow, he whispered an apology in her ears. Then, in another flash, they lay side by side on the beach beneath the *bateau*, his embrace settling over her, his voice murmuring, *"We must be convincing ..."*

She shook herself from her reverie. René was a good man. *Who does not intend to marry.* Her fingers traced the edge of her collar as she considered Claude. Claude was very much like his brother. She could trust him to do well by her, could she not?

What had René said? *"You will have nothing to worry about. You will have your pick of men."*

She lifted her chin. Pushing a hair back from her face, she let her breath out slowly. She might have her *pick of men*, but for

René, had she met any others more honorable than the one who stood before her? Perhaps her decision had been made for her. She pushed back her shoulders. "I—I will agree to be your wife." He took a step toward her, but she lifted her hand between them. "I will not come to you until then, and you must agree that you will not presume upon our arrangement."

"Tomorrow we will go to Bemidii's village."

"*Non.*" She shook her head. "If I am to marry you, I must prepare myself." She placed a hand on her throat to cover the uncertain throbbing of her pulse.

He smiled and closed the gap between them. He took both her hands in his. "I understand. You want to be a bride." His eyes glittered, and she allowed him to lean forward and kiss her cheek. "You, Brigitte, will be mine to my old age. Someday, after I have become a partner, we will return to a civilized land. I will buy a farm, and we will continue there. You and I and our descendants."

A flush raced over her, and she lowered her gaze.

He laughed. "Come. Let us enjoy our supper."

CHAPTER 19

"No Indian woman, unless a half breed, should be taken by any white man whatever in their service under the pain of 100, Halifax penalty to be paid by the proprietor in whose department it should be allowed."
— Decision of the Proprietors of the North West Company at Kaministiquia, July 14, 1806

Sitting with his Indian guide in a lean-to of logs and pine boughs, René clenched his teeth as he tugged off wet moccasins and pushed his feet closer to the fire. His toes ached from cold and wet, and his stomach clenched with hunger. He might even eat a share of the duck entrails his guide now roasted. It couldn't be less appetizing than the bird itself. The guide had only pulled a few of the longest pinfeathers before he split it open and threw it unwashed in the kettle with two handfuls of parched corn.

René wiggled his toes near the blaze as the Indian took the duck off the spit. He tore the duck in two and handed half to René.

"*Wiisini.*" René accepted the man's offering with a nod and ripped it with his teeth. Forcing it down half chewed, René allowed the roasted guts to take the biggest pinch out of his own.

"*Merci.*" He wiped the grease on his pants. It was a small meal, but enough to help him think of sleep, so he settled in for the night.

By morning, though the fire had died to coals, René was dry and warm. When he stepped out of their meager shelter, a heavy frost blanketed the ground. Another Indian had arrived during the night. He and the guide emerged from the lean-to, and the newcomer gave each of them a chunk of pemmican. René washed down the remnants with a few gulps of water from his skein, then looked to the sky.

"Lead on." He nodded his head toward the south.

They arrived at the post on the Clam River late in the afternoon. The post was only a building some twenty-feet square, built with corner timbers set in trenches and sides built of mortised, stacked logs. A ridgepole supported a roof a little over six feet above ground. Inside, a window made of the thinnest parchment skin allowed a fraction of light to seep in but deterred the wind and rain.

The clerk, a long-bearded Scot named McGregor, raised his head when they came through the door. "Dufour. A civil man." He peered at René's companions.

René followed his gaze. Lowering his pack to the dirt floor, he held out his hand. "McGregor."

The man grinned. "A visit from our new partner. I am honored."

"Have you anything in your kettle? It would honor me to eat something better than half cooked duck and pemmican." He patted his belly. "Our growling stomachs could be mistaken for roaming bears."

McGregor grunted and reached for trenchers. He brought three that looked as though they'd been scraped clean once or twice before, but not scrubbed. He passed them to the waiting men. The Indians wasted no time ladling corn mush from the pot over the hearth and heading to a corner table. René brushed his sleeve across his plate before filling it. He carried it back to the counter where McGregor stood with his arms spread, leaning on the rough-hewn top.

"Your Ojibwe should keep an eye. There has been constant fighting between our hunters and a nearby clan of Sioux. Warring over hunting grounds, as usual." He dipped his head, indicating René's mush. "Fresh meat arrives irregularly under such conditions."

René nodded as he shoveled the food into his mouth. He gave a glance about. A few hides, still unsalted, lay folded in a stack on the floor. The distinct smell of urine drifted to him from one corner of the room, and René spied two men lying on cots against the far wall. He pointed with his spoon and scooped another bite.

"What ails them?"

"Fever. Diarrhea."

René swallowed. "An ill way to start the season."

The burly trader shrugged.

It came as no surprise to René either, not with the foul conditions about the camp. He'd witnessed these types of discomforts many times before, and he'd lived in worse squalor himself on occasion. The men would muddle through the misery of winter. Through it all, some would do well and bring in many pelts, while others would barely survive with little to show for their experience. René pushed his empty trencher aside and belched. He'd seldom succumbed to such illnesses. Still, other men would die before their time.

"There is a rumor," McGregor said. He reached for two tin cups and filled them with coffee, pushing one to René. "It is said ye brought a Montreal woman to the St. Louis without any man." He raised his cup and narrowed his eyes above the rim. "I was surprised to hear it."

"I was surprised to do it." René took a satisfying sip. When he lowered the cup, McGregor was smiling, his eyes bright with curiosity above his thick, red beard. "She is not mine. She looked for her father."

"Who is he?"

"He was a man named Marchal."

"Marchal. I recall him. Didnae he die a few winters back?"

René gave a nod. "It is unfortunate for the girl that we did not see you at rendezvous. We might have saved her a journey to *le fond du lac.*"

McGregor's laugh rumbled deep. He sipped his coffee and set it down with a thunk that sloshed liquid out of the cup. "I suspect ye d'nae mind so much." His rumbling laugh grew to an outburst.

René pulled his lips tight, but it was impossible to keep a lopsided smile from creeping out.

Finally, McGregor calmed down. He reached across the counter and slapped René's shoulder. "Ye will nae linger at your circuit any longer that ye can help, aye, *partner?*"

Daylight waned through the hide parchment windows. "Thank you for the meal. In the morning, we will examine your books." He gave a nod and picked up his pack. The stink of the room filled his nostrils now that he no longer thought only of a meal. He would find a place outdoors to sleep.

René pondered McGregor's chiding. With luck and half a prayer, he did intend to complete his early circuit and return to Fort St. Louis once more before winter's grip fell upon them. There, he would rest for a fortnight, write letters to the agents, gather supplies for the winter's adventure, and tally totals he'd procured thus far in the Fond du Lac district. Then he would set out again. And …

Brigitte crept into his thoughts while he considered the coming month. Never had he thought he'd miss her as badly as he did, so relieved he'd been to have gotten her safely from Montreal. As the first cool weeks of autumn passed, however, thoughts of seeing her again soothed him like a balm against the harsh living his work required. She was a strong woman, stronger than most. She had conquered the great lake with a spirit as true as any voyageur's. She was already learning the ways of the wilderness. Still, his conscience niggled.

René gathered pine boughs for a bed and leisurely set about building a lean-to over them.

What if Brigitte suffered in the coming cold? The St. Louis fort was built for the needs of men, not women. Still, it was a safe place, and Claude's house could be warm if his fires were tended. His wife might have even become a welcome companion to abate Brigitte's loneliness during the forthcoming long, dark season if they had come to understand enough of one another's language. Brigitte would come through the winter well, as long as Claude kept his promise to watch over her while she worked to forge a new life.

René frowned. A new life indeed. *And what will that mean to you, Brigitte? Another young voyageur like Gervais? Some* sauvage *who will claim you and love you, then—when his ardor is cooled—turn you into a workhorse?*

He sniffed, then blew warm breath into his cupped hands before working a piece of twine about a pole to hold it firmly in place.

That was what became of the Indian wives if they did not marry a *bourgeois* or at least one of the Métis hunters who knew something of another way of life. He hoped Brigitte chose well. She was destined for better things than what he often saw in the wilderness.

A smile crept out as he thought of her *cran*. Such spunk, such courage was hard to find in a woman, especially in a gentlewoman. She would argue that she was not a gentlewoman, of course. She would say only women who moved in circles like that of—what was the cur's name? Caroux—*non*. Caron ... Clom ... *Clarboux*. *Oui*, that was it. Such circles as his. But, indeed, she was gentle, kind, sweet, and lovely. A gentlewoman.

By nightfall, René was able to settle comfortably into his new shelter. The three days following, he worked in the Clam River post with McGregor, transferring records, tallying new furs that arrived in the hands of Ojibwe trappers, and enduring the teasing of McGregor—though he did not mind it terribly. Then he and his guide moved out.

René's body warmed again as he trudged through mile upon mile of soggy trail. Sweat ran down his spine, despite the dampness in the air that cooled droplets on his brow. He could ignore the hardship. He thought only of the work, of carrying the pack, of the beautiful girl he had known for a short time.

If my life were different ... if there were not men better suited for her than I ... if she had been my woman in more than pretense ...

Perhaps he should not let himself think in such a way. But, ah! It was pleasant to do so. How her spirit and determination inspired—the fire in her eyes when he challenged her, the softness in them when she grieved, and the questions, the laughter, the mystery in their brown depths. His mind drifted away the miles to the Bois Brule post. Days ... miles ... a journey until he could rest and see her again.

Brigitte raised a hand to the band of fine beadwork tied about her throat. Keeheezkoni stepped back to look at the effect. She smiled at Brigitte. The band matched the bracelet on Brigitte's wrist. Keeheezkoni had made them both, just as she had the new pair of moccasins intricately beaded in a pattern of blue, red, yellow, and green flowers.

Bemidii's younger sister, Shenia, stood just behind her mother's shoulder and offered a shy smile too. "You like?" she asked.

Brigitte nodded, hardly able to fight the emotion tightening her throat.

"I teach you to make after you marry."

Brigitte nodded again, thankful for the barriers breaking down between her and the young woman. She looked to Keeheezkoni. "You will come to the wedding?"

Keeheezkoni's face clouded, and she stiffened. She shook her head as she gathered the leftover combs and ribbons.

"*Dada*? I wish it."

The woman would not meet Brigitte's gaze. Perhaps Keeheezkoni still resented Brigitte's mother for stealing Brigitte's father away. She laid a hand on Keeheezkoni's shoulder. Bemidii's mother looked up. "Because of my mother?"

"*Ina.*" She squeezed Brigitte's shoulders gently, but still she refused to answer why she would not attend.

Brigitte thought less of the coming ceremony than of the loss of Keeheezkoni's warm gaze. She was not Brigitte's mother, but as she and Bemidii grew to know one another better, it felt as though his mother might be, to her, the woman she had lost.

"You go now." Keeheezkoni's hands fell away, and she busied

herself.

Brigitte looked at Shenia, but the girl also dropped her gaze, so she ducked out of the lodge and wound her way out of the village back to the fort, her feet warm and comfortable in the soft moccasins. Though Keeheezkoni refused to bless her marriage, she had still given Brigitte these gifts. If only Bemidii were here to see her in them, she might not feel quite so alone. Perhaps she would be used to being Claude's wife by the time her brother returned.

She let herself into the house and gazed around the main room, viewing it with new eyes. Claude must have banked the fire so they would return to a warm dwelling after the ceremony. All was tidy and welcoming. The hearth had been swept. A fresh loaf of bread was wrapped in cloth on a trencher in the center of the table. The candles' wicks had been trimmed, ready to light when needed. In only a short while, she would no longer be merely a lodger here, but mistress.

Claude's wife.

Brigitte ran her hands over the fabric of her dress, smoothing the yellow calico Claude had given her to sew.

She'd felt as fine in the blue Indian dress René saw her wearing at Fort William.

She wished René had been at the fort when Claude asked for her hand. Would she still have said yes? *Brigitte Dufour.* She bit her lip. Had she made the right decision?

A knock on the door beckoned her. Claude had gone ahead to the blockhouse, so she answered it. The granddaughter of the medicine woman stood outside. "Your *niinimooshe* waits."

Her sweetheart. Brigitte flattened her palms against her cheeks, and the girl smiled. She settled a warm rabbit fur robe around Brigitte's shoulders and turned to walk ahead of her. Brigitte and Claude would come together then, as God intended. In that instant, she felt like a bride.

At the blockhouse, Claude would be waiting with several of his men, the medicine woman, and a few Indians. Again, Brigitte felt her brother's absence. If Bemidii were present, he might give her away, but he was still off hunting and might not be back for days.

She gathered her courage. She must present herself as a bride. *Oui, a bride. But a sweetheart?*

The wind had picked up, batting her dress against her legs and whipping tendrils of hair free of her braid. She shivered, pulling the robe tighter and wishing for a moment that it was spring. *By then I will be long-married. Perhaps with child.*

Her heart pattered faster than her feet as she hurried down the path to the blockhouse. She and the Indian girl entered with a gust of wind that nearly pushed them through the door, then slammed it with a bang behind them. Everyone in the room looked at them—at her—as the girl stepped to the side.

Claude stood by the door. His brown hair was pulled back in a queue with a black ribbon, a knotted cravat at his throat. He smiled, and Brigitte didn't miss the way his gaze drifted over her. For a moment, she saw René's smile, and a pang cut through her.

"Are you ready?"

She eased out a breath. She would not back down now, even if she had her doubts. René expected her to marry, and indeed she must eventually. Claude, at least, was a man René trusted. Therefore, she could too. Her doubts were foolish anyhow. Every bride must have them.

He stepped forward, took her arm, and turned her toward the medicine woman.

The medicine woman's eyes were closed, and she sang some low tune as she burned tobacco. Brigitte did not remember much of the meaning behind the *Anishinaabe* ceremonies of her childhood. She could not clearly hear the woman's words, but it did not matter. Her decision was made. Whether or not the nuns, the priests, *Tante* Eunice, or God himself approved was no longer meant for discussion—so she whispered to her heart. She clenched her hands, then opened them. Pulling in a slow breath, she forced herself to look at Claude again. His eyes glittered. A corner of his mouth rose in a beckoning smile.

The woman continued to speak in Ojibwe— "You will share the same fire"—and Brigitte tried to listen, but her mind spun with many thoughts.

Was René sitting by a warm fire even now? Did Bemidii warm his long hands above a flame? The shaman's voice sounded far away as the mystery of Claude's eyes pulled Brigitte in with a shine of pleasure.

"You will walk the same trail."

She had carried a canoe on many a trail, watching the legs and feet of the voyageur in front of her. René was always waiting for her when they stopped.

The woman spoke again, and something sparked in Claude's eyes. He looked away for a second, breaking the spell. Brigitte glanced down at their hands as he took hers, twining them together. A prickling ran up to her hairline.

The door opened, sweeping the room with a violent breeze. Cinders sparked in the fireplace, falling on the hearth and shooting up the chimney. The wisping smoke of the tobacco dissipated.

Claude released Brigitte's hands as heads turned, murmurs and motion sweeping over the gathering. Their guests shuffled apart, and another party entered the building.

Hunters and porters spilled through the door. Men in layers of fur and tall, blackened moccasins, their bodies reeking of travel. Red cheeks surrounded by thick beards. One man pushed through the others, tall and dark and fierce. His eyes found hers.

René.

Her heart leapt to see him, to know that he was safe, and … she swallowed through her tight throat. He had arrived in time to see her wed to Claude. Wouldn't he be pleased? Her hands knotted into fists at her sides.

A clatter of voices turned to a din. Claude raised his hands and quieted them. How different he looked from the others in his gentleman's clothes, clean-smelling and shaved.

Her gaze settled on René, broad-shouldered and austere in his fringed leather hunting clothes, his beard grown thick and his hair longer. Some would find him frightening, but she was not afraid of the dark, burly trader.

"What is this we find? A party? A festivity before the doldrums of winter?" René's gaze stole about the room as though he would corral everyone in his jest. "Brigitte. You are well, I see." She opened her mouth, but he looked to his brother and gave him a curt nod. "Claude."

"René, you are just in time to wish us well."

"Oh? You are going somewhere, or there has been an illness?" He spoke to Claude, but his gaze sought Brigitte's complicity.

She licked her lips but could not calm the fluttering of her heart. "You see, I have taken your advice. Now you are here just in time to help me celebrate my marriage to your brother."

"*Oui.*" Claude's smile seemed almost a grimace. "You have arrived in the very midst of our ceremony. You see, we have brought the medicine woman to bind us as one."

René's gaze swept over them again. "So you have."

His tone taunted her. She curled her fingers into the fabric of her dress. Why did he not seem pleased? Why did he not smile and congratulate them?

He tugged at his gloves and strode to the fireplace, nudging a log farther into the blaze with the toe of his moccasin. Brigitte glanced at the medicine woman who frowned, her eyes like black beads in her leathery face.

"The deed is done," said Claude. He jerked his head at the shaman. Her chin raised and face set, she gathered her things.

About the room, the men who'd just arrived started talking again. They laughed and jested, but her whole mind fixed on Claude and René. Was something wrong? Was the wedding to be over so soon?

"Claude," Brigitte leaned to him, "what is happening?"

"Nothing, my dove. Go now, and wait for me at the house."

"But, our vows—"

"Hurry now."

She nodded, confused. Perhaps she had expected too much of the ceremony. She turned to go. René blocked her path. She offered him a smile, some bridge to reacquaint them. "I am happy you are returned safely. I had hoped to see you sooner."

"Had you?"

"*Oui.*" She nodded.

"It is good to be back. I should have come before now. I would have, had it been possible." He looked past her at Claude. As she stepped past René, he laid a hand on her shoulder. "I will come to the house. We must talk."

It was then that she saw Keeheezkoni waiting by the door. Bemidii's mother wrapped Brigitte in her thick robe and walked her into the cold. It was not the conclusion to her wedding that she had expected.

CHAPTER 20

The fountains mingle with the river
And the rivers with the ocean,
The winds of heaven mix for ever
With a sweet emotion;
Nothing in the world is single,
All things by a law divine
In one another's being mingle—
Why not I with thine?
—Percy Bysshe Shelley, 1792-1822

René glared at Claude as the door closed behind Brigitte and Keeheezkoni. Flames guttered in the candles and lamps scattered about the room. Claude walked to a cupboard and pulled out a small jug, tugging the cork free. René's anger burned as he waited for his brother to drink.

"What is it? You look like you are ready to kill something." Claude passed the jug off to one of the trappers who'd blown in with René. The man took it and wandered off to his companions.

"So I am."

"Whatever for? Has your new promotion been so hard on you?"

"Where is she?"

"Brigitte has gone home."

"Your *wife*. Where is *she*?"

"Brigitte is my wife. That much should now be obvious."

René launched toward Claude and grabbed him by the shirt. He pulled him close, his voice hissing through his teeth. "I want to know what happened to Mina, and why Brigitte is going through with this charade."

Claude clutched René's forearms and shoved, freeing himself.

"It is no business of yours. Mina has left me, and Brigitte has agreed to be my wife."

"So it seems. What I want to know is *why*." René could hardly believe the girl he'd come to know would do such a thing. It had stung Brigitte even to pretend to belong to him on the voyage. Now to willingly commit adultery seemed so unlike her. René could hardly contain his shock or his anger.

Claude sneered. "Is it so unlikely that she and I would find one another … companionable?"

René clenched his fists.

"She is a desirable woman, as I'm sure you've realized." The glint in Claude's eyes mocked René. "If you hadn't been so slow yourself—"

René lunged forward, satisfied to see his brother flinch. "Do not test me further."

"Why shouldn't she marry me?" Claude's voice was patronizing, calm. "You expected her to marry someone else? Who? When Mina left—"

"Why did she leave? Where did she go?"

Claude waved his hand. "Home, I would imagine. To her people."

"You sent her away with another child coming."

"I did no such thing. She left on her own." Claude's stare burned into him.

René knew better. "Mina recognized your lust for Brigitte and was angry."

Claude's jaw bulged, and his eyes narrowed.

"Brigitte is a proper, Christian girl."

"Is she?" Claude asked.

"You didn't know?"

Claude lifted his lips in a smile that stopped halfway. "I will have much to learn about her."

René's gut tightened. He wished to put his hands around his brother's throat. What stopped him were the nagging doubts about Brigitte. After all, didn't she have some blame to bear in this deception?

Claude shrugged his shoulders. "Stop fretting about her. She is not a child, as I am certain you are well aware. She cannot remain on her own. You have said it yourself. I, at least, am not a *sauvage*."

René was not so sure. "Have all the words been said?"

"You saw."

He had seen only that they stood before the shaman woman, and Brigitte had seemed quite pleased with her lot. "Do you even care for her?"

Claude's shoulders relaxed, and this time his smile looked easy. "She is easy to care for, *non*?"

René hesitated, but caring for Brigitte was something he could not deny. He nodded. "*Oui*."

Claude clapped him on his shoulder. "Marc! Where is my rum?" Taking up the jug as it was handed back to him, he lifted it in a salute. "It is good to see you again, brother. Very good."

René took a drink as well, trying to douse his anger, but the questions kept climbing back, weighing him down, needling him. Claude seemed in no hurry to go home to Brigitte, despite his eager assurances to René. Claude appeared more than content to drink with the men and listen to their regale.

The imbibing irritated René. What must Brigitte be thinking as she waited for her husband? Would he come to her drunk? She should at least be forewarned.

Something took hold of René, some spirit—a demon likely— who urged him to interfere. He would go to her, prepare her for Claude's state of mind. Encourage her to be brave.

She *was* brave. Always.

René would also ask her the questions that nagged him. He looked again at Claude who laughed with an Indian hunter. He seemed to have forgotten René's presence. Perhaps he should take Claude home. The notion churned his gut.

Still wearing the heavy coat he'd arrived in, René strode out the door. Claude didn't even glance his way. Frigid sheets of wind blasted him, sheering away uncertainty. He bent his head and marched to his brother's small house. The soft glow of candlelight met him as he cracked open the door.

"*Salut.*" He slipped inside and waited.

"Claude?"

"*Non.* It is René."

She appeared from his room—*her* room. "René." Her smile was tremulous. Her hands twined together. "Come inside by the fire. Warm yourself."

For the first time, he was able to gaze at her without any other eyes upon them. She looked soft and lovely in her pretty dress. The realization only served to aggravate him further. "I am sorry to disturb you."

"It is all right. Come. *S'il vous plaît.*"

He followed her to the fireside, where she indicated Claude's chair. He pulled the fur cap from his head and removed his coat. Then he sat while she took another chair near him. She looked down at her hands pressed together in the lap of her gown. "I wasn't expecting you. I thought it would be Claude."

Her cheek flushed in the soft light, yet the fire was not so warm. How comely she looked, dressed like a bride in her yellow calico, her long braid draped down over her shoulder, waiting to be loosed.

René cleared his throat. "He will come soon, no doubt."

"René."

"Brigitte."

They spoke at once.

"I am glad you are here." Her breath rushed out with her words.

"*Oui.* So am I. I ... Brigitte, are you sure about this step you have taken?"

Her eyes flashed at him and then to the draw of the firelight. She nodded, but he saw hesitation, or so he hoped. "Should not a woman be a little unsure of such things?"

"I suppose she should. Especially if—"

"If?" She leaned forward and looked at him fully. Did she expect him to reassure her? He could not. He leaned his elbows on his knees, clasped and unclasped his hands. "If she bears her betrothed no love. If she fears or mistrusts him. If he has another wife."

She jumped to her feet. Marching several paces, she twirled to face him. "I do not know which of your comments to address. Why do you even suggest such things? Of course, I care for Claude. I trust him. Should I not? And what can you mean by *unless he has another wife*?"

René cringed at the fire—*non*, the fear—in her eyes. He fought the temptation to stand, to comfort her. "I do not mean to alarm you. I only wondered how you came to this decision."

"The way most do, I imagine."

"Really? And what of Mina?"

She blinked rapidly and gave a slight shake of her head.

René's stomach churned.

"Mina?"

"*Oui*. Claude's—" He could not say it.

Her eyes grew rounder if such a thing were possible. They glowed like white saucers in the firelight. Her lip trembled. She whispered, "She was his woman?"

His frown deepened as he stood. He took a step toward her, worried she might faint. "His wife."

Her knees buckled, and he reached for her, but she steadied herself and put her palms up, holding him at bay. She stumbled to the chair and dropped to it. "You are lying." Her voice shook.

"Lying …" He murmured the word, confusion rippling through him. "*Non*. When have I ever? I tell you the truth. You mean, you did not know?"

She shook her head.

"How could you not know?"

"How could you not tell me?" She looked at him again, her eyes about to spill over.

He stooped beside her, this time touching her shoulder. "I thought …" He moaned. "I would not lie to you, Brigitte. I would not bring you so far from your home to trick you so shamefully. I thought you knew. I thought Claude told you. I thought Mina—"

"No one told me. Claude only said …" She closed her eyes. "He said her husband was employed with the company. She hated me. Now I understand."

She hung her head and sobbed. René pulled her against his shoulder. After only moments, she pulled in a breath. She straightened and wiped her tears. "I have been a fool." More anger than pain seemed to rip through her words.

"He said Mina left him. Is that true?"

She nodded. "Why would he lead me to believe such a lie?"

What was he to tell her? That Claude lied because he desired her, because she was desirable? "I am not sure. Claude is sometimes … impetuous."

She whimpered, and tears fell again, whether for longing or for shame, he couldn't tell. He reached for her hand as the door opened, and his brother stumbled in.

CHAPTER 21

"It is customary in the country to find a one with whom to pass the time more amiably. As I was often parted for months from the boy's mother, it was only natural that I should find pleasure in the company of another. A fairer partner than Waasnodae, I could not have hoped for."
—Journal of Etienne Marchal

René drew back his hand as Brigitte leaned back in her chair, leaving a cool draft between them. He stood.

Claude studied them, his eyes glassy with drink and the smell of rum rolling off him. His smile was tight, unwelcoming. "Brigitte, how good of you to wait up for me." He swayed slightly as he made his way toward them.

René squared his shoulders. "You did not tell her the truth."

Claude gave a casual wave of his hand. "What truth is that, brother?"

"That Mina is your wife."

Claude snorted. He laid a hand over Brigitte's shoulder, and she cringed. "Here is my wife. Mina and I never stood before a priest."

"Neither have we." Brigitte glanced up, her voice grave.

Claude stepped away with a laugh. "Such a wit you have, my dear. We stood before the *Anishinaabe* holy woman. It is the same thing."

René simmered. "It is not the same."

"It is in the manner of the country," Claude said with a snarl. "Brigitte, go to our room, and I will come to you there."

"*Non.*"

He let out a humorless chuckle and reached for her hand.

René shoved Claude's hand away. "You will let her have her say. Her will is not yours."

"She is my wife."

"*Non!* I am not." Brigitte stood. She fisted her hands and glowered at him, and René felt a surge of pride. "You have lied to me, Claude. You have tricked me. Mina is your wife, and well you know it."

"Am I alone to blame? What about my brother? Did he bother to tell you I had mated with a savage?"

She quailed.

René steadied her. "I thought she knew. I thought so since before we left Fort William."

She glanced at him, questions and trust melding in her eyes before turning back to Claude. Then her face paled. "Mina's children. They are your *bébés.*" She covered her mouth.

"Mina has returned to her people. It is likely I will never see her or her children again." Claude spoke to René as Brigitte turned to stare into the fire, her expression a mixture of horror, remorse, and sorrow.

René stepped between Claude and Brigitte. "We will speak of it tomorrow. Brigitte is tired. She must go to her room and rest."

Claude's eyes narrowed.

"I will sleep here by the fire. Do not try to molest her."

"What do you take me for?" Claude shouted. "I am not such a devil as that."

"Then you will have no trouble proving it."

Claude moved toward Brigitte, but René stiffened his stance. Claude narrowed his bloodshot eyes. Then he spun and strode from the room, slamming the door to his quarters.

René stood beside her at the fire. "*Je suis désolée.*" He faced her and placed his hand on his breast. "I am very sorry. I should have said—"

"It is not your fault. I was blind. Naïve. Wishing for security. Perhaps too much."

"But you care for him."

She dashed a finger beneath her eye. "*Oui.* Perhaps. Not so terribly."

"*Non?*"

"A little maybe." She choked on a sob, betraying herself.

Her vulnerability stole into his heart. She had done no wrong. Though he shouldn't, René held her. "Shh …" How slight she felt against him. He swallowed a lump in his throat.

She struggled to compose herself even as she clung to him. "I am angry for being so foolish. I was never so foolish as now."

"You were not foolish. You were deceived."

She turned her gaze up to him. "I insisted we stand before the shaman, of course. This *mariage à la facon du pays*—in the manner of the country, as they say—I was afraid of being wrong in the sight of God." She huffed. "Yet I commit adultery. What would Sister Agathe say of such a thing? What would she think of all I have done?"

"The *mariage à la facon du pays* is acceptable here in the wilderness. It matters not what the sister says. If two pledge their troth before God, as Claude and Mina have done, it is enough. It is Claude who sinned, who is guilty of a crime."

Brigitte pressed her cheek against his chest. Could she feel the pounding that her closeness stirred?

"Ah, such blackness lies upon my heart," she whispered against his shirt. "I could tear it out, if only I knew how. Tell me how, René. Tell me how."

He laid his hand on her head. "Your heart is not so black if it feels this agony."

"Claude has little children and a *bébé* coming. I am filled with rage to think of it. Claude is no better than—" She raised her head again and shot him a fiery stare.

René tucked his chin. "*Oui,* I remember how you felt that day at the convent. You do not have to stay with him."

"But where will I go? I live in this house. *His* house. Perhaps I may go to my brother."

"Your—" He drew his hands to her shoulders and put a space

between them. "Your brother?" He frowned. "Who is it you speak of?"

He listened, incredulous, as she told him her tale of Bemidii. René was glad for the truths she'd uncovered, yet he soured at the thought of her living among her relations. She was not like them. She could not accept all their ways. "There are other houses, other ways to survive."

"Tell me what they are. I cannot work for Claude, not anymore."

René frowned. "*Non*. You cannot. We will think of something else, I am sure."

She squared her shoulders away from him and clenched her hands together. "I am sure of nothing."

He sighed. "It has been a trying day. Tomorrow, we will sort it out. Until then, you must go to bed and rest."

She nodded. "You are right." When she faced him again, a sad smile lifted one side of her mouth. "How is it you are always right?"

Was he? He knew better. His own fault in the matter proved it. And gazing into her eyes the way he was, he knew what he wanted to tell her to do, but she was young and vulnerable, and he too unrefined for her. The years between them, though not unsurpassable, weighed upon him. So did the thought of leaving her for months on end like other men did with their wives. She deserved more. If he told what lay upon his heart, then she would know just how wrong he could be.

Brigitte slept, but barely. She woke early and turned her thoughts to God. Pushing back the blankets, she crawled from the warmth of her bed and fell to her knees. "I have sinned, my Lord. I have caused a man to ..." Her throat pinched closed.

To say the words grated her, but the admission scraped out on her tongue. "To put away his wife. I know not what I ought to do now. Mina has gone away, and Claude says she will not return, but I beg you to bring her and the children back to him." Brigitte stretched her arms across the ticking and laid her head down while her knees grew cold and shivers raced up her body. "Forgive me. I am an *imbecile*." She shoved a fist into her mouth. She would not cry, but, ah—the sin!

Her legs ached with stiffness by the time she arose. Blood buzzed like angry wasps through her veins. As she rubbed her hands over her thighs, her thoughts turned to Claude. Soon he would awaken. His head would be clear of the rum, and he could speak cleanly, honestly.

Warmth surrounded her as she dressed for the day. René must have kept the fire alive. As she left her room, she discovered him stirring the red-hot coals and adding more wood. She stepped beside him as he drew to his feet. From his appearance, he'd slept as little as she.

"I will fix something for you to break your fast."

He nodded.

She prepared a meal of corn cakes and chicory coffee, and they ate without conversation. When they finished, she finally broached the subject heavy on her mind.

"I do not know what to do, but I am willing to take your advice. You have never led me astray. I trust you and will do what you say."

"You credit me far too much. I am as perplexed as you."

"Surely you must have some idea of what is best."

"*Oui,* it is best you are cared for. Best you are safe, with a roof over your head and food in your belly. It is best you have discovered your relation."

"Then you think I should stay with Bemidii."

"I did not say that."

"But you believe it."

He sipped the coffee, his face hidden behind his cup.

"*Je vous en prie, allez-y.* Tell me. Please."

He hesitated before setting his coffee mug on the table. "If you wish to stay, perhaps you will be safe and cared for." His gaze lingered. "You may find love among your brother's clan."

She laid a hand against her warm throat and dropped her gaze. Why did his words embarrass her? He had said as much to her at other times.

Claude's bedroom door opened with a creak, drawing her attention. He stepped into the room and paused. Then he sauntered near and stood next to Brigitte's chair. He took her chin gently and turned her face upward.

"Good morning, my dove. I must apologize for my behavior yesterday. Things did not turn out as … as either of us would wish."

As he leaned toward her, she jerked her chin free.

He straightened and smiled at his brother. "René, I owe you an apology as well. You are overseer of *le fond du lac*. I should have killed the fatted calf. Both Brigitte and I should have awaited your return to begin our lives together." His gaze shot between them, and Brigitte's breath quickened as she felt herself weighed between the Dufours.

"There will be no such beginning, Claude. You are wed to Mina."

Claude drew up a chair and sat. He rested his elbows and let one leg slide forward in a posture of nonchalance. "I have never stood before the *Midewinini* with Mina."

Brigitte clenched her jaw. He would pretend that all the evening's revelations were mere portages to be gotten around? She stiffened. "It matters not to me whether you stood before the medicine woman with her or not. You have children with her. You are her provider. I could never be with a man who takes such responsibilities so lightly."

"You would rather be with someone else? Who?" He flashed a dark look at René.

René scowled. "Do not divert the subject. You have called Mina your wife, and so she is."

Brigitte gripped the arms of her chair. "Claude, I am a Christian. Is the same not true of you?"

One side of his mouth lifted. "I am sure our backgrounds are quite similar."

"But that is not the question."

"*Christian*. Is it nothing but a term? Are we not all spiritual beings? Frenchmen? The Indians? Even the rank voyageurs who brought you here, do they not all pray and sing of God?"

"We do not all believe the same thing. For instance, this easy notion of putting away one wife for another, just as my own father did. I am not so sure that all beliefs see it the same. I do not see it as you do. That much is certain."

Claude leaned forward with his cup between his palms, his elbows resting on his knees. He shrugged. "You must understand, Brigitte. Men and women will still come together and make families whether or not a priest or holy man can be found. They vow together before God, if you will, to pledge their lives. I think your Christian God must understand."

"*My* Christian God?"

"God is God."

"If that is true, then all would believe the same things of Him, of Christ." René's voice rumbled. "Yet many do not regard Him the same. Their beliefs contradict one another."

Brigitte scooted forward, pulling her knees up and tucking her dress around her legs. "And is changing the things we believe to suit our circumstances nothing more than self-indulgence?"

Claude laughed. "You confuse self-indulgence with necessity."

She frowned. "Necessity?"

"Of course. You find it necessary for your own safety and well-being to marry, do you not?"

René had made that much clear to her. She nodded at Claude.

"Then how can you deny yourself that very *indulgence* when a man willing and able offers to care for your every need? Why wait for a holy man of your choosing to come and help you solve this matter? You might live in the wilds for years without seeing a priest or even one of the Protestant missionaries I have heard tell of."

"You think it matters not if I am a Christian, or if I choose to follow the beliefs and practices of my mother's family instead? It is all the same, as long as my conscience guides me?"

"*Oui.*" Claude leaned back.

She blew out a sigh. "I see, and yet it is not the same to me."

"Brigitte." Claude's tone turned beseeching. "How can I keep you here with me the whole winter and not want more? You may wrestle with uncertainty, but I see you as my wife."

"But your children—"

"Are gone. Am I to live alone, waiting for them to come to me? Man was not meant to do so."

René rose, his brow twisted. "You have a silver tongue, Claude. Brigitte will stay with you no longer."

Claude sneered. "Oh? And pray, where will she go?"

"I will take her with me to Fort William when I return in the spring."

"The truth comes out. You have desired her for yourself."

A bolt of shock struck Brigitte. She gaped as René lunged for Claude, shoving him to the floor. Hot coals tumbled onto the hearth.

"Do not *ever* speak so foully of my regard toward her. Do you understand? Brigitte, come."

She stood, her heart pounding.

With two long strides, René reached for her *capote* and handed it to her. She shrugged into it, her wits scattered like ashes on the hearth.

Claude sat up. "That is how you treat me?"

She pulled her gaze away as René steered her toward the door.

"This is not at an end, René."

René reached for the latch as a pounding met them from the outside. He swung the door wide.

The apprentice clerk stood in the doorway, his face flushed. "Monsieurs Dufour, there are Indians. Sioux. Four of them at the gate." A crisp wind gusted across the hard-packed floor.

Brigitte pressed a hand to her chest.

"Do they wish to trade?" René asked.

"They carry no furs."

René leaned toward Brigitte. "Wait a while longer." His voice was hushed. He took three strides to the fireplace and plucked his pistol from the mantel, tucking it into his belt as Claude rose to his feet. Claude gave Brigitte a passing glance as he retrieved his own pistol. Together, the brothers left the house. The door closed in their wake, leaving Brigitte in silent dread.

CHAPTER 22

"I tell you, the Sioux were there, lurking about the fort,
making our hair stand on end. We sat about the fire,
watching the eerie dance of our own shadows on the wall.
The following morning, we saw their tracks in the snow, and
when Lejeune and Chevier arrived, they told us they heard
no less than 30 shots from the direction of Lac la Croix."
—A Trapper's Regale, la Fond du Lac Region

René hastened across the grounds with Claude, directing the few men around them to be on alert. He nodded at the guard, then he and Claude waited as the wind bit their faces and the gates swung open.

Four Sioux warriors bearing austere expressions entered, blanket robes wrapped over their shoulders. Two wore porcupine roach headdresses. Another had strips of quillwork wrapped around his two long braids. A pair of feathers dangled from the scalp lock of the fourth.

The Indians strode past the guardsmen, stopping in front of René and Claude. The man with the braids lifted his chin. "We speak to the *bourgeois* Dufour."

René set his hands on his hips. "I am Dufour, partner with the North West Company. It is good of you to come and meet with us."

"I am Akecheta."

The man with the feathers leaned forward and spoke sharp words to Akecheta.

Akecheta studied René, then his eyes settled on Claude. "You are the Dufour whom we seek. You are the husband of Mina."

The man behind Akecheta spoke again as he glared at Claude.

"*Oui.*" Claude waved his hand toward René. "We are both

Dufours. Brothers. René, allow me to introduce you to Mina's brother and her uncle."

Akacheta lifted his chin. The man with the feathers—Mina's brother—crossed his arms beneath his robe, his stare digging into René.

Around the yard, men began to appear, several of them Ojibwe hunters who bore no love for the Sioux. If they didn't step lightly, there would be a blood-letting. Whose blood would spill remained in question.

René bowed, hoping to diffuse the situation. "We are honored you've come."

He glimpsed Claude, who gave them a stiff bow at the neck but pressed his palms to his sides as he did so. "Please. Come inside."

Claude led them to the blockhouse, and René followed. "Henri, bring food." Claude barked the order as he pushed a bundle aside on a long table and indicated a chair for the older man, but Akacheta remained unbending as they gathered around.

"You have sent Mina back to us. She tells us you have tired of her and have taken a new woman. Your children play at her brother's fire instead of their father's, and your seed again grows large in her belly."

Claude's color rushed back.

"What do you wish my brother to do?" René saw no point in beating around the bush or making excuses. "My brother says Mina left of her own will."

Mina's brother spat a flurry of words in Sioux. Fire lit his eyes. His jaw went rigid, and he clenched his fist. René needed no interpreter.

Claude spread his hands. "Mina left me. She grew tired, not I. She took our little ones and ran away. The Great Spirit sent me another."

The Indians murmured, their anger fueled. René halted Claude with a touch on his arm. He cleared his throat, and the Indians skewered him with their attention. "Does Mina regret her decision to leave? Is it her wish to return?"

"She desires her husband to come for her, to prove himself. She wishes he would send away his other woman."

Her brother spoke again, his eyes narrowed further, if possible, on Claude.

"My nephew says he will rid you of the nuisance this other woman has become."

René's heart lurched.

Claude's brow lowered. "Now see here—"

"There is no need," said René. "If you will allow us a moment to speak."

An Ojibwe woman arrived with meat and bread on a walnut trencher. She placed it on a side table, averting her eyes from the Sioux men as she passed them. They helped themselves to the food while René pulled Claude aside.

"What will you do?"

Claude huffed. "It is all blown out of proportion."

"Is it?" René spoke between clenched teeth. "They know as well as I that you are Mina's husband. You have tried to deceive everyone. Now you will have the whole nation down on us, as if there isn't enough trouble between the tribes."

"I will calm them, make them see."

"*Non.*" René took a breath, forcing steadiness back into his voice. "You will not put Brigitte at risk. You will think of something else."

Claude rubbed a hand over his eyes, his back to the Indians. "*Oui, oui.* All right. I will go with them if I must."

"They will kill you." René's jaw relaxed, the reality of what the Sioux might do assuaging his anger toward Claude.

"They may, and they may not."

René stroked his beard. "I do not like it. I cannot let them take you, but I cannot let them harm Brigitte."

Claude smirked. "You care so much for her?"

"Her father is dead. Her safety seems always to lie in my hands, as is yours."

"You cannot let go, can you, René? I am ever your *petit frère*. You would make our *mère* proud." His tone was less than complimentary.

"Do not stray from the point."

"I see no other way to please them and to protect Brigitte."

Mina's brother barked from across the room.

"We will take you both. You, Dufour, and your other woman," Akacheta said. "You will come and speak to your wife, and it will be decided what is to become of the other woman."

Claude glanced at René, his fingers twitching. René felt equally uncertain about what would happen but worked to lay hold of his nerves.

"I will go with you," Claude said, pulling back his shoulders as he faced the Indian. "I will speak to Mina. The other woman will stay here with my brother."

Akacheta spoke to the other men. They murmured and nodded, but a black look hung on her brother's face. René mistrusted what that look meant. He'd seen the face of vengeance before.

Akacheta spoke to Claude. "We will leave now. You come."

"I will get my necessaries." He passed René, giving orders to several of his Métis company men that they should accompany the Indians to wait at the gate. Claude led René to the storehouse. "I dare not return to the house. You must tell Brigitte. I will return as quickly as I can, but it might be several weeks."

"Do not be a fool. You cannot return to Brigitte. They will kill you, and what's more, they will try to kill her too."

"I doubt it."

"You would risk it?"

"What choice do I have?" Claude stopped in the doorway, and his stare settled on René.

René spoke through clenched teeth. "Your *choice* is what brought her this trouble. I will not allow you to endanger her further than you already have."

"I am doing what I can to protect her." Claude marched inside with René on his heels. He reached for a pack.

"You will worry her sick."

Claude frowned. He pushed clothing and supplies—even a few trade items—into his bundle. "It is all I can do. The Sioux camp is more than twenty miles up the river. A good distance to assuage them if I am with Mina."

"And *if* you return? What then? Will they believe you have no further interests in Brigitte?"

Claude stopped packing and gripped René's shoulder. "You must take her away. She must be kept safe, so you said. Take her away with you. When it is safe, you can return her here." He shoved a knife into his belt.

"You ask the impossible." René planted hands on hips and followed Claude as he continued to pack. "To flee would only heighten their suspicions. They will think I hide her for you, and thereby danger will increase for both of you."

Even as René spoke the truth, the solution that had been winding through his thoughts grew more urgent. To Brigitte, an unthinkable solution, no doubt.

Claude shrugged. "What other way is there? Let her be gone for a while. Take her to one of the inland forts until spring, perhaps."

"And what about you? What of your safety?"

"I intend to be free of Mina, but we will see what happens, won't we?"

The false smile on Claude's lips made René's stomach clench. He feared for Brigitte, but more so for his brother. "Claude…" His voice softened. "Why not keep Mina as your wife? She is a good woman. She has given you children and takes care of you. Can you not see that you do them both wrong, Brigitte and Mina? Brigitte's own father did the same to his first wife. Brigitte will never have you now."

Claude's smile became a smirk. "Ah, René, but can you not see that she is worth the risk? Have you no idea how Brigitte appeals to me? An intelligent, beautiful girl of French descent? One with whom I can return to Montreal, or even Quebec someday? You have no such aspirations, I know. But I do. Mina is a good woman, as you say, but I never planned to keep her once I become a partner."

"You haven't become a partner. You might never become a partner."

"Is there some reason why you think so?" Claude's jaw tightened. "Now that my own brother is a partner, is there any reason why my promotion should not occur eventually?" He crammed gear tighter into his pack.

René sighed. "It is beside the point."

He punched a finger at René. "It is *exactly* the point. I have plans for my future. Brigitte suits them better than Mina. And besides, I want her. You understand *want* at least, don't you?"

The fist in René's stomach constricted. *Oui.* He knew want. The image of Brigitte bathing in the moonlight flashed before him. He pinched his eyes closed and pushed the thought out. "You are right about one thing. She is an intelligent woman, a worthy woman. She deserves a man who treasures her for more than his wants."

Claude chuckled humorlessly. "You have gotten sentimental. Watch out for that." He refastened the single button at the top of his *capote,* then tightened the dull sash around his waist. He slung a leather satchel across his shoulders before picking up a long rifle and his pack. "Take her tonight." He headed out the door with René close behind. "Slip away before they know she's gone. Should things go wrong—should Mina demand they return for her or should they come simply for vengeance sake—she will be safely away."

"She will stay here at the fort, with me. Someone must take over your duties. I will tell them she is my woman, not yours."

Claude's brow lifted. "You will play the old game? Very good, and noble, I might add."

René walked in silence. *A game, but must it always be so?* "Tell me, Claude." He grasped his brother's shoulder, forcing him to stop. "Is it only lust, or do you love her?"

"She is desirable, is she not?"

"She is." He walked stiffly past Claude.

"René," Claude whispered harshly. René looked back. "If it helps you to do what must be done, I love her."

René strode toward the waiting Sioux, barely concealing his anger.

CHAPTER 23

*"My sorrows were many, until I met my husband who
became Shenia's father. Then my heart became open again."*
—Keeheezkoni, Anishinaabe Woman

Brigitte crouched at the hearth and stirred the fire, banking orange coals against newly added wood. The heat pressed almost too intensely against her face, yet it felt good. It dried her eyes and punished her skin.

Who were the Sioux at the gate? Only hunters? After witnessing Claude and René's worrisome exit, she did not think so. Had they come because of Mina? Were she and her children well?

Brigitte pushed at a charred log, sending sparks up the mud-daubed chimney. To think that Claude had deserted Mina and his own children. Such a man she would have spit upon in Montreal, as she had when she thought René had abandoned the infant girl on the nunnery steps. However, she could not bring herself to think quite so harshly of Claude.

Claude should not have dealt with Mina so carelessly. All would be well if he had behaved more prudently. If only Claude had not tried to deceive Mina or Brigitte, she would not be burdening René yet again.

Oui, and such a burden she was.

She strode across the room with a sigh. Dust motes danced in a beam of light cast from the room's only window. On the table lay one of Claude's ledgers. She ran her fingers across the sun-warmed cover as her thoughts continued to skitter.

What kept Claude and René so long with the Sioux? Were they in danger? Must René always be forced to rescue her? *He defended me—again.*

He'd allowed her to remain on the voyage, saving her from a

marriage to Tristan, held her when she cried for Gervais, given her warmth when she was cold, spoken tenderly to her when she talked of her *père* and how she missed him, protected her from the others by calling her his woman.

I am in love with him.

Truth, like nettles, stung her heart. It pounded against her ribs. It had never stirred so for Claude. René had saved her even from his own brother. Her heart beat for longing. Longing for a man she continually burdened.

A wildness of emotion washed over her. She buried her face in her hands and held her breath, frightened by the power of her own nature.

The door opened, startling her.

"Aamoo."

"Bemidii." Sunlight glinted behind her brother's silhouette. Fresh air ushered in around him, cooling her. He held a brace of rabbits in one hand, but that did not prevent her from rushing to him and falling against his chest. He dropped the creatures to the floor. His hunting shirt smelled of grease and campfire, but she did not care. Her dress was clean. Her body was clean. Nevertheless, her soul felt dirty, more mired than any hunter's clothing. "You are back."

"I am back. I only just arrived this morning. I came from the village so not to be waylaid from seeing you." He chuckled, but she shuddered. "Perhaps I should not have gone away at all."

"You had to." She spoke into his shirt, but he nudged her away until he could see her face. She looked into Bemidii's eyes, eyes so dark she could hardly see his irises. "Bemidii …"

He frowned. "What is it? What darkness lies upon you?" He closed the door and drew her farther into the room.

Where to begin? She shook her head. "I have done a wicked thing." *Mon Dieu, I am a filthy person, unworthy to be called Your child.* "Oh, Bemidii …" Her vision swam.

"You frighten me. You must tell me."

Her throat tightened. "Mina has been greatly wronged. I—I do not know what will happen." Her voice broke.

"Continue."

In bits and pieces, she told him the whole sordid story, from Claude's duplicity to Mina's leaving to René's arrival, then the Sioux.

Bemidii's face grew dark and his shoulders rigid. The muscles of his hands flexed into fists. He turned to the door.

"Where are you going?"

"I will not wait for the Sioux to avenge my sister."

"Bemidii, *non*."

He looked back, his face contorted. "Why do you stop me?"

She shook her head. "You must not. The blame is as much mine."

He squinted. "Why do you say so? Did he not trick you?"

"Yes, but ..." She reached for him but lowered her arms with a heavy sigh. "Oh, Bemidii, I am guilty of destroying Mina's home and family. *Me*." She pressed her fist against her chest. "The weight of it is almost more than I can bear."

Wind rattled the window as Bemidii watched her. When his expression calmed, he held out his hand. "I will wait if that is what you wish me to do."

She pulled in a deep breath and nodded. "*Merci*, Bemidii." She laid her fingers in his palm.

The door opened again, and René stepped through. He halted when he spotted Bemidii. His gaze swept to Brigitte.

She stepped forward and held out a palm toward her visitor. "René, you have known Bemidii, but you have not known him as my brother."

He nodded. "*Oui*. I know him. We spoke several weeks past, just before I left the fort. He did not tell me then who he was."

Bemidii peered down his nose at René. "And you did not tell me then that you were not the man of my sister."

René raised one brow and turned his glance toward Brigitte.

"I am sorry for interrupting. I did not know your brother had returned. I will leave you to speak."

She took a hurried step toward him, halting him with a touch. "What of the Sioux? Were they … is Claude still with them?" She stood rigid, waiting for his answer.

René nodded. "*Oui*. They are Mina's relatives. He has gone with them."

Her breath caught. "I—I am sorry, René."

"It is not your fault." His voice rasped. He turned to go, his back to her as he reached for the latch. "I have promised them that Claude will make things right with Mina." His shoulders slouched, and Brigitte waited until she feared he would tell her the Sioux had refused the promise. "I have told them you are not Claude's woman, but mine."

Her lips parted, but she could not find words to speak. He lifted the latch and let himself out, the door closing without a sound. Brigitte and Bemidii stood in the wake of silence.

After some moments, Bemidii shifted to look at her. Tenderness lay in his gaze. "Your heart carries a load and has no place to go. Your concern is great for the woman and her children, and that is a good thing. It is a strength in you that you care so. Yet, the load you carry, is it not for more than this difficulty?"

"I fear for Claude."

Bemidii frowned and shook his head. "It is not of that Dufour I speak. Tell me truly, little bee, is not this thing that settles heavy upon your heart love for another? I have been away, but even when I watched you at Fort William, and again on the journey from Grand Portage, I saw how things passed between you and this one who pretends to claim you."

She stepped back. "You must not talk so." She swallowed. "But how … how did you know?"

"You wish it was he who stood with you before the medicine woman."

"*Non*."

"You do not wish it?"

"I could never really be René's woman, not even if I wished it. Now more than ever, for the trouble I have caused with Claude. He may never see his brother again, and it is because of me." Tears burned her vision.

"You are the woman of the man you love." Bemidii tapped his chest. "In here."

"Bemidii, you do not understand."

"Maybe I do not. But does not your heart tell you this is true?"

"My heart is not to be trusted. I have wronged them both. I pray for forgiveness."

He pushed a strand of hair back from her eyes. "You should pray for more. You should choose this man you know is right for you."

How could she pray for René's love when she had caused such grief? When so much error stood between her and God? A tear slipped down her face, and Bemidii pulled her to him again.

"I fear it is too late."

"The time is never past to act."

"Bemidii, please, you must not say anything to René about what I said."

His embrace tightened.

"Please."

He sighed heavily. "I will do as you say, but it is folly."

René let himself into the warehouse and moved behind the counter where Claude kept his account books stacked in order. Everything about the place was arranged thus, from the hides dried and stacked on tables to the jars of beads, pots, and bolts of cloth on the shelves.

René opened one of the books. His brother's tidy penmanship scrolled across the page. *Oui*, Claude was good at his job, and, if he should become partner someday, he would deserve it for his work.

Why could he not be satisfied with that, with Mina at his side as she had faithfully been for these past years?

René flipped to the most recent entries in the ledger, where the slant of the lettering changed. Brigitte's additions, no doubt. On the day they met, she had held chalk in her hand, tallying up the inventory of the convent pantry. This was the first time he had looked upon her writing. Her letters were delicate, made with a lighter touch, unlike Claude's bolder strokes.

René had wished to speak with her, to go to the house and comfort her. Now that privilege fell to her brother. Her brother's hand held hers when René wished it had been his own, perhaps to stroke her cheek.

"She wishes for security. She wishes to have a family." Bemidii stood inside the door.

René had not heard the Indian follow him into the room, but he wasn't surprised. Yet, he was irritated to be torn from his reverie. He spoke to Brigitte's brother without lifting his gaze to look at him. "She has you."

"She wishes her own man and her own children. She wishes the warmth of her own fire, not the fire of her brother and a kin she has not known."

René tapped a quill pen, pretending to concentrate on the ledger.

Bemidii moved around the counter and stepped near. His breath hovered close to René's neck. "You should marry her."

René's gaze shot up. "You do not know what you ask. Has she not been humiliated enough that I have told others she is my woman? How much more should she be forced to bear?"

"She told me what happened with the one you call *brother*." Bemidii's lip curled at the word. "If you had not returned when you did, he would have taken her as second wife." Bemidii folded his arms. "Could it not be that your God has returned you to the fort for this purpose? You have saved her for the moment, but will you not satisfy her need to its end?"

René closed the books with force. "She had already decided for Claude. I cannot expect her to change her heart so quickly."

"But you would like to marry her." Bemidii's voice softened. His tone was not lost on René.

He drummed his fingers on the book and gazed fully at Bemidii. "Leave it alone, my friend. I am not able—"

"Bah." Bemidii waved his hand. "You are able. I have watched her many days, just as I have watched you when we traveled the long voyage from Grand Portage. You are better for her. You have been a protector and more. Now that you know who I am, you call me a friend, but it is you who are her friend. You are wrong if you think she could not care for you more than she cared for your brother. And you fight your own heart when you pretend you do not have feelings for her."

René ground his teeth. What could he say to that? He did care for her. Feelings for her stole over him with greater vigor each time he stepped into her presence. He left quickly after delivering her to the St. Louis post, knowing that if he didn't, he might tell her how he felt and embarrass her. There were times he'd had to pull his gaze away while watching her, curbing his thoughts. He fought doing so less and less.

It was bad enough, this unrequited love for her. If he were honest—which he very much wished *not* to be—he would admit to having been drawn to Brigitte from the beginning. Any other man would have left her to her fate in Montreal and gone ahead without her. In honesty, René had wanted her with them. Many times since, he'd been visited by her image bundled in a *capote* and moccasins, crouched by a fire, sunlight shining off her blue-black hair. He'd wanted to release that hair from its long braid and run his fingers through it, bury his face in it while it wrapped around him.

Lust perhaps? Not completely. There was more to his feelings for her. Yes, he wanted her. Wanted even to marry her, but Brigitte would faint in shock if she knew.

"I suppose I care for her a great deal. I would not have been so careful with her if I did not. Are you happy to hear it?"

Bemidii's lips stretched into a wide smile, an expression René had never seen on the Indian before.

"It does not mean—"

"You should marry her, my friend. Take her to the holy woman. Then take her to your bed and leave no room for her questions."

"You go too far, Bemidii." René jerked the book off the counter and returned it to the stack.

"I am her brother. If our father were here, he would say it."

"I refuse to press her against her wishes."

Bemidii strode away. "Never have I met two such people who cannot urge their own hearts to do what is right." He slipped from the building as quietly as he'd entered.

René turned to the supply stock, pretending his mind might easily return to work while they waited to find out if Claude lived or if he intended to keep Mina as his wife. But as he weighed powder and shot and counted blankets and beads, his thoughts kept returning to his conversation with Bemidii, giving in to the wonder of whether or not he was right. And if Brigitte would be willing.

CHAPTER 24

"Therefore, if any man be in Christ,
he is a new creature: old things are passed away;
behold, all things are become new."

—2 Corinthians 5:17

René added the smaller hides to a growing bale and cinched it tight. After he'd hoisted it high onto a shelf, he rubbed his hands together and blew out the lamp. All day long, he had wrestled with Bemidii's admonition, wondering if, indeed, Brigitte would accept him. Wondering even if her heart might be open to more than friendship. Taking her as his wife was the only way to assure her safety, but how would she receive such a suggestion? *I will reason with her.*

He knocked on the door before letting himself into the house. It had always been as much his home as Claude's, but he didn't wish to startle Brigitte again, even though she had slept by his side, something she had not done with Claude.

The day had warmed, and no fire burned in the hearth. Brigitte sat in a chair facing the cool hearth with a light shawl wrapped around her shoulders, a book in her hand.

"*Bonjour.* I hope I am not interrupting."

"*Bonjour,* René."

He pushed a hand through his hair and stepped farther into the room. "I see you will soon need a fire." He kept his tone light.

She nodded.

"I can assist you with that."

She steadied the book before her.

He squatted at the hearth and began laying kindling. "You are quiet."

"There is much to think about. Sitting here, doing little, it helps."

He turned a stick absently in his hands. Did she worry for Claude, or was it his announcement that morning that made her solemn? "Where is Bemidii?"

"He has gone to the village, but he will return tomorrow." She rustled in her chair. "He has promised not to harm Claude, should he return."

René sighed. Claude and his endless trouble-making. He'd had no business asking Brigitte to be his wife. *According to the custom of the country.* What was that to Claude but a way to slake his base desires, a way to gain something he had no right to?

René hadn't realized he was shaking his head until he noticed Brigitte staring at him. "I trust he will keep his word. Brigitte … it is probably better if we share our thoughts."

"*Oui.*" She nodded. "I am deeply sorry."

He faced her on his knees. "As I have already told you, you must not blame yourself for his predicament with the Sioux. It is not your fault."

She huffed and closed the book. "I *am* at fault, and I continue to be a trouble to you."

"I thought by now you would have come to realize that you are no trouble to me. You have traveled a great journey as a voyageur, a true woman of the north." He offered her a soft smile.

She dropped her gaze to her hands curled together over the book in her lap. "I have been foolish once again. It seems all I have done since first we met is cause problems with my decisions. Please tell me the truth, René. Will Claude die because of me?"

He reached across the space between them and laid his hands over hers. "You must try not to worry. He will use his gift of persuasion when he speaks to the Sioux. Come closer as I build the fire. Your hands are cold."

She nodded, not looking at him as she drew her chair nearer the rough hearth.

He laid twigs and struck the flint. As the small flame grew, René continued adding twigs until the fire danced. So did his courage. He sat back on his haunches. "Claude tells me he is in love with you." Now she looked at him. "He tells me you are his."

Tears rimmed her eyes. "I know not if he loves me, nor do I care. I only know that I have been the cause of great trouble, and now there is no fixing it. You would have every right to be angry with me."

René fought down the taste of bile. "I am not angry with you. He is my brother, and I love him, perhaps too much. It is he who angers me. He does what he wishes, whether or not others approve."

"And you do not."

"Humph."

Her chin tilted up. "You are forever giving of yourself for his good."

"I go my own way often enough, but I swore to our mother that I would look after him."

"He is a grown man, René."

"Whose headstrong choice may yet get him killed. He lied to you, Brigitte."

She nodded. The muscles of her throat moved up and down.

He drew his eyes away with effort. "I have been indulgent with Claude on too many occasions."

"Because of your love for your mother."

He folded his arms across his chest and wished Claude were there to take a thrashing. After all, how much did René owe his brother? How far did the promise to their *mère* go? Hadn't he always looked to Claude's interests even above his own? Didn't he hope to see Claude rise in his business ventures above himself? Should a promise to the woman who bore him go to such lengths as this—to protect her other son from God's hand of discipline?

René looked at Brigitte, worrying her fingers in the fabric of her dress. "I was a lucky son to have such a mother. When I remember her, I find myself thinking of you, how you spat at me when you thought I'd abandoned the babe."

Her lips pinched off a smile, but a moment later, it escaped. For that brief instant, she looked happy, at ease. "I was very upset."

"*Oui*. As you should have been, had you been correct."

The brief flicker in her eyes faded back to seriousness once again. "And because of that, you must wonder what I feel about Claude abandoning his children."

"Isn't it the same?"

"*Oui*, it is. And for that reason, if for no other, I understand your anger. I feel it myself. I remind myself that I am not without sin and that God will restore Claude to Mina if He wills it. It is no small thing to ruin the life of a child."

A soft rush of color heightened her honey-colored skin, and René fought the urge to caress her cheek. Ah, but she was meant to become some child's beautiful mother.

She raised her chin. "You once told me you believed there was something of God in everyone. You do not think God has placed something of Himself in Claude, something that will call his heart to goodness?"

René considered it as he rose and took the chair beside her, pulling it close. "I believe God puts a prick, a calling, the knowledge of a need. It is up to each of us to respond. As to good, I think we are mistaken to be content merely with good."

"But isn't it goodness God seeks in us?"

"Is that what you were taught?"

She nodded, but her brow twitched.

"You think goodness enough? Then tell me, Brigitte, why did the Christ bother to die? Could we not achieve a measure of human goodness without such blood-letting?"

Her frown deepened. "Is that not what this pricking you speak of is about? God urging us to do good?"

"*Non*." René shook his head. "I think it a call to something even greater. Something goodness alone cannot replace. Goodness is never enough. A gaping hole in a beaten *bateau* can be patched by effort, but it will need to be repaired over and over again. It can never, never be made new but by total replacement. It is the same with our hearts."

He stared into the glowing flames and spoke to himself and to God. "Some find this is true when they understand their goodness is not enough to patch the hole. They meet God then, and He makes them new." For just a moment, he forgot she was there beside him, but a soft sigh drew him back.

"Have you been made new, René?"

He smiled. "I am a sinner."

"But are we not all? Are not each of us the dirty clay with whom God chooses to work?"

"*Oui.* So we are. Perhaps it is that I am being made new, despite my ineptitude for goodness."

She had spoken correctly when she called them all dirty clay. He had waited a lifetime for God to help him mold his brother into something their *mère* would be proud of. Now Claude had committed this deceit. Would his wayward brother ever yield himself to God to be remade? *Oui,* there was plenty of dirty clay there for God to work with, should Claude ever stoop to acknowledging his need or listen for some greater calling.

René looked up to see Brigitte watching him, her face soft and eyes tender. "You are full of goodness, René. You should never think otherwise."

His heart squeezed. "Brigitte, while we are sharing our thoughts, yesterday—"

"You told Mina's people that I was your woman. You protected me yet again. See, René? You are good."

"*Oui.* I did tell them so." He rubbed his hand over his beard. "It seemed the best thing to do."

She nodded. "I trust your judgment. If we are to go back to our old ploy to keep Claude safe, I am willing to do so."

He studied her for a moment, not daring to tell her it was for her own safety as well as Claude's. He didn't want to frighten her. If he asked for her hand now, wouldn't that frighten her too? Instead, he stirred the fire and added another log. "Just as before, I did not consult you. You are not upset? "

"You did as the moment required. I understand."

"*Oui*." He wanted to tell her it was for her he did it, but she had smiled and accepted the ruse as it was. For tonight, he would let it lie. For tonight, he would crush down his hopes a while longer. He reached for her hand, and she gave it. Together, in silence, they watched the fire burn.

CHAPTER 25

"Until the days when the hunters depart, there is much cause for regale. There is singing and dancing and always the sound of the Indians' drums. The occasions must live in memory for, when one embarks to the forest, the solitude is overpowering."
—Journal of Etienne Marchal, Voyageur

Wearing her red leggings beneath her dress and a buckskin jacket, Brigitte made her way across the commons to bring René his midday meal. Mud oozed around her moccasins as she inhaled the scent of wet earth and clean air stirred by an autumn breeze. With a smile, she tilted her head to the sun's warmth.

René had taken over Claude's work at the post and formed a routine with Brigitte that would establish them as a couple in the eyes of all, should word travel back to Mina's relatives. René came home in the evenings, sleeping in Claude's room while Brigitte remained in her own. He left the house each morning to work in the stores and warehouses. Each day, Brigitte brought him his lunch and dinner and stayed for a short time to tidy shelves and sweep the floor. Occasionally, she assisted him in making entries of the hides brought in by the trappers and payment made. It was an amenable arrangement as the days drew on into fall.

Life had settled for the moment, and she wondered how long it could last. Sooner or later, René would have to journey to the inland forts, which were in his district of oversight. He should have gone already. She didn't like to think of him leaving her again. Meanwhile, the days ticked away, and still no word came of Claude or Mina. Today, René busied himself with work in the company store while Bemidii joined the hunters.

Brigitte slipped into the storehouse and spied René examining a pile of pelts. How wild he looked in buckskins, his beard grown thick and black, his hair grown long enough to club behind his head. She would fear his dark looks had she not come to know him and trust him so. He remained always kind and forbearing, although sometimes something like a shadow passed in his gaze. When it did, her heart turned over in a staggering rhythm.

He caught her glance and smiled. "You are just in time. I am ravished."

Her cheeks warmed. "I hope you like it. It is a fish stew. Keeheezkoni shared some herbs with me."

"My stomach growls. Do you hear it?" He took the bowl from her hands and drew it to his lips. He closed his eyes, inhaled, and moaned. "You are a miracle worker, Brigitte." She was unable to hide a smile as he drank from the bowl. He finished with a belch and smiled. "Exactly the thing." He set the bowl down. "Come. I need to get out of this fort and breathe. Let us walk together."

"Except for the day Bemidii took me to my father's grave, I have only gone between the fort and Keeheezkoni's lodge since we arrived."

René looked at Henri, who counted and stacked hides into bundles on the other side of the room. "I leave matters of the fort in your hands, Henri. I am going out for a while."

"*Oui*, Monsieur Dufour. Very good." He bobbed his fair head.

"Come." René held out his arm, and Brigitte slipped her hand through. Such closeness she had not shared with him in a long time and a hunger for it opened wide. They left the store and headed toward the gates of the fort. She kept her face aside lest René see the effect of his nearness upon her.

They wandered down the shore toward the river. A crisp wind blew off the lake, and she drew closer to René's side.

"You are cold?"

"Not very. I will warm as we walk."

"See the hills."

Past the mouth of the river spilling into *lac Supérieur*, beyond the bay, hills rose in the west, swathed in bright, changing color. "A beautiful sight. Autumn has always been my favorite of the seasons."

"Mine as well." He sighed. "A very fleeting one."

She peeked at the smile hidden in his beard. His contentment flowed into her. "A day such as this will make it last in memory."

"You are right. We must capture it. Winter comes soon enough."

The footpath followed the river inland, leading them south into a maze of wilderness. Within minutes, the stockade disappeared behind them.

Like those days during her journey from Montreal, she fell breathless with the beauty of her surroundings. What must it be like to travel *this* river? Would there be falls and portages, sandbars and churning currents? When her ruse with René came to its end, would she ever experience such sights again? Would she pass this way but once in her lifetime? How many more gurgling streams and snow-covered hillsides waited to be seen? Did René wonder such things?

He nodded to the southeast. "There are other streams spilling from the lake's southern shore that cut through cliffs of orange clay, yet their waters are clean and pure." He stared up the wide river toward a distant bend where it curved away between wooded banks with tops crowned in cedar and pine bowing to the flowing current. "Someday, perhaps, I will paddle you up the river, and you will see the wonders of the interior. Would that please you?"

Her heart quickened. "*Oui*. I would like it very much."

"I will take you to the St. Croix and the Folle Avoine post." His voice sounded farther away than a distant whisper. The dreaminess of it warmed her more than the walk. "Look, there is a deer."

They stilled, and Brigitte held her breath as the doe drank from the water's edge not more than twenty rods away. Its hide had turned an orangish color, like the trees, and the doe's eyes were soft and full. Her ear flicked before she loped off.

For today, fears for Claude, for the trouble that stirred between the Sioux and the Ojibwe, for the unknown future, all abated. Brigitte was safe with René, comfortable in his ability to watch and guide her. They walked along farther until he drew her to another stop along the river.

He held his fingers to his lips, then pointed at the ground ahead of him.

Tracks. Not animal. Human. Her gaze sought his.

He leaned close to her ear and whispered, "See the shape of the moccasin? It is Sioux."

A current trickled through her. Her gaze flitted through the trees heavy with foliage. René jerked his head for her to follow.

They continued along the river's edge, just inside the curtain of trees, and the tentacles of fear let go as she rested in René's confidence. Her gaze skimmed to the west while they pressed on southward. A flicker of movement across the inlet captured her attention. She squinted. There it was again. A man. She tapped René's shoulder and pointed.

René pulled her down beside him. "He isn't one of our hunters." The man appeared at the edge of the river in a small canoe and disappeared again behind the trees, only to reappear a little farther down the shore. "It is likely he who made the tracks. I think he is alone."

"What should we do?"

"We will wait for him to leave. Then we will return."

"Is it safe?"

He didn't answer right away as his gaze traveled over her face. Finally, he expelled a soft breath. "It is never safe."

A shiver raced through her, only this one wasn't brought on by fear. In fact, it was a wholly pleasant feeling.

"Come. He is gone now."

So he was. She'd almost forgotten to watch. René took her hand and pulled her to her feet, leading her through the trees without letting go.

As the track narrowed, René reluctantly released Brigitte's hand, allowing her to walk before him while he watched ahead of her, behind them, all around. She seemed to have forgotten their previous danger, and for that he was glad. He would worry enough for them both.

Her braid swung down to her hips, hips his gaze lingered upon far too long. He had desired women before, but he'd learned to force aside his passions, to direct them into the hunt. He could do so again now, only he didn't want to. He wanted her, but more than that, he wanted to protect her, to care for her, to talk to her late in the night beneath the stars. He wanted to hold her and whisper to her that she was loved.

His chest burned, and the heat of it spread to the rest of his body. He could hardly look away to watch the forest. She embodied this life. How had it happened, this terrible need raging through him to love her?

At last, the bastion of the fort came into view, and he stepped beside her, catching her arm when she tripped on a branch. He tried not to think of the softness of her flesh beneath her buckskin jacket as he steadied her.

They neared the gates of the fort where two unfamiliar hunters stood near the entrance. From the bastion, a man waved. "There must be some news. Come, we will find out together." He reached for her hand and thought she trembled.

They entered the gate, and René stopped a man who was passing. "What has happened?"

"It is our clerk, your brother."

"He is here?"

"Inside." The man pointed at the countinghouse.

A roar of laughter came from beyond the door.

Claude lived. René bowed his head, relieved for the moment.

As he raised it again, an aroma of meat and herbs assailed him.

Brigitte straightened and pulled in a breath. "Well then, we have worried for nothing." She gave him a stiff smile. René had seen her gather her courage just that way before. Did she do so now? "Smell that? Are you hungry after our walk?"

"Not really."

"René." She leaned closer, gripping his arm as they strolled across the compound. "*Merci.* I am not sure if I have said so. I thank you for all you have done for me. I know not what I would have done without you." She glanced toward the countinghouse, then back to him. "I realize it was not only Claude who was spared from the wrath of Mina's relatives. You saved us both."

He stopped and faced her. His hand rested over hers, tucked into the crook of his arm. "I would take you away in a moment to spare you."

Her eyes widened as the countinghouse door flung open and people spilled forth.

The way parted, and Claude's face lifted to them as he made his way through the mass. "Ah!" He beamed a smile so wide one would have never known his life had been recently jeopardized. "There is our esteemed partner, my elder brother. And Brigitte." He opened his arms.

René loosed her arm and reached for his brother's hand. "Claude. You have returned to us."

"Did I not tell you things would work out?" A glint in his eye heightened René's suspicions, but more noticeable was a slight limp.

René flicked his glance to those gathered around, and they swiftly drew off. "You are well?"

Claude folded his arms. "Well enough."

"And where is Mina?"

"She remains with her family. She only just had the babe."

"She has had the child?" Brigitte's voice held conserved enthusiasm.

"*Oui*. Another boy." Claude's chest puffed out. "He is named for me." He studied Brigitte and lowered his voice. "I have missed you greatly, though I tried not to worry." This last part he said with a brief glance at René. "You remained well? You were comfortable and had plenty to eat? The wilderness can be cruel."

"René took care of me." She seemed to stand taller as she said it, and René felt a surge of pride.

A lift of Claude's brow accompanied a measured smile. "I am certain he must have."

René reached for her hand and drew her close again. Her fingers clutched his. "Are you settled?" he asked Claude.

"My bag is in the house." Claude's gaze roved between them. "Where it should be."

René turned his head to speak into Brigitte's ear. "Go to Keeheezkoni's lodge. I will bring your things to you later."

She nodded, and he gave her hand a gentle squeeze before releasing it. She looked at Claude. "It is good you are safely returned." She dipped her head and turned to leave.

"We will speak later," he called after her.

René glowered. "You will not speak to her alone, now or ever."

Claude smirked. He nodded toward the store, and René followed him. Inside, Claude poured himself a glass of whiskey and offered some to René. René declined. Claude tossed back his glass and set it down. He licked his lips and sighed. "You haven't taken the post from me completely, I hope?"

"It is yours, as long as you do well by your duties."

"And you are giving orders that my duties are not to include speaking to Brigitte?"

"*Oui*. That is correct."

"And if I disobey?"

"You will lose this post and more."

Claude chuckled.

"You doubt me?"

"I am not in a position to doubt, only to ask." Then he lightened his tone. "Let us not bandy about such things." He waved away René's annoyance and clasped a hand on René's shoulder. "I am home. Tomorrow we shall have a *fête* to celebrate my return and the coming season. I suppose you will be away soon, so you may as well enjoy it, eh?"

"Tell me about your injury."

"There is nothing to tell. So, what do you say to the *fête?*"

René acquiesced, but he took note of the glaze in Claude's eyes. Not of drink, but determination.

CHAPTER 26

"There is a voice in each of us, impelling us to seek comfort and council from a Being higher than ourselves. From One who knows and discovers all, even exposing the deepest fears and needs of our hearts. Anyone can deny this, of course, if he is a hypocrite or has never suffered sorrow or want."
— Agathe, Sister of the Congregation of Notre-Dame

René rested the adz against the ground and leaned on it while he rubbed the sweat off his brow. He brushed wood chips off the log he was shaping for the corner post of a new structure, then he hefted the tool again. He worked in quietness behind one of the storehouses where he could think above the activity. He glanced to the side only briefly when Bemidii approached.

Brigitte's brother dropped to the ground against the pickets and ate meat off a trencher as he watched René's progress. After several minutes, he called out, "The sun is high, and you have been here all morning. Why do you not rest?"

René heaved several deep breaths. "Winter is coming. Have you no work to do to prepare?"

"I have made many arrows for the hunt. My knives are all sharpened. Now, I eat like a bear and build my reserves for the days ahead." He grinned. "One of the men shot a young buck, and there is a feast. You should eat."

René could smell the roasted venison, wafting on the breeze. "There is work to do, and I have energy to spend." His feet straddled a log, and he lifted the adz, swinging it downward to take a clean bite out of the wood.

"You have a fire inside you, and you hope to burn it out with such work. But it only kindles more."

René glared at him and swung the ax-like blade again. "You

have some cure to suggest? If not, leave me in peace."

"You are bitter because you love my sister, but you have failed to tell her so. You are angry that your brother still desires to claim her, though he has no right. And yet you, who are free to do so, hesitate. In this, you fight a battle you cannot win. You must tell her, my friend Dufour."

René panted and dropped the adz. "If you must know, I intended to make my offer, but Claude returned, and—"

"And you are running out of time. She must marry. If she does not, and the Sioux return ..." Bemidii rolled to his knees, then stood with a grunt. "It is not yet too late for you both, but there will always be others who step in your way." He narrowed his gaze. "The other Dufour is restless for my sister, and I offer you this warning. My hand will not be stayed a second time." He strode away. René stared after him, his thoughts a storm, for Bemidii's words were true.

René returned to his work, but after a few more swings, Claude appeared, as if René's thoughts had called him forth. Today, Claude looked like the *bourgeois* he wished to be. While René had abandoned the fine clothes and trappings of a North West Company partner, Claude wore his fashionable suit and cravat, and he sported a smart-looking cap. Even his limp was less pronounced today. Whatever ailed him seemed nearly mended.

Perhaps Claude should have been given the partnership in René's stead. Yet, that was not the way God had ordained it. Even so, Claude depended upon René to gain future promotion. The notion tasted like gall.

"René, you stink. I can smell you from here. Have you bathed at all since I went away?"

René ignored his goading.

"I can have someone fetch you a bath."

"I appreciate the thought, but I will only develop a new stink in a few days."

"And *your woman* will have you smelling like a dog at the *fête?*"

Sarcasm laced his voice.

So, he wasn't certain if Brigitte and René still played a game. René cast him a scowl and swung the adz, huffing out a breath rather than answer his brother.

Claude shrugged and set his foot upon a log. René noted that he wore moccasins, the only sign of his dress that belied his place in the lake country. Claude tore off a piece of carrot tobacco with his teeth and stuffed it into a pipe. "Women are nonsensical creatures most of the time. Impractical, wanting this and that, emotionally bent on traditions."

"If you think so, then I am more than glad I arrived from the interior when I did to stop your farce of a marriage."

"To spare Brigitte?" Claude threw back his head. "Ha! You sound as if you know about such things, yet isn't it I who have lived as husband the past four years with Mina and her brats?"

René scowled. He leaned the adz against the pile of logs and braced his legs apart to stare at Claude. "Have you?"

"Have I—"

"Lived with Mina as husband."

A puff of smoke swirled up from the pipe in front of Claude's face. "In a manner of speaking. Do not try to make more of it."

"Has Mina gotten herself rid of you for certain?"

"We understand one another." He puffed again, his eyes narrowed.

"What does that mean? I can hardly believe her brother or her uncle are satisfied with your *understanding*."

"Don't be ridiculous, René." Claude took to pacing. "All would have worked itself out if you had not broken up my wedding. I would have been Mina's husband when I was with her, and I would have been Brigitte's husband—her *Christian* husband—when I was with her. Someday, when I am through with this miserable country, it would have been Brigitte alone."

René's blood surged. Like a November buck in the woods, he was ready to plow his brother to the ground. He gritted his teeth.

"You would have used Brigitte so cruelly?"

"How am I cruel? I am enamored of her. You must understand my position here, René. It is important I make liaisons in this country if I am to perform my duties as *bourgeois*, but that does not mean I cannot have another wife, someone who is more my equal." He shrugged with a wave of the pipe. "I would fulfill my responsibilities to Mina. It is the custom of the coun—"

René buried his head in Claude's stomach, smashing him to the ground and landing atop him. Claude's hat and pipe flew off, and his eyes widened in surprise. René leaned back to grip hold of Claude, but Claude freed an arm and punched him in the chest. René hardly felt it as his anger boiled. He clasped Claude's collar, tightening it in his fist, and slapped him with his other hand. Claude's face turned red as he gripped René's wrist. He gritted his teeth, grunted, and squirmed.

Finally, Claude flailed, and René released him, pushing himself off in a single, swift movement. Claude was weaker than René remembered. He glared at his younger brother lying panting in the dirt, then reached down and pulled him to his feet. Claude shook his head and wobbled. Then, his eyes darkened with fury, and he swung at René, catching him on the chin. René's head cocked back, but he steadied himself. His fist sent Claude flying into the dirt. His cravat twisted and his coat ripped. Claude drew his legs up against his body.

"Get up." René ground out the command.

Claude rubbed his chin and smirked.

"Get. Up. Now."

Claude sat up with a grimace but didn't rise. He dusted debris from his sleeves as he rubbed his already bruising jaw. "What is the matter with you? Do you really expect me to turn my back on Mina while I am still clerk here? The Sioux will slit my throat if I abandon her, yet even they understand a man's needs. They are willing to be satisfied with gifts and promises that I come to her when I can. She will be first wife."

"And you said *I* stink."

"What's the matter, René? Are you in love with Brigitte? Are you in love with my woman?"

René hauled Claude to his feet and shoved his face close. "Perhaps I am. Perhaps I will not let you forget it."

"What will you do? Forget your vow and marry her yourself? You were the one who told me she was a good Christian girl. Would she really marry you?"

René shoved him away. Claude stumbled, groaning. His limp returned as he stooped to retrieve the pipe and his hat before it skittered away in the wind. "I am through taking care of you and making your way for you."

"You have been taking care of me?" Claude laughed.

René wiped a sleeve across his face. "*Oui.* You did not know it, but I have. Now, no more. I will marry Brigitte if for no other reason than to save her from you."

Claude sneered. Then, his expression flattened. He hunched with a gasp.

"What is it?"

Claude grimaced. "It would seem Mina and her brother have beaten you. There is no need to save Brigitte from me."

René frowned. "*Que voulez-vous dire?*"

Claude glanced down below his waist.

Horror grabbed hold of René.

Claude straightened as best he could. "*Oui*, the Sioux have emasculated me. So, you see, I will always be faithful to Mina, even if only physically."

René's face flushed. He shook his head. "Claude, I am sorry such a thing has happened."

"Are you? If you wish to help me, you will remember that you owe me a chance at a partnership."

René reached for the adz. "My days of owing you are over."

"You will do it for her."

René hesitated. God in heaven. He would do it for Brigitte if she asked it.

"I see you are caught, brother." Claude sighed. With hands on his hips, he looked up at the blue sky, then back at René, his brow puckering. "We have not always seen eye to eye. I am sorry it is so. You are right. You have done much for me. I am not ignorant of it. Perhaps it is as much your fault as mine that I am … ambitious." He lifted one side of his mouth.

A chill ran down René's spine. He swept up his buckskin jacket—one Brigitte had mended not many days ago—and shrugged into it. "I cannot stop you from pursuing your ambition, but I will tell you one thing for certain. If, ever again, Brigitte should bring any complaint against you in any way, I will make you suffer for it. As I said before, my pledge to our mother is fulfilled. I will make your way easy no more."

René brushed past him. As he did so, he caught the deepening frown on his brother's face and felt wholly free of his yoke at last.

CHAPTER 27

*"There is not a day that my heart does not recall the dip of
the oar, the note of water rushing over the rocks, the blaze of
the sun on the crest of the trees."*
—Journal of Etienne Marchal, Voyageur

The afternoon stretched before Brigitte. Not since her early
weeks at the St. Louis fort, when time stood still and little
worry marched across her thoughts from day to day, had Brigitte
rested so well as she did in Keeheezkoni's lodge. At night, Bemidii's
sister slept softly beside Brigitte, her beautiful lashes lying still upon
her cheeks. Her brother's pallet, as well as her stepmother's with
her husband's, lay on the other side of the *wiigiwaam*.

Keeheezkoni had offered to teach Brigitte some of the old ways,
and she was an apt and eager pupil. She enjoyed the conversation
between the women and the scents and sights of her surroundings.
Yet, even in the restful village, there were eyes upon her.

She had not escaped the notice of Tristan Clarboux, the overtly
friendly nature of Gervais, nor the impetuous desires of Claude
Dufour. Now, the attention of the hunters and warriors in Bemidii's
village strayed to her. There were some whose gazes were so intent
she had to turn away to hide her blush. Only René did not treat her
as something to be possessed.

If she had married Tristan, would she be a mother now? If
poor Gervais had lived, and their friendship had bloomed into
something more, would she be his woman now? If her marriage
to Claude had been a true marriage, might she be wondering even
now if a *bébé* fluttered in her womb?

All questions to wonder over as she sat stitching on a shirt,
but none of these things had come to pass, and in her heart she
was greatly relieved. The same could not be said of her feelings for

René.

I love him, Father. I think I always have. I would be a wife to him, but for my foolishness with Claude and his own vow not to marry.

Bemidii pushed back the door of the *wiigiwaam* and jerked his head, "Prepare yourself and come with me to the festivity."

"I am thankful Claude is safe, but I do not wish to spend time with him. I will not attend."

"You are more thankful than I, but do not worry. You have many friends. You will enjoy the feasting with me and the other Dufour."

She grinned at him. "You are always ready for a feast."

His eyes crinkled with mirth. "There is work aplenty. I will take my pleasure here before I go with the *bourgeois* on the long trek."

She rose to her knees on a soft bearskin. "You will go away with René when he makes his winter rounds?"

Bemidii nodded. "It is settled. Come. Forget women's work today. Join me." He dropped the flap over the lodge and disappeared.

Bemidii was right. The days grew short, and soon René would go away again while she would stay in Keeheezkoni's lodge. Brigitte donned the blue skirt Ojawa had given her and trailed her fingers over the beaded sash.

René would leave for the inland posts any day. If Bemidii left with him, then she would seek out his company, as it might be long months before she saw her brother again. Her heart thrummed as she slipped into her beaded moccasins. She would seek René's company as well. Perhaps she would borrow a piece of ribbon from Shenia.

Bemidii raised a brow and gave her a smile when she stepped out of the lodge. "Perhaps you are no longer our father's *Aamoo*. You are *Waabigwan*."

Not the bee, but the flower. She flushed.

He jerked his head for her to follow, but before they moved, Bemidii tweaked her chin with his thumb. "René Dufour will be pleased."

She blushed and motioned Bemidii on. She followed him toward the sound of fiddles and pipes.

They passed through the rear gates and found the revelry underway. She and Bemidii mingled with the other folk gathered in the courtyard for celebration as meat pies emerged from the bakehouse, along with generous amounts of fish, venison, butter, peas, Indian corn, potatoes, and tea.

The afternoon meandered away with gaiety. Brigitte squared her shoulders, intending to enjoy it while she kept her distance from Claude, but the rich food she partook of lodged in her throat. She had never been one to drink, but today she wished she could. Her stomach churned with unsettled emotion. Where was René? She should have seen him by now. Had he already gone?

He would not have gone away without telling me.

She stuck close to Bemidii as the hours waned and evening drew on. Dots of light on a purple canvas sprang out overhead. Having seen Claude mingling on the other side of the compound, she excused herself and wandered into the store to see if René was there, but he was not.

She looked to his house. Was he inside? She took a step forward and then thought better of it. What if Claude should see her and follow? She scanned the crowd but did not see either Dufour about. Disappointment carved a hollowness inside her.

The thought of Keezkeehoni's warm lodge beckoned Brigitte. She turned toward the rear gates, then spun around, changing her mind. *I need to get out of this fort and breathe the air.* The very words spoken by René filled her with resolve. She hastened across the yard to the front gates instead. With a nod at the sentry, she slipped beyond them.

Her racing heart calmed at the sound of the waves washing the shore. A full moon rose over Superior, and she shivered. Still, she turned her face upward and pulled air into her lungs. She closed her eyes and imagined the long shadow of Superior's north shore stretching toward Grand Portage and Fort William, hundreds of leagues distant. Hundreds of leagues that separated her from another world that might someday separate her from René.

"Aamoo!" Bemidii strode toward her across the wet sand. "I am happy to see you did not spirit away."

"I am here, Bemidii. I found I wanted the quiet of the shore."

He met her and smiled, reminding her of their father. "I see it on your face. You seek a journey."

"*Eya*." She nodded. "I miss it. Bemidii, do you ever wish our father was here?"

"As a boy, I dreamed of going on the hunt with him. I have accepted it was not meant to be."

"I always thought to see him again."

"He is here." He pointed at his heart.

"*Oui*, but I miss him." Must all she loved forever live only in her heart?

Bemidii touched her arm and drew her attention. He nodded up the darkening shore. Brigitte squinted into the distance. Movement on the water. Eventually, the shapes of men, pulling on their oars. The voice of their *avant* called over them.

"It is late for a party to arrive."

"It is." Bemidii stepped ahead of her. The boat flew toward the shore. Men leapt clear, splashing into the icy water and pulling it ashore.

"Carefully! Get these *pièces* inside. Stewart, you and Moose turn the *canots*." The man giving orders had a voice that rang familiar.

She and Bemidii drew near as workers began carrying their load ashore. Her mind left its melancholy, and she narrowed her gaze. She laid a hand on Bemidii's arm. "I know that voyageur."

She took another look. *Oui*, 'twas the *avant* from her boat on the journey from Montreal. His visage and barking orders had frightened her then, but the *avant* had been their guide and René's friend, and he'd been very kind to her when Gervais was lost.

"Monsieur Jacques!" Brigitte waved.

He straightened beside the *bateau*. A moment later, a smile spread across his moonlit, grizzled face. "Ah, it is the *petite voyageuse*, our very own *femme du nord!*"

She was glad to see a face from those days.

He wandered toward them. "You are to be here the whole winter, eh? A *hivernant*."

"I must have my adventure, just like the rest of you."

They shared a laugh. "*Oui, oui.* It is sure to be a full season for all of us, but in springtime we return to *rendezvous*, eh, *petite voyageuse*? And how is my friend René? He has made you an honest woman, *non*?" She lowered her eyes, and the man laughed. "Still so shy? Where is the new partner? I must see him if he is here."

"He is somewhere in the fort. There is a *fête* for his brother who has just returned." She held her hand out toward Bemidii. "Monsieur Jacques, I have had good fortune since last we met. I have discovered my brother. This is Bemidii."

Jacques straightened. One eye twitched as he examined the tall Métis next to her. He perused him, hands on hips. "You say you are her brother, eh?"

"You say you are her friend?" Bemidii asked crossing his arms.

A slow chuckle rumbled through the older man. "Ah, I see it." He held out his palm, and Bemidii shook his hand. "René has busied himself with a party and left you here with your relation, eh?" He turned his attention back to Brigitte.

"Our clerk, his brother, narrowly escaped great trouble with the Sioux." She tried to speak the words dispassionately but found she could not look Jacques in the eye as she did it. "But all is settled now."

"Some dispute with them and the Ojibwe?"

She shook her head and swallowed. "*Non*. It was his wife. She was … enraged."

Jacques frowned. He scratched his bearded chin. "She is Sioux if I remember?"

Brigitte nodded, wishing they could talk of other things, but it would likely not be the last difficult conversation she would need to bear.

"Never can trust them. Would not surprise me if she tried to slit his throat." Jacques grunted. "Dufour sets high store on his brother. He will not take any Sioux actions lightly."

"The *bourgeois* clerk has only himself to blame," Bemidii said. "René Dufour will realize it."

"Let us hope it is so. With the season underway, trouble with the Indians will only make it more difficult." Jacques excused himself then, giving his crew more orders, his voice gruff and demanding.

Bemidii remained with Brigitte, and they continued their walk up the shore. They spoke of Bemidii's coming excursion into the wilderness until he turned the subject. "You are afraid of what this man Jacques says? Afraid of Mina too, perhaps?"

"*Non.* Perhaps I should be, but I am not. Surely, Claude will come to his senses." She sighed. "The quiet stretches around me. I am reminded of the days after my *Tante* Eunice died. I saw nothing in the future then either." She strolled along the shore, moving around a piece of smooth driftwood.

"You are young, Aamoo. You have much to look forward to."

"You are hopeful, I know, but—"

"Look." Bemidii pointed toward the fort. In the glow of light spilling from the open gates, a figure strode toward them. *René.*

Revelry had taken over the fort, but René had not felt the joy of it. A blade of agony sliced through him. Things would not be the same between him and his impetuous brother again this side of eternity. Perhaps not on the other.

He rolled his quill pen in his fingers, disgruntled at the thought, and looked out the window above his desk in the store. The courtyard was full of activity—campfires burning, and the shadows of people eating, dancing, carousing.

He set down his pen. "I suppose I must join them." As partner, he owed his workers that much attention. As he rose from his chair, the door was flung open.

"Monsieur Dufour!"

"Jacques." René smiled and went to meet the hearty Canadian. Jacques stepped aside as several of his men marched past into the store with bundles on their shoulders.

"Our first take of the season. Deer mostly, and a few muskrat. We will wait on the beaver until they are thick with winter fur, *non?*" He gave a belly laugh and grabbed René's hand. "It is good to see you again, my friend."

"And you," René said. "I was not expecting you until next month."

Jacques hooked thumbs in his sash. "Winter comes soon enough. We have a beginning, and we brought a little meat too, but I see there is no shortage today. I could smell the feast from outside the gates."

"Please, you must enjoy it. It is a celebration for my brother's safe return from a visit to the Sioux."

"So I was told by a young woman on the beach." He raised his brow, and the comment lingered.

René's heart skipped. "Brigitte is outside?"

"With one of the natives who says he is her brother."

"Ah."

"That is all you have to say? Why are you not out there with her on such a fine night?" Jacques winked. René grinned, and Jacques slapped him on the back.

"Perhaps you are right, and I should excuse myself of your company, pleasurable as it is." René reached for the door.

"Do not hurry back on my account. Moose!" Jacques called to his man, as René slipped out. New energy pulsed through him as he walked across the courtyard, not pausing to speak to anyone he passed.

As he walked toward the beach, he saw Brigitte beyond the glow of firelight. He gave a nod to the sentry in the bastion and ordered the gate closed. She was instantly engulfed in only the light afforded by the moon as she stood with Bemidii.

The atmosphere reminded him of the night he'd spied her bathing. His chest ached at the sight of her beauty. He should have stopped the nonsense of pretending at the start. His heart condemned him, for he'd loved her from the beginning, and he had left her to Claude. Such a coward he was. Claude had been a fool, but at least he'd been a courageous fool.

She watched his approach from the water's edge. His feet moved, impelled by a force outside himself. The sounds of laughter, shouting, and singing fell away in the distance.

As he neared them, René glanced at Bemidii, his black eyes a-glitter in the moonlight.

Brigitte hugged herself. Moonlight shone on the water and lay upon her cheek.

"It is good you are not alone," he said softly.

She nodded. "*Oui.*"

Bemidii stepped back and bowed his head. A moment later, he faded into the night.

René stepped closer to her side, and they watched the heavenly light glint off the ripples on the horizon. Their shoulders touched, and she moved to put a space between them, but he reached out and stopped her. He drew her close and felt her stiffen, then relax. She sniffed.

"Brigitte." He turned to her and lifted her chin to the moonlight. Tears glistened in her eyes. "Why do you cry? If it is for Claude, he can no longer be saved from his choices."

"I do not cry for Claude." Her lashes swept down. "I do not know why I cry. Perhaps it is because I have grown used to you, and soon you will go away, as you must."

"Brigitte." He considered his next words carefully. Her gaze was his again. "My brother. He is changed, yet his wishes have not. Others will not give up on you." He pulled in a breath and eased it out. "Unless you are married."

He'd drawn her attention again, but she huffed.

"The idea repulses you."

"It is not the idea. I would marry someone trustworthy and noble if there were such a man …" Her voice trailed off, and she glanced to her feet.

He reached for her hands. "Will you be *my* wife, Brigitte? Many have thought you my woman. I would not have you pretend such a thing any longer."

Her head snapped up, moonlight glistened on her tears, welling afresh. She shook her head. "You pity me."

"*Non*. That is not true."

"It is true. You are sorry you let me talk you into bringing me to this land. You are forgiving over Claude because you are kind, but you pity my foolishness and ignorance. You pity, you—"

"You are a brave woman. Why should I pity you? I admire your strength."

"It is because of the others you mention. You have always saved me, and now you feel you must save me yet again like you did so long for Claude." Her voice climbed and strangled.

"Though it is true I would spare you from the likes of such devils as Clarboux and even my own brother, you are wrong about my reasons, Brigitte." He caressed her arms.

"Then why?"

With his thumb, he wiped her tears, cradling her cheek in his palm. He leaned close, only a breath away. "Marry me. Tomorrow." Closer still, he bent his head. Her eyes widened, and her lips parted, which only beckoned him to touch them with his own. She stilled. Her mouth tasted salty and warm, soft and compelling. He took her face between both hands and kissed her again.

She whimpered. He broke the kiss and breathed her name as he laid a hand against her braid, drawing her to his chest. "It is not pity I feel. If I feel anything at all but tenderness, it is regret that I have kept my true feelings from you so long."

She pushed against him gently, and he released her. Her gaze sought his.

His chest ached. "You wish it were not so. I am too old, too rough to love you."

"René—"

"You must believe me. I do not pity you. I could not. But if you do not care for me, I will not press you."

She laid her hand against his chest, her eyes wide. Her voice, barely a whisper, lifted. "You love me?"

He cradled her to him. There was no holding back his feelings now, even if she should reject him. "My sweet Brigitte. I have fought it, for I have known others would please you more. But I cannot help it. *Je t'aime.* I love you." He kissed her again, and she received it, matching it with a hunger of her own.

The notes of an Indian flute reached them through the darkness, and at last René found the strength to pull apart from her, but he kept her in his arms. "Will you marry me, *ma fille douce?*"

The moonlight captured a small smile that broke from her lips. She nodded. She laid soft fingers against his lips. "Long it is I have loved you, René. I will marry you. *Je t'aime.*"

René pulled air into his lungs. He grasped her face in his hands again. Laughed, sobered, and kissed her well.

Many minutes later, they walked hand-in-hand along the shore. The moon rose higher. In the distance, the silhouette of Bemidii playing on a flute trilled soft notes into the night.

CHAPTER 28

Many rivers run, as I run to you,
Many sparrows fly; your wings sing close to mine,
Many are the trails; our two ways go as one,
Many are the nights I lie within your arms.
—Flute Song of Bemidii

At dawn's light, Brigitte roused. She had slept only a few hours beside Shenia. When daylight crept upon her, her heart quickened, waking her with a joy that made it pound. She slipped quietly from the *wiigiwaam*, a smile playing on her lips as she thought of the day to come.

René was to become her husband. Her true and only husband. Her lover, as well as her protector and friend.

Her heart yielded to a praise she could not have kept inside. *"Merci, Dieu,"* she whispered into the dawn.

Retrieving a kettle, she hummed a voyageur's tune as she walked to the river's edge. Frigid water splashed over her hands as she filled and carried the kettle back to the camp and hung it to boil over the fire Bemidii had kindled, all the while, pondering the preparations she must make. Thankfully, Keeheezkoni had promised her aid. Bemidii's mother would not stay away from this wedding as she had the erroneous wedding with Claude.

Despite the way Brigitte's breath hung in the air, a warm and wonderful feeling filled her, so different than the uncertainty when she'd prepared to marry Claude. She longed to laugh and sing, but the morning was too early still. Not everyone had risen to begin their day. *Ah, René, I will love you so.* Such thoughts made her smile again.

Later, she would don the yellow dress and arrange her hair. First, she would help Keeheezkoni with the breakfast while the water for her bath warmed.

The fire crackled as morning sun burned through the mist. The coagulated meal in last night's pot bubbled and softened. Brigitte was reaching for a spoon when something soft touched her shoulder. Keeheezkoni stepped closer, lifting the kettle of warm water and beckoning Brigitte from the fire.

She followed Keeheezkoni back inside the lodge. Everyone else had risen and gone. Her stepmother motioned for Brigitte to kneel, then undressed and began to bathe her. She blushed as water trickled over her limbs, and Keeheezkoni sang softly. Then she told Brigitte what to expect from her husband. Brigitte's face heated even more to think of what was to come, but she grasped hold of the moment with Keeheezkoni's tender ministrations. She had missed much when she had believed she should marry Claude.

When Brigitte was dry, Keeheezkoni perfumed her skin with herbs. Afterward, Brigitte reached for the yellow dress, but Keeheezkoni stayed her hand. "Shenia!"

The girl dipped her head through the door. Over her arms, she bore a dress of creamy white deerskin. As Shenia held it before her, Brigitte gasped at the beauty of it. Before she could study it long, Keezkeehoni nodded at Shenia and touched Brigitte's elbows. Brigitte lifted her arms, and the women slipped the wedding dress over her head. She had not worn anything so soft since leaving Montreal.

Once it was on, Brigitte glanced down the front at the blue beads dangling from the fringe of her bodice. Her arms, still raised, dripped fringe from the elbows past her waist. The hem, too, hung with long fringe that would reach from her knees to the floor once she stood. With her elbows still lifted at her sides, Keezkeehoni wrapped Brigitte's waist in a blue and white beaded belt.

"It is my ceremonial dress, saved for special occasions," Keeheezkoni said with a smile. "Today you shall wear it in memory of your mother's people."

Brigitte's throat tightened over Keeheezkoni's generous offer. In light of their past, her offering could not have been kinder. Brigitte blinked back tears. "*Miigwechiwi'*, Keeheezkoni. Thank you."

Keeheezkoni's eyes also glistened. "Bemidii's sister has become like my own daughter." She reached for Shenia's hand and squeezed it.

"And a true sister," the younger girl said.

Keeheezkoni backed away from Brigitte, and Shenia stepped near. She held a comb and ribbons in her hand, and Brigitte turned around, understanding. The girl spent long minutes combing and oiling the strands of Brigitte's hair. She parted it in the middle and wove one of the ribbons through a tiny braided lock, but the remainder of Brigitte's tresses she left undone.

Keeheezkoni shuffled closer. She held a pair of long, beaded earrings shaped like blue and white flowers and a bracelet that matched.

The women moved back and nodded, their faces beaming. "My sister's new husband should be very pleased," Shenia whispered.

Brigitte flushed to think of René looking upon her with open affection, even desire.

"You are ready," Keeheezkoni said. "Come. Your bridegroom awaits."

"He is here?"

The older woman nodded. She took Brigitte's hand.

"Keeheezkoni …" Brigitte hugged the woman, her heart spilling over. "Thank you."

Brigitte followed her out of the *wiigiwaam* into the sunlight. The morning haze had burned away, and Bemidii waited, straight and tall, reminding her ever so much of their father. He wore a new shirt decorated with dyed porcupine quills. He raised a brow and lifted his chin in the manner Brigitte had come to know as his approval. His smile gentled over her, and she could only blush again at the satisfaction in it. Her heart surrendered fully to the joy of having his attendance with her.

When he reached for her hand, she grasped it. They strode

along a path between lodgings and cook fires as word ran ahead through the village. People stepped out of their lodges to watch. Some, already outside, drew closer and formed a gathering in the center of the village. Bemidii led her toward the western edge, where the morning sun slanted against the white birch and poplar trees, glistening off the leaves like gold coins.

And there stood René.

Brigitte barely acknowledged the two men with him. His friend, Jacques, and Henri, the apprentice clerk, stood beside him.

Her husband-to-be looked more handsome than ever in his new fringed buckskin. His long, black hair was pulled into a queue, and he had trimmed his beard. Her breath quickened, and the rest of the people faded away as she focused solely upon René.

Bemidii leaned close to Brigitte. "Our father would be very proud."

Her skin heated, and her knees shook. Her heart raced. Then René stepped forward and held out his hand.

She stepped toward him. When his fingers wrapped around hers, the pulsing in her chest steadied.

"*Tu es belle.* You are beautiful. So beautiful." She pulled at her smile, but it could not be controlled. His teeth shone white in his handsome face as he smiled back. "Come, let us marry."

He led her toward the medicine woman, who waited beneath the birch trees along with Jacques, Henri, and some others from the fort. Villagers gathered nearer. The men smiled and nodded. Some patted René's shoulders as he stood among them. The medicine woman stood before René and Brigitte and spoke in solemn tones.

Bemidii stood taller. "I give my sister in marriage to the *bourgeois* Dufour. As a gift, I go with them as hunter when he must travel to the other forts, so that he may take care of my sister's desires."

Jacques chuckled.

The medicine woman laid a cord over René's and Brigitte's hands, and she bound them together. "Each of you will be shelter for the other. You will feel no cold. Each of you will be warmth for the other. *You are two, but there is only one life before you.*"

Brigitte fell into the depth of René's gaze, swallowing her in bits and whole, and she knew at last that she had found her place in the world.

A cheer erupted, and applause fell over them.

René cradled his bride's face in his hands, content to look into her eyes. His fingers crept beneath the veil of her hair, and he kissed her.

Drumbeats shook the sky, and people sang. Ending the kiss, René and Brigitte turned to face the crowd. Keeheezkoni hugged Brigitte and kissed her cheeks. René shook Henri's hand as Jacques pounded his back. Bemidii stepped before him, and the two stared at one another before Bemidii stretched out his hand, and they clutched one another's forearms. Other women from the village stepped forward to congratulate Brigitte, then Bemidii whispered in her ear and glanced at René with a smile. René squeezed her hand.

Jacques winked. "Tomorrow I go up the river, while you must enjoy your honeymoon."

René's smile grew. *Ah*, his honeymoon. He put his arm around his bride's waist and chuckled. "I will listen to the wisdom of our friends."

"At last." Bemidii gave him a wry smile, and René laughed aloud.

The way parted for them. There was much to discuss with his new wife about their future, but first, there was this day and the hours that they would spend together. He'd not imagined such a day would ever be his.

Keeheezkoni led them to her *wiigiwaam*. After René and Brigitte entered, she closed the flap, leaving them alone with a bed of furs and food.

Brigitte lowered herself to the bedding and blushed. Her hair framed her face and tumbled into her lap. She pushed it back over her shoulders and returned his gaze.

Every nerve in René's body tingled. He cleared his throat. "We have been alone before, and many times have slept in close quarters, but I find it strange, now, for my thoughts and feelings to be free."

"And welcomed."

He smiled. "*Oui*. Welcomed." He shrugged out of his jacket and knelt in front of her. He took her hands and kissed her knuckles. "They are welcomed then, truly?" he whispered, searching her eyes to see if she really felt as he hoped.

Her lashes swept her cheeks, and she blushed. "Most welcomed. Most desired."

He reached around her shoulders and drew long ribbons of hair forward, smoothing them in his palms. "I have often longed to see you like this again."

"Again?"

"Once, during the summer voyage on the lake. You had washed your hair. I saw you coming out of the water."

"You saw me?"

He nodded, letting the silken strands of her hair flow like water through his fingers. He trailed his fingertips down the sleeves of her dress, feeling the quivering of her flesh beneath the fringes.

"And you respected me."

Passion roared hot through his veins, lighting him on fire in ways he'd always suppressed. Now he let the heat course freely through him. His breath grew shallow. "I desired you. Even then I loved you."

Her eyes widened, then softened as her gaze warmed to match his own. She licked her lips, tugging his attention to them. Their talking ceased. Their bodies melted into the furs beneath them, and the summer's memories were swept through an open door of freedom for their love.

Brigitte turned her head to the fire burning low in the *wiigiwaam*, warming them against the evening's cold breath. Soon the first ice would appear in their water buckets each morning.

René sat upon the hides, his elbow propped on one drawn-up knee while he bit off a piece of bannock. Brigitte rolled onto her stomach and rested her chin on her hands as she admired the muscles of his bare arms and chest. "The morning will come too soon."

He smiled.

"And the next day and the next."

He brushed the crumbs from his hands and moved down beside her. "This bothers you?"

"You are a partner of the North West Company. You have a charge."

He stroked her hair. "Only as long as you are willing to go with me." His hand rested on her waist. How easily his touch aroused her senses.

"You are sure? You were gone for only a short time before, and it felt like a lifetime."

"Where I go, you travel with me, unless you ever wish to stay."

"I am a *femme du nord,* or have you forgotten?" She gave him a sly smile, and he kissed her again.

"What a valuable woman I have wed."

She raised her head. "I will go wherever you lead me, René. I trust you. I have always trusted you."

"Then we will go to the Folle Avoine together, and so on to the other posts."

She laid her cheek on her hands and thought about that. Months would pass before she might again see this place or the others where they'd been—the great lake, the heavy forests puddled with lakes and seamed together by rivers. If she had ever imagined returning to Montreal, that thought seemed farther away than before. Perhaps it had always been mist.

"*Oui*," she whispered. She looked at him. "Together. I should write to Sister Agathe. It is time she knows what happened to me."

"We can leave your letter with Henri, and he will send it along with the first traders moving east or north. Perhaps we will send it with something for the *enfants* as well."

Brigitte rose and threw her arms around him. "You are a good man, René Dufour, and I am sorry I doubted you when first we met." She kissed his rough cheek.

His arms snugged her about her waist. "I am sorry for that too. And that I judged you a spit of a girl with a mind too big for her *oncle's* britches." He growled as he nuzzled her neck.

She huffed. "I filled them well enough after a time."

"You are not your uncle, and you look much finer when you are not wearing men's britches," he said, setting her insides on fire. "Now, wife, let us cease chattering about what is yet to come, and consider what is already before us." His voice was husky, and Brigitte once again forgot the world outside.

They did not join the others in the village, nor did René return to the fort until the next day. He had to repair to his business with the company, after all. For the next several days while René worked, Brigitte helped Keezkeehoni smoke fish and mix pemmican for their journey.

At last, the morning of departure came. Their *bateau* was loaded nearly to the gunwales with wares for trade. They carried as much food as they could and brought their own packs, as well as those of Bemidii.

Dawn stretched over the edge of the lake. Fog lay low upon the water and crept over sand and reeds. Brigitte stood in her fur-lined moccasins and wrapped in her *capote* while René and Bemidii secured their load. She was in charge of the ledgers, and her only task for the moment was to keep them safe and dry.

Just before the time came for her to climb in and settle in the middle of the *canot,* two figures appeared from out of the fort. Brigitte held her breath as Claude approached, and with him was … *Mina.*

The woman's eyes caught Brigitte's, and she lifted her head proudly. In her arms, she carried a child. Claude's son.

René leaned on his paddle. Bemidii folded his arms.

Claude stepped forward and gestured at Mina. "I know we have said our goodbyes, René, but winter is always long, and I would not wish to spend it parted with trouble between us. As you can see, Mina has returned to me." He glanced at Brigitte. "I asked her to stay and take her rightful place. Perhaps"—he looked at René again—"perhaps you would care to meet your nephew."

Mother's pride shone from Mina's eyes as she awaited René's attendance. He gave a nod and stepped over to peer at the child. His shoulders loosened their tight posture. "He is a handsome boy."

Claude smiled. He glanced at Brigitte again. "And perhaps his aunt would also care to say hello." His voice was gentle, his tone apologetic.

Brigitte faltered as she looked to Mina. The mother scrutinized but did not resist Brigitte's approach. She peeked at the dark-headed infant.

The baby's smell—soft and sweet, sour and wild all at once—drifted into her nostrils. Smooth skin, much the shade of her own, appeared velvety. Her heart strummed, and her breath grew shallow. She lifted her gaze to Mina's. Something passed between them. A woman's understanding. A woman's longings. A woman's heart cries. Brigitte raised her finger to stroke the babe's cheek. "He is beautiful," she whispered. *"Il est beau."*

Mina did not smile, but her brow twitched, and she looked pleased nonetheless. Brigitte backed away to stand beside her husband.

"We wish you well." Claude dipped his head. "We will see you both"—he glanced at Bemidii—"all of you again soon. Perhaps then we will have a *fête* to celebrate your union."

Brigitte nodded, smiling.

"The sun rises. We must away." René reached for Claude's hand, but when Claude grasped it, René pulled him into an embrace. A moment later, they broke apart, and Claude stepped back. René took Brigitte's hand and helped her settle into the middle of the *canot*.

He nodded once more to the couple on the shore, and Brigitte watched them disappear as the craft caught the current and slipped free.

René and Bemidii pulled with their paddles, driving them upstream. Brigitte looked over her shoulder once again, but Claude and Mina had faded in the haze made golden by the rising sun's rays. Along the banks, small creatures stirred. Two young men netted fish in the river.

Her gaze wandered as they rounded a bend, and at last, the signs of village and fort fell away completely. Vapors danced on the river that stretched new and unknown before her, yet there was no other place she'd rather be in the world. The men paddled silently. Only the gurgle of the water's current and the morning song of a thrush cut through the dawn's stillness.

All day long they paddled. Occasionally, Brigitte took a turn, stretching her muscles. At nightfall, they drew the *canot* onto the bank and made camp, just as they had done together many months past. Bemidii worked near the fire, cutting some fish into the pot to cook with their peas. Then he wandered away to spread his bedroll on the open ground beneath the thick bows of a cedar tree.

The first stars lighted the northern sky against a backdrop of dusky blue. Light that, moments ago, lay on the western horizon faded away. René and Brigitte strode to the overturned canoe where their blankets were spread on a soft hide beneath, facing the river where a fine evening mist descended in the twilight. Dropping to their knees, they loosened their garments and lay down. She pulled their three-point blanket over them and tucked her head upon his chest.

"It is said that the Americans may soon take over these lands, and the French trappers will no longer be able to work here." His voice rumbled.

"Then what will we do?"

He shrugged. "There is much left of this country neither you nor I have seen. There are beaver, deer, fish. Lands we cannot imagine, rivers too vast and numberless for us to touch upon in our lifetimes. There will always be other places for us."

"And what of Claude? Where will the company send him? He, with a wife and children. Her people—"

He silenced her with a kiss against her temple. "Claude must find his own way now. He understands. Do you?"

"You speak of relinquishing your responsibility for him, but what of other responsibilities? Did you always choose your path only because of what would serve your brother? Did you never choose your own way until now?"

"Sometimes I chose for myself, yet much was for him." His short beard brushed her cheek. "Because of my promise to our mother, I always believed my life lay in serving my brother's needs. That time is over. Truthfully, I think it was over years before I recognized it. Now God has shown me a new responsibility, one I take happily." He ran his fingers through her hair. Her braid untangled. "Your needs and mine are intertwined. We are one, Brigitte, and we have only to meet the needs of each other."

Brigitte curled close in the curve of René's body and listened to the rhythm of his heartbeat. "Then you are not sorry." She didn't ask it this time. She trusted it.

"And you?"

She shook her head. "How could I be? You love me."

"We have both found where we belong, and it is not to the company or to our pasts, but only to each other and to God."

She hugged him tighter. "You are a good man, René. I am very happy."

He chuckled soundlessly, but she felt the gentle roll of his laugh. "Because I am wed to a very fine woman. One who loves me and will also love our children one day."

She lifted her head to look into his eyes. The night sky deepened, making his irises hard to see. "You will never leave us."

His arm tightened around her. "We will have children, *ma chérie*. Many children. You, I imagine, will be like a she-bear with her cubs, and I will never leave them or you."

She pushed back a wave of his thick hair and kissed him. He kissed her back, arousing her desire. A chorus of frogs rose up, and the smell of the open water sharpened her senses. Stars stitched a blanket over their heads—a blanket that stretched forever in a sky that would look the same—like home, wherever their voyage carried them. Together.

THE END

Made in the USA
Middletown, DE
06 October 2018